MW01419477

To W.

THANK YOU & ENJOY

Willie
Thank you so
Much for Reading
good friend

UNTRUTHFUL SPEECH

Ron Cisneros and Michael Padjen

This is a work of fiction. Names, characters, places, events, and incidences are products of the authors' imaginations or are used fictitiously. Any resemblance to actual persons, living or dead, or actual events is purely coincidental.

ISBN: 978-1-09834-746-8 (softcover)
ISBN: 978-1-09834-747-5 (eBook)

This book is dedicated to the lives lost to Covid-19
and to all whose lives have been permanently changed by the pandemic.

Thanks and love also to the blessings given to us in the past year;
our four new grandchildren; Carsyn, Sonora, Solielle, and Enzo.

May the world return to a place where we can gather, celebrate, live,
and break bread without the threat of a virus taking these joys away from us.

PREFACE

The blue Ford entered the parking lot and came to a slow stop near the bike trail entrance. It was late, and the trail was seldom used due to damage caused by recent record wind and rains. The parking lot was also under repair and closed to the public, but the gate had been torn down by teenage vandals who wanted access to the isolated area for purposes of getting high and having sex. Eagle Lake was adjacent to the bike path and was used for fishing and other water activities. The quiet of that evening was broken only by distant horns of small boats pulling in for the night.

The Ford's lone inhabitant was an agonized soul who sat quietly, regretting drinking had never become a personal vice. Surely, a drink right now would settle some nerves. Rolling down the window and slowly taking in a breath of the cool air would undoubtedly be a better alternative, but would it be one of the last breaths of life? Peering out the windshield, the occupant could see the tall pines swaying back and forth as if they were keeping the rhythm of an anxious heart, ready to flee its solitary darkness.

Cars and trucks hurried past the lot, with their drivers daydreaming of the upcoming weekend or glancing at their mostly unimportant text messages. As each vehicle went by, breathing would halt, followed by a momentary sigh of relief.

Reaching to the floorboard, and under the passenger's seat, a gun's handle was felt. Fingers caressed the rough topography of a thousand machined pyramids, and cleaning oil smell wafted from its barrel. The time was near, and the tears came, first on the cheek, and then salty in the mouth. Blood red eyes stared at the reflection in the rear-view mirror. Another breath, then another tear. Will I be able to do this? Trembling fingers wrapped tightly around the grip of the revolver. The time for redemption was drawing near.

Part I

The Package

CHAPTER 1

May 2019 – Massachusetts

Mack inhaled the warm outside air. His nose filled with the smell of spring. He exhaled with relief and was happy to see how easy it was to breathe after his battle with the late spring flu. He sat on his back porch excited to see new blades of grass popping out of the topsoil of his freshly seeded lawn. It was an encouraging sight to see the final stages of the newly constructed home come together. The couple would soon be entertaining family and friends to enjoy the new pool during the hot summer months.

Mack Griego taught at the University of Massachusetts Amherst, classes in business and accounting, while Stephanie, his wife, owned and managed a coffee house. The establishment was a local place where the college students frequently hung out and studied. The coffee was fresh and the Wi-Fi was fast.

Mack and Stephanie's backgrounds were as different as Rush Limbaugh and Morning Joe, but as husband and wife, they fit like a single barrel bourbon and a drop of water. How they met would be a story apt to grow in drama as they got older, like how a fish gets bigger upon each rendition of the catch that got away.

Stephanie was raised and born in Needham Heights, a suburb of Boston. She was from an upper-middle-class Catholic family. Her father worked for General Electric as a Corporate Compliance Attorney.

Her mother was a stay at home mom, raising four children and devoted to her church. They attended Saint Joseph Parish, which managed to slip by all the abuse scandals targeted at so many Boston Catholic churches. Stephanie had a good childhood and was close to her two brothers and one sister. After high school, she was accepted to the Northeast University School of Law and, after passing the bar exam, took a job as a public defender in Boston.

Unlike Stephanie, Mack often moved due to his father's military career until the family retired in Austin, Texas when he was in middle school. Mack was happy with the stability and became a high school football star, which provided him an athletic scholarship at the University of Texas. He knew football would not be his career; he was good, but not NFL material. He focused on his education, graduated, and decided to stay and finish his MBA at the University of Texas. After receiving his MBA, Mack found himself wanting to teach as a career, but wanted out of Texas. Although Austin was as liberal as Texas gets, overall, the state was very conservative, as were his parents. Mack was eager to leave the state and seek out more liberal-minded people.

After Mack's graduation, Randy, a close college friend who was aware of Mack's plans to relocate, invited him to Massachusetts, which had a political climate more suited to Mack.

Upon arriving in Boston late in the day, Mack and Randy set out to spend the evening having a good time at some local bars. Walking out of the last bar before heading home, they both witnessed an assault taking place in the parking lot.

Mack, a little drunk, still thinking he was a running back, shouted "Hey!"

The assailant ran off with Mack giving chase, while Randy attended to the victim.

Mack still had his playing speed and caught up to the man quickly. The adrenaline was pumping hard, and Mack knew this would be an easy tackle. What he wasn't expecting was the assailant deciding it was fighting time. He quickly turned around to confront Mack as he pulled a gun out of the front of his pants. Mack didn't have but a second to decide. He didn't break stride, driving his shoulder into the perpetrator's stomach, wrapping his arms around his waist, and throwing him into the ground. The gun went off.

For just a moment, Mack figured he or the guy on the ground had been shot. Fortunately, the bullet ended up in the brick façade of the building across the street. Once he gathered his senses, Mack kicked the gun out of the way. Looking down, he realized he was staring into the eyes of a teenage boy. "Let me go you mother fucker", the young assailant shouted.

Randy, finally making his way to Mack and confused by what he just witnessed, asked. "What in the hell were you thinking, Mack? This kid had a gun."

"Hell, I didn't know until he turned around. I had to take my chances and go in for the tackle. If I had slowed down, he would have shot me. Something took over."

"Dude, I think maybe it was stupidity, but I have to tell you that it's about the most fucked up, crazy-ass shit I've ever seen. I didn't know you had it in you; you've always been such a pacifist."

"Neither did I. I just chased down and tackled a guy with a gun pointed at me. I hope I never have to do that again."

"Buddy, a word from the wise; you don't chase guys down here and not expect to get shot. Boston isn't artsy-fartsy Austin."

The police arrived and took the teenager away; both Mack and Randy gave their statements and contact information.

Several months passed, Mack took a job at a local accounting firm while working on his Ph. D. part-time at the University of Massachusetts Boston. He and Randy remained friends, but it wasn't easy to get together with their busy schedules. A few months after the assault, Mack received a call from Randy asking him if he received his notice of arraignment. Mack checked his mail and saw his notice was there. They agreed they'd like to be there and meet at the courthouse on the arraignment date.

The court day had arrived, and both Mack and Randy sat quietly near the back. "All rise," the Bailiff shouted. The Judge entered the courtroom and heard the charges from the Bailiff. She then turned to the Defense Attorney and asked how her client pled? "Not guilty," Stephanie answered in a confident voice.

Neither Mack nor Stephanie could tell you today if that was an accurate rendition of what happened, but it was their story of how they met each other.

CHAPTER 2

Mack and Stephanie eventually married and had two sons. Their eldest, Steven, died three years earlier from Acute Myeloid Leukemia. It was a deadly form of the disease caused by an uncommon chromosomal abnormality he carried. He lived only six months from his diagnosis, a painful and dire time for the entire family. For some time, the suddenness of Steven's death created a world covered by a veil of grief for the family, rarely allowing them a glimpse of a normal life. It felt like a nightmare that might never end.

Steven's death more severely impacted Nick, who was three years younger and a senior in high school. Nick missed his big brother terribly. Steven wasn't just a brother, but his best friend, mentor, the one always there to take care of a bully, teach him the finer points of sports and girls, buy him a beer, or take the blame for something stupid he had done.

Before the cancer, Nick had been a top-level student and planned on a medical career, just like Steven. The death soured him on that idea. His feelings for the medical establishment and Big Pharma had changed significantly. He viewed them, rightly or wrongly, as a supporting factor in his brother's death, not from direct action, but their inaction. He saw them as not interested in finding a cure, but only making additional profits from marginal improvements. Nick decided some time away was needed to reflect on his feelings and his future. He would make his final decision at the end of the school year regarding the direction in life he would be taking for the short-term, despite already being accepted at UMass.

Until his pending graduation, Nick also decided he would do whatever possible to make sure no one's brother, sister, mom, or dad would ever die the brutal death Steven did. No one deserved that ending.

Nick became a voracious reader of medical journals, blogs, Facebook group dialogues, and advocate sites. He found a tremendous amount of research was taking place, but most of it was into treatments to prolong lives or replace other medications that stopped working. In many cases prolonging meant only a few extra months of life, and in a majority of those cases they were months of extended suffering only. The cost of the added time could also be so expensive it would bankrupt the families. Ultimately, he concluded politics and money were the drivers of drug creation and lack of actual cures. This belief fueled his rage and his opinion Steven's death wasn't necessary.

Nick quickly became a determined patient advocate himself. He was aggressive and angry, creating personal blogs and social outreach pages on Facebook, Instagram, Twitter, and all the other relevant social networks he could find. Nick advocated relentlessly until after his high school graduation. By that time he was burnt out and needed to get away from it all. He eventually decided to volunteer with the International Volunteer Programs Association (IVPA). Maybe taking a year or two off could help him get his head together. The IVPA had a great teacher's assistant program in Bangkok. He was confident time in Thailand would take the edge off his anger and help guide him back to some normalcy. All he had to do now is tell his parents he applied.

CHAPTER 3

May, 2018 - Boston

Nick heard a light tapping at the bedroom door. He was not in the mood for company after a heated fight with his mother about his plan to enter the IVPA.

"Nick, can I come in? It's dad," the gentle voice on the other side whispered.

"Yeah, dad, come in."

"You OK?"

"Dad, why doesn't mom understand me wanting to take a break from school, this city. You did the same thing back in Texas."

"I didn't take a break from college. I took a break from my dad and Texas." Nick was keenly aware of the conflict between his dad and Gramps.

"Gramps? He wasn't so bad. He taught Steve and me to shoot. He took us camping and fishing; you know survival skills."

Starting to become annoyed, Mack said. "I'm sure he also told you his war stories about his time in Vietnam killing innocent civilians, too."

"Dad, Gramps never told us stories of killing anyone, and I'm not joining the IVPA to kill anyone. I need to do this. I know you and mom lost a son; I lost a brother. I think Steven would be proud of my choice; I wish you and mom would feel the same."

Mack was conflicted about his relationship with his dad, who was the son of an immigrant who left Mexico to live the American dream by working in Utah's copper mines. His grandfather wanted to do what most immigrants at the time saw as the American dream; provide his family with the opportunities they would never enjoy in Mexico. He and his wife raised a large family in a small town named Copperton.

Jose, one of their children, was Mack's dad. He joined the Army after high school and spent four years in Korea. After his commitment to the Army ended, Jose enrolled in college under the GI Bill and graduated with his bachelor's degree. It was while in college he met and married Mack's mother, who was Irish American. Jose then enlisted in the Navy as an officer and later became a Navy Seal fighting in Vietnam.

Mack and his father never really saw eye to eye about any war, and Jose didn't comprehend why his son couldn't understand guns and power saved the world from tyranny in World War II and would continue to protect the world from Communism. Their beliefs eventually separated them. Mack chose a different route than his father's and understood his son needed to do the same.

Nick did see his grandfather in a different light. Maybe it was because when Gramps lost his relationship with his son, he focused on being present for his grandkids.

He and Steven got to spend summers with Gramps in Texas. Grandma Griego died when they were young. So, it was just the three of them hunting and fishing or doing whatever the hell they wanted to. Mack would have killed Gramps if he knew all they did, including their first beer.

Nick felt Gramp's heart was in the right place, serving his country, protecting American lives.

Gramps wasn't a replacement for his dad, but both Steve and he had a great relationship with him they cherished. Sadly, they lost him when Nick was entering high school, and Steve was graduating.

"Son, I understand what you are feeling, and you need to take the time to discover what you think you're supposed to do. Understand, your mother and I are worried and fearful of something bad happening to you. It has only been eight months since we lost Steven; we don't want to lose you, too. Just give your mom some time. She'll come around."

Mack, at this moment, was feeling a little closer to his father.

Nick sat in his room and re-read the letter from the IVPA. *"You have been accepted to The International Volunteer Programs Association (IVPA) Cross-Cultural Solutions Thailand."* He didn't realize at that moment of clarity; God might be laughing at his plan making.

February, 2019 - Boston

Nine months later, Nick's plane landed in Boston. His two-year commitment with IVPA had been cut short by circumstances he would soon sort out. Mack and Stephanie were at the airport to greet him and take him home. They weren't sure why things had changed so much with Nick's plans, and didn't understand much of what Nick had done during his time abroad. All they knew was when Nick completed his shortened first assignment with the IVPA, he told them he had earned enough money to supplement a backpacking trip across Europe and Asia for another six to eight months. He planned to pick up odd jobs to fill in his monetary needs along the way. When Nick returned, all they could get from him was, "Just traveling and learning." The only other information they had were photos he occasionally emailed to them while on his adventure.

Mack and Stephanie immediately saw a change in their son, both physically and mentally. His physique had transformed into that of an athlete, and he projected a tough demeanor, very unlike the grieved high school graduate who left nine months earlier. They didn't know what to make out of it, or if they liked it.

When they arrived at the house, Nick immediately told his parents he needed more time before going back to school. He told them he had always wanted to work on a lobster boat and could use the extra cash. Mack questioned Nick's decision, but realized he couldn't change his son's mind. He understood the experience would be useful to him.

Despite his mother's objections, Nick let her know the decision and plans were already in place. He would be leaving in a week for his new job on a lobster boat named the Serendipity in Bar Harbor.

CHAPTER 4

April, 2019 – Bar Harbor

Nick didn't communicate much after going to Bar Harbor, but after two months working on the Serendipity, he called his parents to tell them he would be coming home in May for a few days to take a break. He didn't commit to when he would leave his job and enroll in college, only that he would see them soon.

Later the same day, a new hand named Derek came on the Serendipity to look at the rig. He was scheduled to be part of the crew for the next trip. To Nick, Derek seemed older and have more experience than him working on lobster boats. However, since Nick was the veteran deckhand, he expected Derek to follow behind. Although he wasn't expecting a new hand, Nick could see they would get along fine.

The month of May came quickly. Mack and Steph were thrilled they would be able to see their son soon. They had been concerned he'd change his mind about coming home, especially considering the changes they saw in him, but now it looked more and more like he would be there any day.

The grass was luscious and full, and Mack was cutting it twice a week, getting it just right. Much like Mack, Stephanie was waiting eagerly for their son's arrival, getting things together for a small welcome home party. She was concerned Nick had not called her to let her know the exact day he would be on his way, but Mack calmed her by telling her they would soon see their son.

Several more days passed, and Nick still made no contact. Mack was getting worried, too. He started thinking about the changes he and Stephanie had noticed, and wondered if there was more reason to be concerned.

Mack tried calling Nick's cell only to get an immediate voice mail message. He had the number of the captain, but again only got voice mail. Mack left several messages for him to call, and asking for the whereabouts of Nick. He continued to call for the next few days. His worry had been building. It heightened with the news of two lobster fishers being murdered in Bar Harbor the previous weekend. Although Nick had not been identified as one of them, his concern wasn't going away. They needed answers.

Mack and Steph were having was they

Right now, they wished they had asked Nick

They would find out soon enough they were not alone in knowing little about the man now employing their son, who went by the name, Skipper. People who met him or worked for him would tell you he wasn't what you'd expect as the captain of a fishing boat. He was slender and tall, with a slightly protruding Adam's apple, but was strikingly handsome in his own way. He looked more like a minister than the rough and tumble fishing boat captain you saw in the movies.

Even his real name didn't fit that of a fishing boat captain; he had been christened Nigel Edward Shackelford, a name more befitting a bookstore owner. That's why he went by the more unassuming title of "Skipper" or "Ed" to his friends.

Most people had heard he was in the British Navy serving as a Midshipman, and his last gig was during the Falklands War back in "82."

What everyone, save a few, didn't know, being a naval officer was just a cover for him. He was there representing MI6, the British equivalent of the CIA. There had been troubling intelligence indicating the involvement of the Soviet Union and Cuba in the war, so Nigel was commissioned to determine its accuracy.

As far as anyone was aware of his personal life, Skipper didn't have kids, and according to gossip, his wife died early in their marriage. Skipper was pretty much a loner but the same town gossip had him spending a lot of time with a researcher named Elli, who worked at Lerdell Labs.

CHAPTER 5

Nigel knew he owed Nick's parents a call. He had been putting it off for a week now, hoping things would shake out, but they hadn't; plus, Nick's dad had been calling all week leaving messages. It was late, but he knew he couldn't wait any longer and finally relented.

In his Americanized version of a Yorkshire accent, the Skipper explained to Mack there wasn't anything new to having his crew disappear for a few days after docking. He told him they had been back about a week and Nick and his buddy Derek left together. The plan was for Nick to drop off Derek in Manchester then make his way home to Boston.

He went on to tell him after working long hours with little sleep for days on end, the crew usually only had three things on their minds; blowing off steam, fucking, and sleeping. Sometimes they got lost along the way. *Too Much Information,* Mack thought.

"Give it another day or two; Nick would show up soon enough. I'll check on things to see what I can find out; I have both their phone numbers."

As Nigel was hanging up on Mack, the front door flung open, closely followed by Eliza Rossi Fernández, one of Nigel's only friends left from the Argentina days, and the supposed "dead" wife. Her finger was pointing at Nigel, and her eyes cut towards the faux leather Italian sofa, where Nick and Derek were sitting.

Eliza pushed her finger towards them to make her point and said, "Waiting is no longer a strategy, guys. It has been a week, and much bad stuff has gone down since things got ugly last Sunday. We may need to rethink this before it's too late. Nick, dealing with your parents may have to be first on the list. Nigel, meet me in the kitchen."

Nigel looked at Eliza as she entered the room, telling her, "I believe we have this handled. Nick understands what's at stake."

With a piercing glare, she turned to Nigel and said, "I hope you're right."

Nigel knew Elli was concerned, but believed Nick could be an asset because he had information on one of the individuals involved in what had taken place a week earlier.

"Has Derek been with Nick the whole time since the incident?"

"Yes, but there is another problem," Nigel said with little confidence Eliza's reaction would be calm.

Eliza turned back, staring at Nigel.

"I spoke with Nick's dad. He's worried, I wouldn't be surprised if he calls the police or shows up here."

CHAPTER 6

Eliza was born in Italy in 1954. Her mother, Maria, was from Bologna; Her father, Giulio, was born in Rome and rose to power as a commander in the dangerous Fascist organization called the Black Shirts. They were mainly disgruntled ex-soldiers, who posed as champions of law and order. Still, they violently attacked Communists, Socialists, and other radical and progressive groups, mostly during World War II.

In 1943, when the Allies invaded Italy, Giulio decided he and Maria needed to escape to Argentina. After changing their identities and surnames to Fernández, they eventually made their way to La Rioja, Argentina, which housed an enclave of escaped Italian families loyal to Fascism. It was also was a fledgling wine region. Giulio took to the art of winemaking and created one of the largest and most successful wineries in the region. It was just beginning to take off when Eliza was born.

Eliza grew up in a storybook setting. She was an only child, pampered by everyone at the winery. She spent her winters being tutored by hand-picked, local academics while enjoying the temperate climates afforded by their location. Her summers were spent running through the vines, picking roses from the bushes at the row ends, and participating in the harvest. She didn't realize her parents were grooming her for bigger things than winemaking.

During her formative years at the winery, she was also influenced to hate Communism and Socialism by her parents and trust more in the Fascism Giulio called "The Italian Way."

By her early twenties, Eliza had worked her way to the top both socially and professionally. Her reputation as a political expert grew. She had earned her Doctorate in political science in near-record time. Though her politics weren't in line with the ruling Peronists, her reputation allowed her to maintain a professorship at the University of Buenos Aires. Behind the scenes, Eliza worked with her parents, backing the military Junta which eventually forced their way into power.

For the following six years, Eliza stayed on staff at the University. She also became a confidante to the Junta leaders. Over that same period, Eliza slowly became disillusioned with the government she had become so enamored with early on. Eliza finally concluded their hate for their political rivals had become far too brutal and inhumane. Death squads had been created by the Junta, and tens of thousands of political enemies were slaughtered in a few short years. By 1982, their arrogance had become uncontrollable. Not only was the Argentinian military ready for a change, but also the ever-loyal Eliza.

Eliza was perplexed about her feelings for a while; however, she gained clarity when she learned an envoy from The Soviet Union and Cuba had met with the ruling regime's remnants. The topic would be the invasion and takeover of the Falklands, and an agreement to possibly allow Russian nuclear missiles to be positioned there. The memory of the Cuban Missile Crises had faded, and the Soviets felt the US was losing its focus in the region.

Also, the Soviet Union was starting to fall apart. They needed a new friend in the Western Hemisphere to offset Ronald Reagan and the US's power there. They were also very aware of valuable and strategic mineral deposits in Antarctica. Unbeknownst to Argentina, their main goal was to set up a base for the colonization and control of this frozen continent and its treasures.

Eliza hated Communism. Always had and always would. Now her government was getting into bed with two of the worst players on the planet. Whatever they were planning wasn't going to be best for Argentina or her family.

Little did she know her change in heart against the existing Junta would turn her world on a dime or what she planned to do next would lead her to a grand partnership with a man named Nigel Shackelford and, eventually, a son named Derek.

CHAPTER 7

1982 – Argentina

Eliza had been on the CIA watch list for some time. They became aware, through some of their embedded sources, of her unease with the Junta she had secretly supported into power five years earlier. She eventually moved from the watch list to being actively recruited after the CIA became aware of the Soviet's meeting with the Argentinian regime. That meeting was all they needed to succeed in bringing Eliza into the fold. She could become a key to getting intelligence on their plans for the Falklands.

The British government needed some vital financial intel, so Eliza was asked to meet an MI6 agent named Nigel to turn over information on a war financing scheme between the Junta and the Soviets.

Nigel's ship, the HMS Bristol, was met by a CIA controlled fishing boat in international waters off the Falklands coast. Nigel would pose as part of the crew until they could find the right time to get him into the town of Camarones to meet with an embedded operative named Eliza.

Nigel spent a week on the boat, all the while being an active crew member. He couldn't believe how much he loved it. By the time the meeting had been set up with Eliza, Nigel wished he could stay longer, and was now contemplating buying a fishing boat after leaving the service. Little did he know how soon that would be.

When his boat docked in Camarones, the captain told him to make his way to a cantina called "La Casa de Dariqe'." He would be looking for someone wearing a Boca Juniors Soccer Team cap and a baby blue basketball jersey with the name "Jordan" on the back. Nigel was wearing a pair of denim shorts and a white t-shirt with the words "I'd rather be fishing" emblazoned on it.

Nigel made his way from the dock up the winding cobblestoned Juan Manuel Estrada where he found the entrance to the bar at the bottom of a set of some crumbling concrete steps.

His eyes took a moment to acclimate to the dark, but when they did he still wasn't sure if he quite trusted them. Across the room at the bar was maybe the most beautiful woman he had seen in a long time. To Nigel this was significant considering the cap and oversized basketball jersey she was wearing.

Eliza was an elegant woman, with deep green eyes and jet-black hair that popped out the back of her cap in a ponytail. She was definitely on the tall, slender side of average. She wore a pair of glasses that not only made her highly intelligent-looking but also very attractive. Even the Tarheels shirt couldn't ruin her look.

Nigel slowly made his way across the room. He wanted to take in this scene as long as possible. As he got close Eliza turned slightly, sensing his approach. When her eyes finally met his she got a little tongue-tied but got out the words "You must be Nigel."

"And you must be Eliza."

"Yes."

Still a little tongue-tied, Eliza blurted out, "You don't look much like a Nigel to me."

"So, what's a Nigel supposed to look like?"

"I'm not exactly sure, but not like you. Take that as a compliment."

"I guess I'll have to take your word."

They both laughed. The chemistry was strong and the banter lively.

By the end of their prolonged meeting Eliza had passed off two Swiss and one Peruvian bank account numbers along with all the codes required to retrieve any money from them. The Soviets and Argentinians were using the accounts to funnel money for financing the war.

Eliza hadn't been sure she would hand the accounts over when she got to the bar. She continued to have some trust issues with the CIA even though they hadn't done anything to raise her suspicions but had set up this meeting. She was concerned it might be a set-up to get her arrested. By the end of the evening Eliza's paranoia was gone. She knew she could trust Nigel.

Nigel would make sure the Americans got one of the Swiss account numbers and the Peruvian account number. Maybe he'd hold onto the other Swiss account for a "Plan B." In the end what he passed to the Yanks was enough to help end the war.

They said their goodbyes. As Eliza was heading out the door she looked over her shoulder. "Hope we get to meet each other again."

"I am sure we will."

CHAPTER 8

As they left, going in opposite directions, a lone figure emerged from the far corner of the bar, following Eliza until she entered her hotel. Eliza had an uneasy feeling the entire walk back. Still, she talked herself out of the paranoia, even though her body tingled with unease. If she had turned around, she would have realized her intuition was spot-on. Not ten paces behind her was Gustavo Peralta, on loan from Cuba to Argentina, a principal advisor to the death squads, and go-between for the Soviet Union and the Junta.

You could not miss Gus. He was an imposing figure, 6'5" and 280 pounds of lean muscle. He usually sported a full beard and a shaved head but these days he had stubble and a thick mustache. The rumor mill said he was a top-shelf assassin on retainer to Fidel Castro. Gus had been instructed to keep a close eye on Eliza. A professional acquaintance had notified Argentinian authorities her loyalties had changed.

The next weeks passed quickly as Nigel worked the boat, waiting for further instruction from his contacts. When the Argentinian surrender finally transpired, Nigel was called into action and sent to Buenos Aries to retrieve Eliza, who was in grave danger.

Eliza was in her apartment. She knew she would be dead in less than 24 hours. The ruling party had been embarrassed and the Soviets were pissed. Worse than that, there was talk Eliza had not only changed her loyalties but was now associated with the CIA and the primary reason the Brits had cut off their money flow. If the Junta's goons didn't get her, the KGB would.

"Bang bang.... Bang, bang, bang." The door sounded like it was going to get knocked off the hinges. Eliza couldn't believe the Argentinians had figured things out so fast. She made herself ready to be either shot or put into prison for a long time.

Then she heard a familiar voice say, "I'm looking for Eliza." It was Nigel, whom she had been thinking about almost non-stop since their meeting at La Casa de Dariqe' eight weeks earlier.

She ran to the door, unlocked it quickly with her badly shaking hands, and, in an instant, was kissing Nigel. When she realized what she was doing she pulled away even though both were enjoying the moment. This was no time to reacquaint themselves in such a friendly manner, knowing trouble was soon on its way.

"Wha, what are you doing here, Nigel?"

"Getting you out."

"Where are we going? They will find me wherever we go."

"Let's get you out of Argentina first, and we'll worry about the rest after that." "I have a plan. Hope you are OK with cold weather, not a lot of people, and water."

Nigel had left out a small detail. Eliza had already been found. Before entering the building Nigel cased the area. About a block down with a full view of the building were two men sitting in a sixty-something Cadillac. Nigel was surprised they were being so obvious but realized they didn't know he was coming. It was the only car parked on an otherwise empty street. He recognized the driver as Gus Peralta. Knowing they were minutes away from getting to Eliza, he decided to take things into his own hands.

Screwing on the silencer, Nigel walked toward the rear of the vehicle, then quickly to the driver's side. If Gus looked into his review or side mirror, Nigel might not have time to get shots off before Gus and his partner got their guns on him. Gus did see him in just enough time to duck as he reached for his pistol. Nigel fired off five shots point-blank. Both men slumped in their seats. He decided, if necessary, he would tell Eliza about this encounter once they were safe.

Within five minutes Eliza had her duffel bag packed. They both headed to the CIA fishing boat moored at the docks. The plans were to get to Rio de Janeiro in a little over two days, with a few Reals and fake passports in hand.

As Nigel and Eliza were making their way on the boat, Gus Peralta crawled out of his car, severely wounded, but not dead. His partner's face was unrecognizable due to the three bullets that directly hit his head. Gus had a bullet lodged in his jaw, and, more seriously, one in his lung. If his other lung collapsed, he was a dead man. He promised himself if he lived through this he would track both Nigel and Eliza down and kill both of them, but surviving was the first thing on his mind right now.

CHAPTER 9

May, 2019 - Boston

Stephanie woke up hearing Mack's voice and asked franticly, "Was that our son calling?"

Mack fumbled with the light switch on their lamp and turned to her.

Stephanie knew that look on Mack's face; she had seen it before. Mack's mind was racing to find the words to tell his wife everything would be OK. All that came out was, "He has been off the boat for about a week now."

Mack quickly got up out of bed. Stephanie again asked, "Mack was that Nick?" Mack was silent as if not to hear his wife's question for a second time.

He made his way to the closet, reached up on the top shelf and grabbed the black lockbox.

He hadn't been in that box for years, so he fumbled with the combination.

"Three, right, nine left, back to three again, nope."

"Three right, nine left, back to three, no stupid all the way around 0, then to three."

The box opened, and by then, Stephanie stood in the doorway of the closet.

"What are you going to do?" asked Stephanie. "I thought you got rid of that thing."

"I'm going to get our son," Mack replied, placing the Wesson 10mm and some extra clips into a duffel bag. "I was planning on selling it but never got around to it."

"Mack tell me what's going on, is Nick in trouble?"

"I'm not sure, that was the Skipper calling, he said Nick had left a week ago.

Something about giving another hand a ride home to Manchester."

Mack rummaged through the closet and grabbed some clothes. He went into the bathroom, grabbed a toothbrush, and deodorant, then stuffed all of it into a duffel bag.

"Wait a minute, where are you going and why are you taking your pistol?" Stephane asked, looking more scared than ever.

Mack was distracted, turned to Stephanie, "What?"

"Where are you going?" This time she was shouting at her husband.

"Steph, I didn't like his voice."

"His voice, do you mean his accent?"

"No, his tone.

Something is wrong; he didn't seem overly concerned Nick had not shown. He didn't go into any detail about this Derek fellow. He just said Nick's is fine."

"You don't believe him?"

"No. I asked about Nick, why would he tell me they are both fine?"

Stephanie could read her husband pretty well. If he believes Nick's in trouble, then she thinks it, too. She grabbed her bag and started packing as well.

"What are you doing?" asked Mack.

"I'm going with you," she said with a sense of purpose.

Not really knowing the game plan, Mack and Stephanie finished packing, loaded up the car, and headed towards Maine. Mack left a message at the college informing his Dean he needed to be off for a week or two and recommended an excellent substitute to teach both courses. Stephanie called Lori Becker, an employee who had worked at the coffee house for several years. Lori was trained to manage the shop in her absence. Stephanie trusted her to operate the shop for as long as it took to find Nick. They made their way to Interstate 90 and planned for the five-hour trip, which would get them there around 7:00 AM. They drove silently for a while, which was making Stephanie crazy.

She finally asked, "What is the plan?"

"Don't know, still working it out in my head."

"Well, can you let me in on what you know so far?"

"When we get to Bar Harbor, we will pay a visit to this Nigel Skipper guy. He can't be that hard to find in a fishing town."

"Do you think he did something to Nick?" she said softly.

"I don't know. At the very least, he can help us trace Nick's steps, or."

"Or what?"

"If it doesn't help or worse, has something to do with our son's disappearance, well that's why I brought my gun, or."

"Another or?" asked Stephanie.

"Or, if Nick is partying in Bar Harbor or Manchester with this Derek fellow, then I will shoot him myself."

"Shoot who, Derek or our son?"

"Our son! for putting us through this, then Derek for corrupting our son!"

For a moment they both smiled, hoping this was the case with Nick. Soon it got quiet again; the smiles turned to frowns because they knew their son was a responsible young man and would call if he could.

CHAPTER 10

1992 - Bar Harbor

"He's beautiful. I think he'll have dark green eyes and an olive complexion just like you."

"You never know, Nigel, it's still too early to tell."

"Nah, I can already see he's not going to have my pasty white, North Atlantic skin tone. What name are we going to give him, Elli?"

"I've been thinking about that. If it was a girl, I wanted to name her Dariqe' after the bar where we first met. I've always loved that name, but I'm not sure now."

"I've been thinking a little too. How about Derek? The names sound almost identical, and Derek is quite common, and American." The sideways smile on Nigel's face showed he'd been thinking about it a lot more than he let on.

"I love that Nigel. Derek it is!"

Eliza, very content and maternal at that moment, drifted into thought. The past ten years had gone by so fast. It started with the escape from Argentina. In the meantime, they fell in love.

Nigel left active duty at MI6 and retrieved the money from the Swiss bank account. He still had the number, passwords, credentials, and fake identification to get him through any security necessary. When Nigel returned to Bar Harbor he purchased a lobster boat he had been hoping to buy. He named it Serendipity. It all felt so good at the time. Things seemed to be falling into place, finally.

Britain and the US had been very thankful to Eliza and Nigel and very thorough in making the real Eliza disappear. She would find out eventually the thankfulness of governments only goes so far. Times change, people change, and most of all, loyalties change.

She and Nigel had been involved in some bad stuff the past few years but it seemed karma had been their friend for the most part.

The only real tough times had been the first three or four years in Maine when Nigel and Eliza could only secretly see each other. The first year was the worst. Nigel had spent most of that time finishing up business in London, retrieving money in Switzerland, and setting up the business and homestead in Bar Harbor. He was gone almost the entire time, and Eliza was very lonely.

Eliza, who was now known as Elli, was set up in her own home, deep in the Maine woods, about 30 minutes away, outside Ellsworth and a mile away from her nearest neighbor. She had some bitterness about not being with Nigel but accepted it. For her safety her entire life and existence before 1982 had been wiped from history. This was her life now. She would likely never be able to go back to Argentina. The worst part was the possibility of never marrying Nigel officially if danger still lurked from days past.

The only saving grace from those years were some of the local friends she made when she was on her own. In particular, one named Eliza had moved into her neighborhood from Cologne, Germany, about three months after her. They became fast friends and took good care of each other, spending a lot of time talking about world politics, Eliza's studies and eventually Eliza's job. Her new friend, Talia, talked a lot about her work as a freelance writer and photographer, which seemed to be a fascinating life.

Elli never mentioned Talia to Nigel. First of all, her new friend asked her not to. That wasn't a problem for Elli because she wasn't planning on it anyway. Talia's worldview was the polar opposite of Nigel's. He wouldn't have allowed the friendship because of his paranoia for her safety.

Unfortunately, most good things come to an end. Talia, her new closest friend, maybe the closest in her entire life, got a job promotion. One of those she couldn't refuse. She would be moving back to Europe; London, this time. As sad as Elli was, it was also about the same time Nigel was spending more time with her. That would help fill in the gaps and the loneliness, and give her more quality time with Nigel.

Talia and Elli stayed in touch for several years, sharing adventures and promises of visiting each other. *That's what best friends do, right?* They talked a lot about their jobs. Elli was incredibly excited about her new research position in a project focusing on decoding the human genome.

They eventually lost touch after Derek was born. Elli had relished their relationship and knew it was something she would never forget, or tell Nigel about. It was the one thing in her life that was private; it was all her own. One day she hoped she would see her friend again. She had always been very fond of Talia and knew Talia felt the same way about her.

She now had Derek to fill some of the voids in her life.

Eliza also had some lingering regrets lying on top of her bitterness. Due to the danger she was in, especially from the Kremlin, she took on her new identity which would lead her into having to live two separate lives. Even though the escape and coverup were well executed, nothing is ever perfect. Her alter ego would likely have to remain in place for the rest of her life, no matter the regrets or her secret wishes. On top of that, she would have to hope karma would continue to be kind.

Her life was now that of Dr. Elli Brunetta. Over the past ten years she had morphed into an unmarried, single mother, PhD., Harvard graduate in biochemistry, and Senior Researcher at Lerdell Labs, one of the top medical research labs in the world. She knew she should be satisfied, but simply wished to be Eliza Rossi Fernandez Shackelford. This name didn't exactly roll off your tongue, but she hoped for it all the same. Elli had brought her hope up with Nigel several times but he would quash it quickly, pointing out the danger it might put her and Derek in.

She also would probably never see her mama and poppa again. Along with everyone else in Argentina, her parents believed her to be dead, killed in a fiery car crash outside her hometown immediately after the war. Most thought it was set into motion by her enemies in the government.

In reality, the CIA set up the crash to help cover her tracks. This murder would have a lasting effect on Eliza and be her biggest regret, something she would carry in her heart for the rest of her life. Someone else had died brutally in that crash. All that was left were a very charred female body and an almost equally charred passport traced back to Eliza. She was ultimately responsible for that woman's death. It had been her decisions which led to someone else dying in her place. How would she ever forgive herself?

Her "other" life was even more secret than that of Eliza or Elli. Along with being Nigel's life partner, she would become a partner of sorts in his lobstering business. Nigel had set it up to help him run a smuggling operation. It moved mostly money, people looking for safety, weapons, and, occasionally, some top-grade weed. Nigel's connections from the past proved invaluable in running an operation that brought twenty times the money his fishing company did.

Eliza spent little time in action on the boat due to her day job but was the brains and moral compass of the operation, even when a "moral decision" required a lesser, immoral action. That business was taking off when she found out she was pregnant with Derek. She reluctantly would have to take a break and be "mom" for Derek, and pretty much Dr. Brunetta to everyone else. Her life with Nigel would have to go on a soft hold for a while. They'd have to be much more careful now that there was a child in the mix.

2011 - Bar Harbor

For the seventeen years after Derek's birth, Elli played her single mom and research titan role passionately. Once Derek had proven to be a reliable, intelligent young adult, she started craving for that exciting alter ego as a smuggler. Even though Elli loved being a researcher at Lerdell Labs, she had to make more money. Derek would be heading off for an expensive engineering education at MIT, while she and Nigel would make their contacts to jumpstart the old business.

They were able to pull this off for over a year. Things changed on the night Derek decided to come home a day early for Christmas break. He had finished his finals early that semester.

"Mom, I decided to come home today! I brought a bottle of…"

Derek quickly rounded the corner into the kitchen, moving so fast he hit his shoulder on the door jamb. That must have jarred his senses. After regaining himself, he saw his mom and Skipper seated at the kitchen table with nautical maps stretched out across it. The scene wasn't so unusual an explanation wouldn't be available, but when he saw the Ruger 9mm pointed at him by his mom, he knew something was very amiss. As his heart started speeding up and his stomach rebelling, he searched for the words to say. Jumping back, Derek shouted, "What the fuck is going on here?"

After some explanation, Derek wasn't as shocked as Nigel and Elli thought he'd be. Of course, they didn't bring up the part about Skipper being his dad… yet. They talked a little bit more before Derek decided he needed to lie down. He was very exhausted mentally and physically, and could barely keep his eyes open. "We'll talk more later."

After his nap, he came back into the room with his mom and Skipper. Derek peppered both of them with the rat-a-tat-tat of unending questions. By late evening Derek had a reasonable understanding of what was going on, except for a matter of fatherhood. They continued to talk over the holidays. Nigel even took him to the boat to show him how they could do what they were doing. He was very impressed.

By the end of Christmas break, Derek had decided he wanted in. He wasn't going back to school. Studying engineering was challenging but tedious. Elli wasn't having any of that, though. Derek was going back to school.

"You're a smart kid, you've got a great future ahead of you. Why would we get you involved in this?"

"Because I'm a smart kid and can help. I'll tell you what; I'll finish school with an engineering degree, which will be valuable to the business. You and Nigel will be getting older and will need help. I think I can make things look more legitimate and set all of us up to have a great future."

Elli realized at that moment; Derek had the same sideways grin Nigel had years ago when they were discussing what to name their new baby. She had been putting it off, but knew she had to tell Derek the truth about his dad. It would only be a matter of time before he figured it out.

"Dammit! OK, I'll talk to Nigel, but I need to tell you something first."

March, 2019 - Bar Harbor

Elli returned from work, was dog tired, and just wanted a bath and a glass of wine. She filled the tub with water so hot steam was rising. With wine in hand, she placed her foot in to get a sense of the heat. Deciding it was safe to put the rest of her body in, her I-Phone rang. The screen said "Unknown Caller" so the temptation was compelling not to answer, but her curiosity got the best of her.

"Hello."

"Hello, Elli, my old friend. It has been too long."

"Talia?"

April, 2019 - Bar Harbor

Derek answered his phone. "Mom, I'll get there as quick as I can. I've never heard you like this. I should be able to be there by tomorrow evening. In the meantime, lay low. We'll figure it out."

Elli looked at Nigel with the eyes of someone he didn't recognize; red, puffed and, more than anything, extremely sad.

The prior evening Elli was approached by a stranger in the grocery store. He must have been no older than mid-twenties. His looks were a little humorous, like a little boy trying to play dress-up as an adult. The jacket was way oversized, the shoes super polished, and he was sporting a knit tie that looked like it came out of the eighties. What she heard coming out of the man-child stunned her.

"Eliza, we know who you are, and everything there is to know about your husband and son. We have a situation that will require your little side business resources, including the presence of Derek." The accent was typical Bostonian but had a little less edge than what you'd hear at Fenway Park.

"May I ask who We is?"

"You can ask, but I won't answer. Suffice it to say, you and your family are in much more danger if your answer is no. I'd advise you to be very thoughtful before you say anything."

"What is it you want us to do?"

"We don't have all the details yet but it will include you borrowing something from the lab."

Elli's heart sank. She knew whatever this was, it wasn't right. Her life, the life of her family, and the LEL's reputation were at considerable risk.

"Borrowing or stealing?"

"Does it matter?"

"Let me know when you have more details. In the meantime, leave my family and me alone."

CHAPTER 11

May, 2019 - Bar Harbor

Derek arrived at the dock early; Nigel told him to treat Nick as if this was his first trip on the Serendipity and NOT let on he was his son. They would be out for a few days with two additional crew members who didn't know what was about to go down. Lobster brought in a profitable return and, with a good couple of days, he could pay his guys well, send them on their way, and accomplish the mission this lobstering trip was being used as a cover for.

Nigel had received instructions from Elli concerning a pickup at Lerdell labs. He hoped the delivery would be at the dock near the labs, but this was not going to be the case. The instructions were now to pick up the package at the bottom of Sols Cliff. It would be tricky to navigate, so Nigel decided it would be best to send out a dinghy to recover the container. However, this presented two problems; sending out the dinghy with one crew member in rough waters would be dangerous and he would have to come up with a story to cover for the diversion to Sols Cliff. Having Derek come along would resolve the first problem.

Derek was now 28 and single. Although he had an Engineering degree, he worked odd jobs in and around the fishing harbor, which gave him cover availability to help his parents.

The morning was no different than any other. Nick showed up when expected and helped the new hand load supplies.

The Skipper was in the wheelhouse, mapping out the plans for the trip.

Nick complained to Derek, "It would be nice if the rest of the guys were here to help."

"Yeah, good hands are hard to find these days," Derek responded, acting as if he was a little disappointed.

"I don't know if you remember, but we met earlier. Ok, I'm Nick. I've been working for the Skipper for about two months now,"

"Yeah, I remember," making no eye contact with Nick.

"Do you know the Skipper or worked for him before?"

"Nope."

"So, this is your first time on the Serendipity?"

"Yup."

The rest of the crew finally showed up. With the supplies loaded and all hands-on deck, the Serendipity set off.

CHAPTER 12

May, 2019 - Bar Harbor

The waters leaving the boat dock were calm, little wind other than the breeze from the boat's momentum. Nick took his favorite spot in the boat's bow while Derek went into the wheelhouse, visiting with the Skipper. The other two hands, Justin Straw and Del Williams, sat in the stern smoking cigarettes and carrying on an argument about who won the billiard game last night. The fresh morning air felt good on Nick's face. The salty mist sprayed up in his face; it's the moments like this he will miss.

He heard the cabin door shut and turned to see Derek shaking his head, joining Justin and Del for a smoke.

The first day was not unusual, baiting lobster traps and icing the coolers. The Skipper told the crew they would be in the area he hoped to provide excellent results and profits. Although his cover as boat captain did not provide the funds, he needed to pay a crew after expenses; he liked paying his team a fair wage. A good catch of lobster can bring up to $7.00 a pound. The first day, actually half-day, the crew brought in about 500 pounds. The next day would be a full-day, and they hoped to bring in an additional 1,000 pounds and head back home.

The Serendipity's storage capacity was 2,000 pounds. If they hit that number, the Skipper could pay his crew $800 each. Not bad for two days' work.

That night the crew settled in and Nick started preparing the evening meal.

He got to be a reasonably good cook and the Skipper taught him how to make great rice and beans. Tonight it was going to be a hamburger surprise. The Skipper did not allow his crew to drink; however, he and Derek would sneak up to the bridge and share a good whiskey.

"So, do you know what we are picking up tomorrow night?"

"No, your mom would not tell me, something important though."

"Yesterday, when you told me we have to stop at Sols Cliff, I was not happy, it's beachless and rocky."

"We just need to get close to the cliffs. The package will be waiting for us there."

"Bad weather is coming in. This could be tricky," exclaimed Derek.

"Yea, I know. That's why we need to head back early tomorrow."

"The crew won't be happy; there is no way we can bring an additional 1,500 pounds of lobster."

"I will pay them for the full load. They shouldn't complain about that."

A rapid knock on the door informed them dinner was ready and they joined the crew for dinner.

"I hear Nick makes a damned good bowl of rice and beans," Derek said, smiling.

"Yes, he does, but I hear he is making some sort of hamburger surprise," Nigel said, smiling back.

The next day lobstering was slow, and they knew they would not reach their target by dusk.

The Skipper came out to the deck and announced they needed to head back due to bad weather coming in. It was 3:00 pm. The moans and groans could be heard for miles. They barely brought in 500 pounds of lobster.

"Damn, we need this catch. We all need the money." Del was speaking for the crew. The weekend had all of them disappointed.

"Don't worry, I understand, I'll make sure you all get paid your full wage."

Everyone was thrilled to hear the Skipper saying he would pay them for a catch of 2,000 pounds. The Serendipity headed towards the coast and started the four-hour run back to Bar Harbor.

Nigel told his crew he needed to make a stop near Sols Cliff before docking at Bar Harbor. He was meeting someone there to pick up a surprise gift for his wife and he didn't want to risk her coming to the dock and spoiling the surprise. He assured them it shouldn't take long.

The crew didn't seem to mind or ask questions as long as they got paid. Bad weather was coming anyway. They were just happy they didn't have to spend another night offshore.

The Serendipity was approaching Sols Cliff, and the storm seemed only to be getting stronger. The boat tossed and turned, and the Skipper was fighting the current, doing his best to keep the boat steady. About one hundred yards from the cliffs they laid down the anchor and launched the small dinghy in the rough water.

Derek was to be the only one retrieving the package but the Skipper had Del accompany him. Handling the small raft would take two to manage. Both put on their life jackets and set off towards the shore.

The little outboard motor fought to maintain speed to get them to their intended landing spot. As they approached the cliffs they saw a figure waving at them from the top. This person was carrying a container. Derek could not tell if it was a man or a woman; the rain gear hid their identity.

Once the figure saw it got their attention it dropped the container in the water and ran off. When the dinghy got close, Derek had Del steady the small boat as he retrieved the container. It wasn't too heavy or too large for Derek to handle. He picked it up and turned towards Del. Derek then heard a crack; this wasn't lightning. In horror, he saw Del fall.

The crew heard the sound of the gunshot. Then another shot rang out, narrowly missing Derek.

"What's happening," Nick yelled out. He too saw Del go down.

Nigel started the motor, screaming to Nick, "Pull in the anchor, we gotta get Derek. Justin, do you know how to handle a weapon?"

Justin responded by nodding his head yes as Nigel tossed him a rifle.

"Just shoot up towards the cliffs. We have to draw fire away from Derek," shouted Nigel.

Bam, Bam, Bam Justin shot towards the cliffs, aiming at any moving target. Derek heard the distraction and secured what he retrieved. The Serendipity and the small dinghy closed the gap as shots continued to ring out. Derek could see Del was dead. From all the blood on Derek's face, he knew it was a head-shot. In the cliffs, the gunman returned fire towards the Serendipity, exchanging fire between the small boat and the fishing vessel.

"Nick, help Derek into the boat," the Skipper shouted commands. Nick reached over the railing in a panic, trying to help Derek get on the boat quickly.

Derek told Nick, "Grab the container so I can get myself on."

Ping, ping Nick heard the shots hitting the boat; they were close, splinters of wood showing where the bullets landed.

Ping, ping "Dammit Justin, don't stop shooting back," shouted Nigel. Nick and Derek looked over in Justin's direction. He lay slumped over a lobster cage; and couldn't shoot back because he was dead.

CHAPTER 13

Nigel, Derek, and Nick pulled in the anchor as quickly as possible. Evenings were ending early that far north, even in May. Between the weather and dusk coming on they had adequate cover, but Nigel didn't want to take any chances. They would have to leave the bodies behind and get the hell out of there. They got back just after sunset and headed to Elli's house, where she was waiting.

Nigel felt Elli had been hiding something from him for a while.

"Elli, you need to come clean. What was in that box? For us to fix this, I need to know everything. I know I fucked up, but you know I would've never brought Derek and Nick or anyone else along if I'd known it was going to be this dangerous."

Elli nodded her head, looking over towards Nick, who was trembling but otherwise calm considering what just happened. "We'll talk later."

"Geez Elli, we have two dead deckhands. All of us could have been killed at the cliffs. Why did you have to bring the stuff down to the cliffs? I did recognize you even with all the rain gear. What else can Nick see or hear that will change anything at this point?"

"In the first place, I wasn't supposed to be the one going to the cliffs. I was supposed to hand things over in the parking garage, and my contact was supposed to bring the package down, but I got called just before the handoff. One of my handlers couldn't reach my contact and had spotted possible "unfriendlies" in the garage. There had always been concern security would see me leaving the building with the box. My handler also told me there was a lot of unusual action near the handoff area, so the plan was nixed. The handler in the garage instructed me to go out of the lab's delivery entrance to the cliffs where they were planning on passing the package off to you. They knew of some camera blind spots and I couldn't be tracked if I followed their instructions."

"OK, Let's hear the rest."

" Elli continued, "Since that night in early April, when the young kid, supposedly from the CIA made contact and extortion was put on the table, things had gone a little crazy. Today was insane. As the days moved ahead, I came to find out someone very high up in the CIA organization had strongly requested a big favor be done for them. When I heard this, I couldn't believe they would approach us after so many years, especially with a request of this magnitude."

Nigel was only surprised it had taken them this long.

Elli explained further. "Derek was brought into the mix to be more of a hostage than anything else. The CIA wanted eyes on everyone at all times and wanted as few people as possible involved. Unfortunately, Nick pushed his way into a bad situation."

Lerdell Labs, is one of the preeminent genetic study labs in the world. Elli was in charge of a study analyzing how feasible it would be to use a new technology called Clustered Regularly Interspaced Short Palindromic Repeats or CRISPR (pronounced "crisper"). CRISPR is a family of DNA sequences found in bacteria. DNA carries the genetic code for most organisms, and molecularly defines that organism.

CRISPR DNA sequences are obtained from bacteria that have been attacked by a virus. The bacteria will have remnants of the virus DNA that had infected the bacteria. The bacteria's use of these sequences plays a vital role in their antiviral defense system, much like the human immune system works using antibodies. In Elli's research the use of the technique was primarily focused on coronaviruses. She rarely talked to Nigel about her work. It wasn't because the conversation would be over his head; it was because Nigel was too busy running a lobstering and smuggling business. Plus, the only thing he knew about corona was it was a beer, and great with lime.

"The entire time, after initial contact from the CIA, all they told me was our smuggling operation was needed to retrieve a package from Lerdell Labs, date unknown. In the meantime, it was our responsibility to learn everything we could about the waters off of Sols Cliff. That is why I told you about and asked you to be sure you understood the waters at Sols Cliffs."

What Nigel and Derek didn't know was they would retrieve a package containing all the study records and samples of two vital compounds. The first was ribonucleic acid (RNA). Its principal role in Elli's research on viruses was as a carrier of genetic information. The second compound was newly discovered CAS enzymes, a family of proteins used for genome engineering from the CRISPR project Elli had been heading up for a couple of years. Elli had been made aware of what would be retrieved early on and, should she tell anyone, would be responsible for her husband's and son's deaths.

CRISPR isn't too difficult to understand on an elementary level. It works like the cutting and pasting tool used in word processing programs. Much of the research done in most labs is on DNA, but in Ellie's research, it was being studied to stop RNA based viruses similar to Severe Acute Respiratory Syndrome (SARS).

The process used was to introduce to the host a solution containing a "guide" or "targeting" RNA, looking for a specific genome section particular to the virus. The CAS enzyme then acts like a pair of very tiny scissors and cuts the sequence out, rendering the virus useless.

Elli's project was different. Her team had discovered a way of inserting several guide RNAs and CAS enzymes, some newly discovered, into the solution. That combination could seek out hundreds of targets, significantly increasing the CRISPR's ability to destroy almost any natural or man-made coronavirus or its mutations.

The CIA wanted control of that technology, as did the GRU (formerly the KGB), Mossad, and, even more so, the Chinese MSS. They were even aware an operative had infiltrated Elli's team. Once the project was near completion, they would make their move. Elli was instructed not to publish anything on the study. There was to be no history of it left and she would not be allowed to start another study, or else. Ellie continued, "Well, I guess I should have come clean earlier. The goons at the CIA, or wherever they were from, told me they'd kill you two if anyone found out."

Derek was still a little shook up and in a sarcastic mood. "I guess that didn't matter, did it? They tried to kill us anyway."

"Honey, why would they do that? They didn't have the package yet, and we were cooperating. They had no reason to try to kill us. I don't think our guards would do that either. They'd just make a note of who was in the boat, then report it."

It was at that point Nick finally broke his silence. "I don't think it was CIA or Lerdell guards."

"How would you know that?" Nigel asked

"Because I recognized one of the shooters. I saw him on the cliff for just a second."

"Are you positive?"

"Yeah, When I got to town for this trip, I went to the Chinese take-out place to grab lunch. I saw him come out of the kitchen, where there were two more Asian guys. They were waving goodbye to each other. One looked like the cook or maybe the owner, and the other was wearing a white lab coat."

"Well, you might be more valuable than I thought." Elli mused.

Elli's phone rang. It was Sam Wilder, the head of security at the labs.

As she listened, her eyes grew wider. "Let me get this clear. You found two dead at the base of the cliff, and one at the top."

She turned on the speakerphone.

"Yeah, Dr. Brunetta"

"Did you recognize them?"

"Unfortunately, we recognized two of them. One was Justin Straw, the other Del Williams. We're trying to contact their families. By any chance, do you think Nigel might know anything? I know he had hired them on a couple of times in the past when he was in a pinch."

"I'm not sure, Sam, I haven't seen him for a couple of weeks now, but you may want to call him. As far as I know, he was only out with Derek and another hand named Nick. What about the third guy?"

"Never seen him. Young kid, wearing a suit and a knitted tie that looked like it came from the eighties. By the way, I need you to know someone ransacked your office, and, according to one of your techs, it looks like some files were taken. Do you know why someone would be going through your office?"

"Gosh, I don't, Sam. Do I need to come to the lab?"

"No, we'll lock everything down for the night. I'll see you in the morning."

"Bye Sam"

Derek again sarcastic in tone, "We obviously have one hell of a shit show going…"

All of a sudden, the front door came crashing in, splintering into several pieces. Two men, dressed in black from head to toe, followed the door, pushed their way through what was left. They carried semi-auto rifles and spoke in Mandarin. One was similar in size to the shooter at the cliffs; the other was much taller and heavier but moved like a deer.

The larger one looked over at Elli, and in English, said, "Where is the box?"

"Mom, tell them. It ain't worth dying for."

Elli pointed across the room, "Over there, behind the sofa."

The smaller one grabbed the box. Both intruders ran out the door. After making it across the yard, they got into a black Jeep Wrangler.

No one in the house saw them drive up or leave, but Derek was happy he had installed a state-of-the-art security system a year earlier. It would surely pick up a lot of what went on out there.

CHAPTER 14

The car warning light came on, indicating to Mack they needed gas. More importantly, Mack could see Stephanie needed coffee. Up ahead, he saw a Sunoco and signaled to get off the Blue Star Turnpike. He pulled to the pumps, got out, and proceeded to pump gas. Stephanie also exited the car, sprinting for her coffee.

"Grab me a cup too!" Mack shouted.

They had been driving for a few hours, and it was three-o-clock in the morning. As Mack was filling the car, his cell phone started ringing. Fumbling for his phone from his pants pocket, he could see it was a call from Nick's cell with the familiar ring of "Twisted Sister, We're Not Going to Take It" he set for his son's ringtone.

"Hello Nick, is that you?"

"Yes, Dad, it's me."

"Son, what's going on; where are you?"

"I'm in Bar Harbor, at Nigel's."

"Nigel, who in the hell is Nigel?"

"The Skipper."

"Skipper, you mean the captain? That man lied to me. He told me you left a week ago. What's going on?"

Stephanie walked out of the Sunoco with a coffee in each hand, and a package of Twizzlers clenched between her teeth. She saw Mack on his cell phone, looking upset, dropped both coffees, and ran over to him. By the time she got to him, she didn't realize she still had the licorice in her mouth.

Spitting them out, she asked, "Is it Nick, Mack, who are you talking to, tell me?"

Mack could only shake his head. He couldn't reply to Stephanie; he was questioning Nick intently. Stephanie wasn't going to be ignored.

"Mack damn it, who are you fucking talking to?"

He placed his hand over the phone and said, "Yes, it's Nick."

Stephanie breathed a sigh of relief.

"Dad, we need to talk, something has happened here."

"Son, we were so worried, we are on our way to Bar Harbor."

"You're coming here, when?"

"We are about three hours away. Once we got the call from your Skipper, Nigel, whatever the hell his name is, your mother and I headed out."

"Wait, mom's with you?"

"Yes, of course. You know I couldn't stop your mother from coming to look for you."

Stephanie waited patiently long enough, "I want to talk to our son, right now."

"Dad, I don't want to talk to mom right now; I don't have time to talk to you or her. I just wanted to call to let you know I'm all right and that I'm staying here for a while."

"Son, I don't know what is going on, all I know we have not heard from you, and your boss lied to us. We are coming to Bar Harbor, and we are going to get to the bottom of this."

Mack could hear someone in the background saying. *"Let them come."*

"Dad, I got to go, but we will talk when you get here; the address is 27 North Chapel, Bar Harbor - bye."

CHAPTER 15

Derek couldn't hold back, "Holy Shit, Dad, this thing gets more out of control every second. We need to call the police."

"That's the last thing we need to do. First, the police could tie us to three murders. I asked Justin and Del not to let on they were fishing with me this weekend, so I have to find out if they listened. I know the cops will be visiting very soon if they didn't. Plus, your mom is in deeper shit if they find out she took all the research and backup to her project."

Elli was tired of listening. "Calm down and take some breaths. We need to think through this and not do anything rash."

Turning to Nick, "You know you can't say anything to anybody at this point. All our lives depend on it. I'm sorry you're involved, but all of us are in a nasty situation now."

"Yes ma'am, but don't be sorry. I want to help any way I can."

Nigel couldn't control his curiosity anymore. "Elli, what was in that box worth killing for?"

"It was all the data, RNA, enzymes, and dosing equipment for the CRISPR project I've been working on the past couple of years."

"In layman's terms, please....?"

Elli explained, "Oh, sorry. Do you remember the breakout of a disease called SARS about 15 years ago? Well, it is a type of virus called a corona virus. Fortunately, it burned out quickly. It had an exceedingly high death rate, like 10%, and was spreading from China. The potential for a deadly pandemic was huge. We are talking millions of lives. The Spanish Flu in the early 20th century was also a similar type of virus. It killed a hundred million people."

"So how does that tie into your project?"

"My project was using a relatively new gene-splicing technique called CRISPR used to fight viruses. It is young in its bio-evolution and can fight only one virus at a time, and has low success rates, mostly because if the virus mutates, the treatment can't keep up. We were on the verge of creating what we called Intelligent Crisper or I-CRISPR, similar to Artificial Intelligence in computers, but at a genetic level. It would be able to identify any virus as corona and attack it. It would also recognize when the virus mutated, modifying its targeting method to attack the mutation. We tested it on coronaviruses and got nearly a 90% success rate in our lab tests. That's about as layman as I can get. Does it make sense?"

"Yeah, it does, so why would the Chinese want it bad enough to kill American citizens on American soil?"

"Your guess may be as good as mine, but my guess is it's not for good. We kept the project to ourselves; first, it was still in the lab, and we were not certain of success. There was little reason to make it public. We were wrong about that, though. It was successful beyond belief. The plan was to slowly release the technology to the world once we finished testing it on humans, but keep much of the key elements in US hands unless a corona pandemic threatened the world. If that happened, we would ride in like a white knight on his white horse, saving the day, while making many countries beholding to us at the same time."

"The other reason is if someone or another country obtained this technology ahead of us, they could release a coronavirus to the world while controlling the spread in their own country or other countries friendly to them. The potential for wreaking havoc in the world in terms of human and financial destruction could be an attractive option. The perpetrator of the disease could use the chaos to control just about anyone or anything without firing a shot while losing very few lives in their own country. That's the evil version. Or they could come in with the cure after things degrade severely, making the world think they had benevolently saved them. Not a savior version, but a ruthless, repressing version. What's your guess?"

Nigel was almost speechless after hearing what Elli had to say. "That's a terrifying scenario. After hearing your guess, I don't need to make one. Is that why you talked so little about your work?"

"Yeah, it is, but now we are all into this thing neck deep. If we don't find a way to get that stuff back, we could be in big trouble, although the consequences we may face from the authorities will be nothing compared to a pandemic."

"We shouldn't call the cops right now then. We may have to stonewall them for a while. When the time is right, I'm going to contact some of my friends, still slugging it out in the spy games. At a minimum, I'm sure they will be able to lessen our troubles. First, I want to see if there is anything we can do ahead of that. Derek, get the thumb drive from the security cameras to see if there is anything helpful there. Nick, come outside with me, and we'll check the yard for any clues. Elli, think through the past few weeks to see if you can remember anything unusual or out of place. Let us know when Derek gets back."

Derek returned in about fifteen minutes. He had brought the video up to the point where the perps knocked down the door.

"I didn't see anyone else outside. The two got out of the Jeep with their masks on."

"OK, fast forward to them going out then."

Intently, they all watched as the two ran across the front yard, the smaller one with his arms around the box, the other, the bigger one, almost running backward with his gun pointed in the direction of the house. When they got to the Jeep, the smaller one opened the back door, placing the box gently on the seat.

"Zoom in closer, Derek!"

The smaller guy then opened the driver's door, pulling off his mask before getting in.

"That's the same Asian dude." Nick blurted out.

The other guy was on the opposite side of the car and got in, pulling off his mask inside. You could see an argument between the two, going on in the car.

"Shit, no make on him."

All of a sudden, you could see the bigger guy getting out again. He had his gun raised and was walking toward the house with a purpose. His partner got out and was yelling at him with his weapon raised too. It was apparent the big guy was coming back for more. His face showed "more" meant death. His partner was yelling at him and letting him know he'd be the next one shot if he continued. The big guy slowed down and was either going to turn and shoot, or blink. He blinked, dropped the gun to his side, and reluctantly returned to the Jeep.

"Derek, rewind to the spot you see his face and zoom in as much as you can."

Derek hit rewind, stopped the video, and zoomed in to where if he went any further, the frame would be too blurry to identify anything.

As everyone looked as hard as they could, Nigel, under his breath, but loud enough for Elli to hear him, said, "That can't be him. He's dead."

"That can't be who, and how do you know whoever he is, is supposed to be dead?"

"Elli, do you remember a guy back in the Argentina days who was the go-between from Castro to the Argentinians, and also was a key player in setting up and training the death squads? His name was Gustavo Peralta. That's him."

"I know who you're talking about, but only saw pictures of him. Why would you say he's dead then? I don't recall any news of his death?"

"Elli, I saw him outside your place the night we escaped from Argentina. He was in his car, ready to come for you, so I took care of the problem. Evidently, he somehow survived. I think helping the Chinese steal your project may not be the only reason he's here…"

CHAPTER 16

Nick hung up the phone with his dad and walked into the kitchen where Eliza and Nigel were sitting. "How did it go?" Nigel asked.

"OK, I guess. I didn't tell my dad much, only that I will explain why I didn't come home when they get here."

What are you going to tell them?" Eliza asked, giving Nick an intense, glaring stare.

"The truth, I have to tell them the truth."

"Nick, you know telling them what happened will place their lives in danger, too." Eliza said with that continued stare.

Nigel looking up at Nick, knew he could only be truthful with his parents.

He had been with him for three months and felt confident he would keep calm with his parents. Nick's reaction to what took place at Sols Cliff and Nigel's home proved Nick was trustworthy. Nigel wasn't concerned with Nick's intentions, but genuinely concerned with his parents'.

"So, what do you think they will say, once you tell them?"

"Skip, they will probably tell me to go home with them and leave this mess to you guys. The last week has been well, a clusterfuck, but I have a chance to do something right, something that may affect not just us but also the world. I can't go home after what I saw and learned. The other thing is if we go to the authorities, we may be putting ourselves in more danger than we are now."

"That does make sense…and your parents?"

"I believe they would want to help once they knew what was at stake. My dad and mom are both educated and activists."

"Activists?"

"You know, tree huggers. If they knew a virus could be created to kill millions of people, and what was in that box could stop it, they would want to help any way they can. They won't be able to walk away from this."

"What about calling the authorities? How are you going to stop them from doing that?" asked Eliza.

"The same way you convinced me we can't let this go public right now. Listen, the last two months of catching lobster is a blur. What is not a blur is what happened in the last seven days. I've been scared shitless; I thought I was going to die - twice! If what you told me is all true, then this is bigger than my parents or me. If we can help stop this, then it's worth taking the risk. Maybe my parents' influence on me has taught me something about being part of a bigger picture; I will tell them that. I will tell them you guys have the experience to make this right, and any outside influence may jeopardize the entire planet. I will make them understand!"

Nigel and Eliza looked at Nick and saw the passion in his eyes. Now they both knew they could trust him. Snores could be heard from the living room where Derek was sacked out.

"You should all get some sleep. Your parents will be here in a few hours. I will keep watch," Nigel said yawning.

If the address Nick provided was correct, Mack and Stephanie were sitting in their car what they thought was the Skipper's house. The home was a typical New Englander style. Other than the front door hanging from its hinges, the rest of the house looked well kept, with good paint, and flower pots aligned on the porch.

The house didn't look like what Mack expected. He thought the yard would be covered in weeds, with useless old boats. However, he would soon realize, this was not the Skippers house.

"Mack, are you ready for this?"

"I'm tired as hell, but yes, we need to find out what's going on."

"Stay calm, and maybe I should go to the door first."

"I said I was tired, not upset."

Stephanie knew her husband and could see the anger in his eyes, but she was angry too. She always relied on Mack's even-tempered personality and rarely saw him upset.

She knew she would be the one Mack would have to calm down. But now they were both angry and worried about their son. Mack fumbled with his pack that was in the back seat.

"What are you doing?" asked Stephanie.

"I'm getting my gun."

"Is that necessary?"

"I don't know this Nigel fellow. All I know is our son has been with him for over three months and didn't come home. Who knows what going on there?

Found it." Mack and Stephanie exited the car and walked up to the door. He questioned where he was when he noticed a fake wreath with ribbons on the door.

Nick swung open the damaged door and let Mack and Stephanie in the house. Sitting at the kitchen table were Elli and Derek. Nigel was standing with a cup of coffee in his hand.

"Coffee?" asked Nigel.

"Dad-Mom, this is Nigel, his wife Elli, and their son Derek."

Mack and Stephanie were not in the mood for pleasantries and wanted answers now.

Nigel smiled at them and gestured for them to come into the kitchen and sit down. Derek got up to give up his seat and waved them in. Mack looked puzzled by Nigel's invitation but moved in closer.

"Coffee?" Nigel asked again. This time he motioned to Derek to get back out there and keep watch.

"Will somebody explain what the hell is going on?' exclaimed Stephanie.

"Yes, of course, but first, do you mind placing your gun on the side table?" asked Nigel.

Mack kept it tucked in his back pants and was surprised Nigel could even spot it.

"I prefer to keep it if you don't mind," Mack responded.

Elli finally spoke, "Be my guest, but please don't shoot your ass off."

All four sat around the table. Nick slid a barstool closer to the group. Nigel poured coffee for Mack and Stephanie and waited for Nick to speak.

"Dad, Mom, I need you to put on your open-minded hats; a lot is going on. I will let Nigel and Elli get into the details, but I want to assure you I'm OK, and Nigel is not holding me against my will. Nigel, Elli, and Derek are good people. They are also not exactly the fisherman and researcher they appear to be"

"Son, where is this going?" asked Mack.

"Dad, wait, let me finish. Nigel is a spy for British Intelligence, and Elli works for the CIA and hates Communists."

"I really wouldn't call myself a spy," Nigel broke in.

Nick continued, "Two of my shipmates were shot and killed by an Asian spy who later came to the house with an Argentinian death squad dude for the package of drugs we picked-up."

This time Stephanie broke in, "Asian killers, death squads, spies, CIA, and drugs?"

"Honey, you forgot British Intelligence," chimed in Mack.

Stephanie was not amused and gave Mack her go fuck yourself look.

Nigel could see this was not going well and Nick's parents needed full details. He had to trust them; he had no choice but to talk.

CHAPTER 17

A week had passed since the tragic day Elli's research had been stolen, two local fishermen murdered, and Nigel, Derek, and Nick had been a breath away from being dead. The two tried to explain it to Nick's parents and give them a crash course on viruses, CRISPR, and genetics. It had been a whirlwind of a week and, at the same time, the slowest and most anxious week Nigel and Elli had ever experienced. Both of them empathetically knew Nick's parents must be experiencing similar feelings.

Nick and Derek seemed almost unfazed by the happenings of the past week. They spent most of it setting up security on the property. Nick rather enjoyed making booby traps, especially the ones that exploded when triggered. No damn Argentinian death squad dude was going to get past his and Derek's handiwork.

Nigel started the week by contacting Justin and Del's families to offer his condolences while seeking pertinent information from them at the same time. He was genuinely sorry and concerned for their well-being but had to worry more about his right now. Thankfully, neither of the spouses had any idea who their husband and wife had been with over the weekend. At least, that's what they said. Nigel would have to accept that for now.

The Sheriff's Department was investigating but hitting dead ends on the murders. They were now looking at the records of every security camera they could find in Bar Harbor. Elli's project had funding from the National Institute of Health (NIH), a Federal organization. Since the project was Federal, the FBI was called in to investigate.

One of the FBI's first discoveries was that all of Elli's computer records had also been destroyed, including the backup copies on the company's secure servers. Most of the camera recordings that would have captured Elli's office and any main escape routes had also been erased, which was a sure sign they were dealing with professionals.

The lead investigator was James Johnson, Jr, who had been called J since his college football days. He was convinced this was an inside job, even though no hard evidence pointed in that direction.

J had been in the FBI for almost 20 years. Since childhood J had proven himself to be an astute individual, growing up in a tough neighborhood in Atlanta called Mechanicsville. He was raised by his aunt and uncle who had three kids of their own. They resided in a primarily black section of the town. They both worked extremely hard at keeping J and his cousins on the right track. J took his opportunities when he could, ending up as an honor roll student and an All-State linebacker for Jackson High. He parlayed that into a scholarship at Georgia Tech, where he starred for four years, while earning a BS in biology and a dual minor in pre-law and police science.

Although he had interests in biological research, he always had law enforcement as his first love and set his secret sights on being an FBI agent, so he chased that career straight out of college. J was accepted to training on his first try. He breezed through Quantico and was placed in a role investigating Weapons of Mass Destruction (WMD), especially the biological kind. Within several years he proved himself as a no-nonsense investigator, with a sixth sense in seeing things during investigations his contemporaries couldn't. He also had assignments in the International Operations Division, known as "legat," and the Organized Crime Division. He was almost the perfect fit for this investigation.

Once Nigel had some confidence he wouldn't be under investigation anytime soon he bought some throwaway "burner" phones and got to work calling old friends from the MI6 days, including a few from the CIA and Mossad. Their networks would reach out all over the world.

Although every one of the contacts asked for details, Nigel would only go as far as to e-mail them a rendering of the Asian guy, give them Gus Peralta's name, and tell them their countries' national securities could be in grave danger. Letting out any further details was not a good idea at this point.

What could he tell them? There was no corroborating evidence because of the destruction of the files. Making accusations of any sort could be extremely dangerous to his and Nick's family and potentially to international relations. Nigel knew he didn't have much time before he would have to come clean. He did have the advantage; the FBI would be holding their investigation close to the vest, so only controlled amounts of information would be leaked to any public or other governmental parties in the short term.

Things dragged on for several days after Nigel finished his phone calls. He finally got his first call back from Talia Levy, an old friend, still an integral part of the Israeli Mossad.

Talia fought in the Israeli army back in the late seventies, spending most of her time in Lebanon. She was the only female soldier asked to be on the public relations photos for the Israeli military. She was the supermodel posing with an Uzi most the Israeli boys fell in love with after passing the age of bar mitzvah.

Back in the day, that was acceptable PR. The Israelis were enormously proud of their female soldiers. Once out of her two-year stint, Mossad asked her to join them. It wasn't because of her looks, although they helped; it was because of her guile, smarts, and courage.

She joined Mossad after the US Embassy was taken over in Tehran, starting as a data analyzer. That's when she met Nigel. Nigel was spending a lot of time in Tel Aviv and was assigned to Talia by MI6 to develop information and data networks in the Middle East.

Nigel and Talia's relationship quickly moved past the co-worker to can't get enough of you sex whenever possible stage. After all, they were spies that could end up dead or reassigned in a moment's notice, right? At least, that was their rationalization for banging in the computer room at the drop of a hat. They joked a lot about it, dubbing it their FORTRAN screwing and sandwich, lunch meetings. Their relationship wasn't love, but was moving in that direction.

Unfortunately, their rationalizations turned into reality when MI6 assigned Nigel to Argentina and, shortly after that, Mossad assigned Talia to Moscow. They had not talked with each other since 1981.

Nigel never told Elli about Talia. He never felt the need. As far as he was concerned, Talia was just one of several work relationships he had before meeting Elli. If something ever came up in a conversation about his assignment in Israel, he referred to Talia as "one of my Israeli colleagues." The same would be true concerning this phone call.

"Talia, how are you, my friend? Long time."

"Oh Nigel, I am good, how are you and your lovely wife, Eliza, or Elli, or whatever you want to call her?"

"You know about Elli? How….?"

"Come now, Nigel; you know you can never leave the game. We keep track of everyone and everything. We know about Elli, your son Derek, and even about your little side operation. Who do you think gave you that job to relocate those two Cuban defectors from Bar Harbor to St. John's, Canada last August?"

"Well, I'll be damned! I have to assume they weren't Cuban defectors?"

"We paid you well enough for you to know they weren't."

"No, ask, no tell."

"That's why we hired you, Nigel. OK, small talk is over for now. I'll get to the point—bad news, and not so bad news. The bad news is we haven't been able to track down Peralta. We know he's in the US and was spotted in Boston earlier this week. No one has seen or heard from him since. The better news is we have been able to locate the Asian guy you were pursuing. As it turns out, he's not a Chinese agent, but a freelancer from Hong Kong who does a lot of work for China. He won't turn away money from anyone, including the US, if the pay is right. He surfaced in Shanghai yesterday. His name is Zhang Wei. The word is he is arranging some sort of auction on the dark web, but we haven't seen anything yet. Nigel, you need to tell me what it is he has for sale."

"Talia, I can't right now. There are people I need to protect. I've gotten two killed already. Plus, Elli is key to properly identifying what we are looking for, possibly the only person capable. Getting you, MI6, or the CIA directly involved could also cause a major global political problem. I promise I'll let you know as soon as I feel I'm in over my head."

"Nigel, I'll be happy to work out details should you decide to go to China, but you need to let the pros handle this. You are in over your head."

"I am a pro. Please give me a little time and help. Can I trust you?"

"For now, but no promises."

"Will you let me know if you are going to pull the plug?"

"Of course, Nigel. A word of warning, people are working at the labs who could be dangerous. You need to be careful. The word is Zhang has someone on the inside monitoring every step you and Elli are taking. It could be anyone. I'll keep you posted on what we find out, but you need to watch your backs. Understand, I am not supposed to be helping you, but this is more important than a bunch of bureaucratic rules. My involvement has to be on a need to know basis. Got it?"

"Thanks, Talia. Yeah, I got it."

"Nigel, why did you never contact me again?"

"I thought you said you knew everything, so you must know about me and Elli's history."

"I know about it, Nigel, but you didn't answer my question. Why did you never contact me again?"

"Another conversation for another time Talia. We'll talk soon." Nigel was getting uncomfortable with the conversation.

As soon as Nigel hung up on his burner phone, his personal cell rang. "Caller Unknown." Should he answer it? He didn't need another robocall asking his opinions about politics. He really could not care less about the subject. He decided to answer anyway.

"Hello"

"Who were you just talking to on your other phone?"

Nigel, startled and suddenly in fight or flight mode, ran to the window and pulled the drapes a little to peek out. How in the hell did this person know he was talking on another phone?

"Nice to see you again, hombre. I guess you thought that bullet in the head killed me."

"Peralta, what the fuck you doing hanging around with some Chinese spy, stealing shit that could hurt a lot of people? After surviving the bullet and the election purge of all you assholes back in the eighties, you should have retired somewhere like Nicaragua, or Peru, or Bumfuck Egypt."

"My friend, I kill people for a living. That's what I do well. Why retire? I'm a hired gun. The guy I was with hired me to be his protection and muscle while carrying out his little escapade here in picturesque Maine. Rumors had it I might run into you, and possibly sweet, dead Eliza. I guess those rumors were true."

"So, why are you calling? You certainly don't owe me a phone call. I could see by our security footage you were headed back to the house for some unfinished business. Why'd you stop?"

"Well, Zhang reminded me he was paying me, and killing you, your family, or anyone else with you, wasn't what he was buying. He also reminded me you and your son would probably be heavily armed, so I may want to reconsider."

"You didn't answer my question. Why the phone call?"

"Mostly to fuck with you, but to also let you know we are watching you. Any attempt to contact the authorities will result in your immediate deaths. Please don't do that. I am looking so forward to killing all of you myself when this is over."

"So, here we are. I know the situation is screwed up, and I know you are very concerned about your son. You also need to be concerned about yourselves. We have to try to resolve this before getting anyone else involved. This project was being carried out in complete secrecy for a good enough reason; people are being killed."

"Wait, why not tell this to the authorities?"

"Because we don't know which authorities are involved. Saying something to the wrong person could put us into even more danger."

Mack looked over at Stephanie as if he were at a loss for words. "Steph, we may not have a choice right now. What are you thinking?"

"I think we ought to kill these mother fuckers before Peralta does, walk away, and never look back."

"Honey, you know we can't do that. Peralta or Zhang would just come after us to get rid of anyone with knowledge of the situation."

Stephanie shook her head, "Maybe you are right, but I need to ask one more question. Nick, why in the hell did you wait a week to call us? We have been worried sick. We didn't know what had happened to you."

"Mom, Nigel took my phone until he knew he could trust me. I called as soon as I had it back."

"Nigel, you are a real asshole."

CHAPTER 18

Mack paced the kitchen floor in disbelief of what he just heard from Nigel. Mack's father was in the service and worked his way up to Lieutenant in Delta Force in the Army and later became a Navy Seal. Mack's father rarely spoke of his time in the Navy, especially in the special forces. Mack wanted a different life for himself and his sons, as he witnessed his father's slow decay at the bottom of a bottle. Mack thought for a moment of the irony of his situation, a college professor getting caught up in the life his father led and now, joining his son in a similar experience.

"Steph, we're not going to kill anybody, but it seems as long this Peralta or Zhang fellow is alive, Nick will always be looking over his shoulder. You need to take Nick and get out of here, go somewhere safe."

"Safe, we are going to go, and what about you?"

"I am not going anywhere," Nick jumped in.

Mack continued his pacing, trying to figure this thing out. He was terrified for his family's safety and terrified of what Nigel told him. Rubbing his eyes then his brow, he turned towards Nigel, "Why did you ever get my son involved in this? He is innocent; only a civilian in your dangerous game?"

"Mack, I never intended for your son to get caught up in all this. He was planning to be on his way home before all this took place. However, it is what it is, and we can't change that no matter how much I wish I could."

Elli looked at Stephanie and Mack, seeing their concern for their son. She liked Nick and in the short seven days, drew close to him and appreciated his passion for helping. However, she knew Nigel was right. They needed to keep moving forward, and time was running out. Feeling for Mack and Stephanie, she had to say something to put them somewhat at ease, "Zhang is not in the country; he is in Shanghai trying to sell the formula to the highest bidder. I don't think you have to worry about him or his men. They are long gone."

"What about this Gus Peralta fellow, will he stay behind?" Steph asked Elli.

"I don't know, Nigel has more intel on him."

"Well, Nigel?" Steph asked again.

"I think it depends where I end up. I trust Peralta is still here in the States, maybe in the Boston area."

"Massachusetts? That's too close to home, why would he go there?"

"Don't know. He is after me. He is not only a hired gun for Zhang, but this is also personal for him. He wants me dead. He could be there in hopes he can learn from you where I plan to be. Lucky you are here."

"Well, Nigel, that's just fine, glad you got it all figured out. So, what's your plan and how does it involve my son." Mack asked, not hiding his sarcasm.

"Elli and I talked, and we have a plan. You two were not supposed to be part of the plan, and we will make adjustments. Derek and I are going to Shanghai; I'm trying to meet with a couple of my MI6 buddies I can trust. We need to find Zhang before he sells the research.

As for Elli, she is staying here.

There is a rat at the lab she needs to uncover. We don't know who or what job they have in the lab, but they can still cause damage. Elli needs to find the source and their connection to Zhang, and Nick volunteered to help her."

"Nope, no way. You're not putting my son at risk," Steph objected.

"Mom, I already volunteered; you can't stop me. You and Dad always taught me to do what is best. All this social responsibility and caring for those other than yourself. Well, this is bigger than us and can harm or kill a lot of people. I can't walk away. I won't."

Mack and Stephanie knew Nick was right. They taught Nick the values of doing his best and helping those who can't. Mack knew his son could not walk away.

"Steph, as much I don't want to agree, we need to help Nigel and Elli. He turned to Nigel and asked, Wŏmen mō bāng zhù nì (*how can we help*)?"

"You speak Mandarin?" Elli asked with a surprised look.

"With a name like Griego I get that a lot. I do speak a little Mandarin, my foreign language elective in college. I've always wanted to go to China."

"Nigel, it looks like Mack is going with you. You can use an interpreter, and Steph, you're staying with me."

"Wait! Wait! Mack, what in the fuck did you agree to do?" yelled Stephanie.

"Staying here and helping Elli is the logical and safest choice for you and Nick.

"I'm going with Nigel and Derek, they can use an extra hand, and my Mandarin may help. I can't sit here and let this formula get into the wrong hands. Nigel, if somehow we let Peralta know you're going to Shanghai, he will follow you there."

"Already arranged. That madman will follow me to hell to get a piece of me. I already have the word out I'm heading to Shanghai; this will get him out of the US. I like the way you think, professor, and I accept your help."

Stephanie relented and agreed to help Elli. This way, she could stay close to Nick. Elli explained to Stephanie she and Nick could help by being a set of eyes and ears in town to report back any concerns. Elli told them she would be at the lab trying to figure out who the snitch was. Although this would be a little riskier, it would isolate Steph and Nick from exposure to lab officials and, more importantly, the government.

The conversation suddenly switched gears when Derek came running into the kitchen, screaming, "Dad, someone is pulling up into the drive."

Nigel and Elli ran to the living room window and peeked through the blinds. A white SUV was at a stop, but no one got out.

"Mack, do you have that gun handy?" as Nigel and Elli both revealed weapons of their own.

A man slowly stepped out of the SUV and carefully scanned the property.

After he looked everything over, he yelled out to the house. "Elli, are you home? I don't want to come any closer. Whoever laid out those booby traps did a poor ass job, but I don't want to take any chances. Elli, it's Sam Wilder."

CHAPTER 19

Derek led Sam along path of least resistance, where he carefully maneuvered through the drive then up the steps to the house.

"Thanks, Derek," Sam said in relief. After entering the house, Sam paused and looked around the room, inspecting the walls, ceilings, and doors.

"There are no booby traps in the house, Sam, you can relax," Nigel said while watching Sam, who seemed to have little reassurance.

"Why all the devices, Nigel?"

"Sam, Derek, and his friend set those up to ward off potential thieves. They're not real," Elli responded.

"Who are your friends?"

"Sam, why are you here, any news about the break-in?" Elli continued.

"No, not really, but that asshole, FBI mother fucker is giving me a lot of shit. He is implying my security sucks and that a first grader could sneak in and steal shit. He also thinks this is an inside job."

"I've heard Agent Johnson is top-notch; and one of the FBI's best agents in this area. He can supposedly spot weaknesses in security better than most.

He wants to meet with me to discuss what was taken and why."

"Elli, you can't tell him, we have to keep this within our organization."

"Really, you have a break-in at your lab, two people are dead, the FBI is involved, and you want to keep this hidden?" asked Mack.

Sam, showing some paranoia, asked, "Who in the fuck are you? Nigel, Elli, who are these people?"

BAM, BAM…glass shattered, everybody in the room fell to the floor. BAM, BAM… wood splintered, lamps exploded…, then a boom! One of Derek's devices went off. It wasn't a massive boom, but enough to send the intruder flying off his feet.

The explosion gave Nigel and Elli much needed time to return fire. The intruder did not return fire, but you could hear the engine roar as the car drove off.

"Everybody OK?" asked Nigel, looking over at Elli, who was alive. Scanning the room, Nigel could see bodies on the floor. Then, thankfully, he saw Derek and Nick get up, acknowledging they were fine. However, the body of Sam Wilder laid silently on the red-stained carpet. The hole in his forehead said all it had to say. Nick looked where his father and mother were standing; he could see the horrific sight of his father holding his mother in his arms. She was not moving.

Stephanie's eyes flickered then opened wide-eyed and in panic, screamed, "What happened?" Mack realized his wife had been shot in the arm, but continued to examine her body for more wounds. Elli rushed over to Steph, pushing Nick aside, who was staring down at his mother. She knelt next to Mack, telling him to put pressure on the wound. She also looked for more injuries, but could not see any more damage. "She will be fine, but does need to go to the hospital and get fixed up."

"Fuck, now my wife has just been shot!" Shouted Mack.

Elli, looking down at Sam's body, "Listen, we are lucky to be alive, except for Sam over there. Nigel, this had to be your friend Gus. Thank God a booby trap went off, or we would all be visiting the morgue. Nigel, you, Derek, and Mack need to make plans to go to Shanghai; we need to make it public to get Gus out of America. I will take care of Steph and get her to the hospital. I will also need to reach out to Agent Johnson for help with posting a guard with Steph and dealing with the local authorities."

Mack was reeling from the attack. "I can't leave my wife now; she needs me. This thing just got real, and we are way over our heads. I have a family to protect."

"Dad, this thing got real for me last week. I knew the risk when I agreed, and so did you and mom. Elli is right; we need to get this assassin out of the country. If we don't, we will still be in danger. I will be here for mom; you need to help the Skipper get this guy."

CHAPTER 20

Agent Johnson made his way to Mt. Desert Hospital shortly after Elli's call. He was working out of Bangor from his field office in Portland; which was only an hour's drive to Bar Harbor and Lerdell Laboratory, and, more importantly, access to an airport.

On such short notice, he needed to find an agent in the area available to stay and watch over Elli's friend Stephanie. He called in a favor and found Agent Miller who was on desk assignment in Portland.

On his way to the hospital Agent Johnson made a few other calls and learned the local Sheriff and his men were on their way to Elli's home. Elli told them Sam was dead. He didn't know much about Mack, Stephanie, or their son Nick. All he knew is he had a mess on his hands, three dead, one head of security at Lerdell Laboratory, and a recently wounded woman. With Nigel and Derek out of the country the Sheriff would consider them as the main suspects.

Mt. Desert Hospital was a twenty-minute drive, but only took Mack ten minutes.

Nigel, Elli, and Derek followed behind in their car to continue their drive to Bangor to catch their flights, after stopping at the hospital.

As the car rolled to a stop, Nick ran inside the Emergency room, yelling for help. He caught the attention of an orderly who quickly brought a wheelchair to the car. Stephanie was pale and had lost a lot of blood despite the pressure Nick had on her wound. Thankfully, she was conscious, breathing, and insisting on walking in herself.

Mack would have none of that and sat her in the chair and wheeled her in. A nurse guided them to roll her into one of the vacant rooms where other nurses were waiting to work in their patient immediately.

Moments after a doctor entered the room, he examined the severity of her wound and ordered her straight into surgery.

"Mack, we got to go; your wife is in good hands," Nigel carefully said.

"Can't we stay for a few minutes? I don't want to leave without knowing she is stable."

"Mack, the surgery may take a few hours; we don't have time. It's an hour drive to Bangor, and our flight leaves in two hours. Nick can call you with updates, and if there is a problem, we can rent you a car, and you can drive back to the hospital."

Mack looked at his son with trepidation. He was leaving his wife and his son to save the world. He couldn't imagine a world without them and thought for a moment, if we die, let's all die together, fuck the world. However, Mack knew the higher purpose and nodded his head in agreement.

"Let's go."

Agent Johnson pulled into the parking lot, got out of his car, and lit a cigarette, inhaling the much-needed nicotine. After finishing his smoke, he flicked it on to the grass and walked into the building visitors' entrance and called Elli's cell phone. "I'm here, where are you?"

"Meet me in the cafeteria," Elli responded.

Agent Johnson looked up at the signs that provided directions to labs, x-ray, surgery, and finally, the hospital's cafeteria. He walked into the cafeteria and saw Elli sitting at a corner table with a young man, maybe 20, with black, messy shoulder-length hair. Innocent looking enough, must be one of the family members Elli described. He walked over to Elli and extended his hand.

"Hi, Elli, and who is this?

"I'm Nick, Nick Griego.

You must be the FBI Johnson dude."

"My friends call me J, but you call me Agent Johnson. Are we clear on that son?" J sternly said.

Elli jumped in, "J, how the hell are you? The last time I saw you was a couple of years ago when you gave us our Active Shooter training. I heard an Agent Johnson would be involved but didn't make the connection. My, you've moved up in the world."

"That was more than a couple of years, Elli. Would you believe it's been over five? Where is Nigel? I thought he would be here?"

"We'll get to that in a minute."

"You haven't asked how my mom is doing." Nick interrupted.

"Hey kid, sorry to hear about your mom. How is she doing?"

"She's been shot. How do you think she is doing?" Nick quickly shouted back.

"Elli, I thought this kid was on board helping. He seems a little emotional."

"His mom will be fine; doctors are patching her up now. Nick, why don't you go ahead and call your dad. I'm sure he would like to hear from you. J and I need to talk."

As Nick left the room, Agent Johnson took an empty seat and sat close to Elli. He didn't want anyone nearby to hear their conversation.

"Just in the last hour the police have been to your house. They didn't enter due to all those devices you guys planted. They had to call a bomb squad from Bangor to secure the area. So, Elli, what will they find in your house once they can gain access?

"Sam Wilder's body."

"Jesus Elli, what is going on that is so damned important three people had to die?"

"CRISPR."

"CRISPR, what is CRISPR?

"It's a biotechnology used to fix or destroy parts of DNA chains."

"OK, so why is this so important someone would want to steal it?"

"We first thought it was stolen for the money it would bring, which is only partially true. The bigger reason is that although it can do a lot of good, it also can be weaponized in an unbelievably bad way."

"Why would Lerdell Labs create such a weapon; they have no military contracts?

"It wasn't meant to be a weapon; it was designed to be a medical procedure to stop future viruses or cure genetically caused diseases that currently have no treatment or cure. We created it to be a medical benefit to the world but in the wrong hands it can be used for just the opposite."

"I think I'm tracking. This technology can kill people by creating a virus we haven't heard of, or seen the likes of."

"That's only partially true. The larger picture is, the process can also save people who get almost any virus. If a virus is created and released, the country with this technology can decide who lives and who dies. Almost as important would be their control over what economies live or die and possibly what world leaders live and die. Can you imagine the power? There is more. Through his sources, Nigel tells us the package is up for sale in China. Many countries want the technology badly and are willing to pay top dollar for it.

Nigel and Derek are on their way to meet up with their contact in Shanghai. Mack, Nick's father, is going with them too!"

"A civilian, why would Nigel allow that?"

"He needed the help, and Mack volunteered. Remember, as far as anyone is concerned, Nigel is a civilian too."

"Yeah, but based on what you have let on from his past, he can take care of himself. China, we may be able to work with, what if North Korea, Russia, or Iran gets in on the bidding or some other leader with a bone to pick with us. Who is Nigel working with over there?"

"Zhiban Jack Wang; J, we have to keep this quiet for now. There may be others involved, and we can't let the media get ahold of this."

"We know about Zhiban."

"Are there others besides that crazy Zhiban?"

"Yes, we believe Wang is working with the CIA or MI6, but not 100% sure."

CHAPTER 21

After leaving the cafeteria, Nick made his way back to the surgery waiting room where he found a young woman, maybe in her early twenties, sitting by herself. She was Asian with big brown eyes, auburn shoulder-length hair tied into a ponytail. However, it was her Redsox baseball cap, skimpy white shorts and tight-fitting tank top that first caught his attention.

Trying not to stare, Nick believed he had seen this girl before, but couldn't place her. She was reading through one of the expired celebrity magazines. On the cover of PEOPLE was a picture of Ryan Reynolds with the heading: *Sexiest Man Alive*. After a few glances at the young woman, he made his move to break the silence, "I thought he was great in Deadpool."

The woman glanced at Nick with a puzzled look then turned the magazine over to see the cover. She shook her head and turned the magazine back over, continuing to read.

Nick, embarrassed by his failed attempt to start a conversation, picked up a magazine, burying his face between the pages.

"I think Idris is ten times better looking," the young woman finally spoke.

"Excuse me?"

"Your cover."

Nick turned his magazine over, and the MAXIM cover read: *Idris Ebla – "I Spend My Life Being Chased By Women."*

The young woman continued, "What is really impressive is that your magazine is six years old and Idris still looks sexy. Hi, I'm Genji; my friends call me Gen."

'Hi Gen, I'm Nick, just plain Nick. So, what brings you to this waiting room? It can't be the excellent reading material."

"Nope, not here for the magazines or the food in the cafeteria. My brother is having surgery for a second time."

"Second time?"

"Someone tried to kill my brother last week. He was shot. Surgeons removed the bullet and kept him here because he was not responding to any stimulation. He had brain waves, so I wasn't ready to pull any plug. Then he started hemorrhaging early this morning.

By the look on the surgeon's face, it looks dire; he might die."

Nick's face turned down towards the pages of the magazine in a blank stare.

He remembered where he had seen this girl before. She was at the Chinese take-out place behind the counter, taking his order. Could there have been more than one shooter on the cliffs, and could Justin have been so lucky to hit someone by shooting randomly up at the cliffs? Nick wanted to ask what happened but knew he shouldn't go there.

This girl is connected somehow.

She may be innocent and have no idea what her brother was up to, but he couldn't risk it. "I'm sorry about your brother. I hope he recovers."

"Oh God, I'm sorry I haven't asked you why you were here."

"My mother, she has been hurt. Doctors say she's fine; I'm just waiting for her to come out of surgery." Nick paused, looked down again at the magazine.

Don't ask, don't ask, he kept thinking to himself, too late.

Gen broke into his thoughts and asked, "What happened to your mother?"

Before Nick could respond, the doctor came into the room. By the look on the doctor's face, Nick could tell it was not good news. Dreading the doctor was coming to talk to him, he was relieved he spoke to the pretty Asian woman. Tears rolled down her face, and she started to tremble.

Nick knew her brother didn't make it.

Seeing Gen's grief, he thought it would be best to leave her alone to speak with the doctor. He decided to go back to the cafeteria to tell Elli about the dead man and the possibility he was on the cliffs that horrible night. Passing by the nurse's station, he asked about his mother to learn she was out of surgery and in recovery. The nurse at the station said she was doing well, but couldn't take visitors. Knowing she was well, he continued walking to the cafeteria. Elli and Agent Johnson were still at the table where he left them.

Walking up to them, he interrupted their conversation, "I have some news."

"Is your mother out of surgery, is she OK?" asked Elli.

"Yes, she is fine and in recovery."

"That's great news, have you seen her?" Elli continued.

"No, not yet. No one is allowed. Elli, that is not why I came back. I have some new information."

J could see Nick was upset, and this had nothing to do with his mother, "What is it, son?"

"There was a girl, a woman in the waiting room. She told me her brother was shot last week. I was present when the doctor told her he had died."

"OK, and this is important; why?" J said, looking up at Nick.

Elli jumped in, "What is it, Nick? You can speak in front of Agent Johnson."

"I saw her at the Chinese restaurant; she works there. I think her brother may have been at the cliffs that night."

Elli motioned to Nick to sit down. She and J moved closer to Nick to keep the conversation a little more private.

Nick continued speaking, "At the restaurant, she was behind the counter taking my order. I also noticed three Asian men in the kitchen. I recognized him later as a shooter at the cliffs when we reviewed the film of him and his partner shooting up Ellie's house. I didn't see anybody else at the cliffs, but maybe her brother was there. There has to be some connection; this can't be a coincidence."

Elli looked over her shoulder and whispered to Nick, "This man had to have been shot more recently if he was in surgery this morning. We can't chase leads that make no sense."

"Elli no, she told me he was shot a week ago. He was in surgery today because he started bleeding again badly. She was so hurt when she heard the news about her brother dying; I couldn't stay in the room and watch her cry."

Agent Johnson shaking his head, looked at Elli, "That makes four dead over your formula."

"We don't know that; we don't know who shot this man, or whether or not he was at the cliffs. It could have been anything, a drive-by, a robbery."

"Elli, a drive-by in Bar Harbor, I don't think so."

"Nick, if you saw this man, would you be able to place him at the restaurant?" asked Elli.

"See him, I can't see him; he is dead somewhere in this hospital."

"Yes, you can. J, we will need your help."

"My help?"

"Yes, your FBI credentials will open a lot of doors, hospital doors."

Agent Johnson knew what Elli was asking. All three got up and made their way to the nurse's station. The crime of a man being shot and killed, the hospital staff would have to cooperate with a Federal Official and not interfere. Nick hoped he wouldn't see Gen again. Seeing her would make him feel uncomfortable because of the short connection they had flirting with each other.

Agent Johnson flashed his credentials to the nurse at the station and asked who was in charge. The nurse looked up at the Agent then down at his FBI identification.

She quickly got up and went through the double doors marked AUTHORIZED PERSONNEL ONLY to see if the surgeon was still with the recently deceased man.

After a few minutes, the surgeon came out through the double doors, still in his scrubs stained with blood. "I'm Dr. Bellows, how can I help you?"

"Dr. Bellows, I'm Agent Johnson with the FBI, and these two are here to help me identify the body."

"Identify the body? His sister identified him last week."

"I may have misspoken; they are here as possible witnesses to a shooting. He had similar characteristics to your patient."

"Characteristics, you mean Asian?"

"Yes, Asian. What did his sister tell you? Does she know how he got shot?"

"You're going to have to take this up with his sister or local authorities.

All I know he was brought in last week with a gunshot wound to his chest."

"We are going to have to see the body."

"Agent Johnson, yes, of course, walk this way."

The surgeon walked them through the double doors and into a small room. This must have been a holding room before the Coroner picks up the body. The room was dimly lit, and the body laid on a gurney covered in bloody sheets. Despite Nick's hopes, Gen was in the room, wiping the dried blood from her brother's face. She looked up at saw Nick amongst the strangers that entered the room. "You, why are you here, did you know my brother?"

Nick's heart sank. He didn't know how to respond and hoped Agent Johnson would say something. It was Dr. Bellows who spoke, "They are with the FBI, they are investigating a shooting. Agent Johnson hopes these two can help with who may have shot your brother."

Agent Johnson wanted to keep the sister out of the conversation and the room. "Miss, sorry for your loss. We are here on official FBI business; we need for you to leave the room."

"Leave the room, who in the fuck are you to tell me to leave. I want to know what happened to my brother. Nick, what do you know, why are you here? Is this why you started a conversation with me in the waiting room?"

Nick stood there in silence; he couldn't give her an answer. He didn't want Gen to know about his mother being in the hospital and connected to Zhang. He had to protect his mom.

Elli asked Gen, "Where was your brother shot? When did this happen?"

"I don't know where this happened. All I know, he was brought to my house bleeding."

"When was this, who brought him?" Elli persisted.

"Last week, Sunday night."

"Who brought him to your house?"

"A family friend, Zhang."

Nick walked over to the table and looked down at the man's face. Gen turned her attention to Nick. "I know you; you have been to our restaurant. I just saw you a few weeks ago. Why are you here?"

Nick's eyes fixated at Gen for a moment, then looked at Elli, "Yes, this is him. He is the man I saw with Zhang Wei at the restaurant."

CHAPTER 22

Wednesday Evening May 22, 2019 - Shanghai

"Ladies and gentlemen, we have begun our descent into Shanghai PVG airport. Please turn off all portable electronic devices and stow them until we have arrived at the gate. In preparation for landing in Shanghai, be certain your seat back is upright and your seat belt is fastened....Blah...blah...blah."

Derek thought the flight would never end. Fifteen hours in the middle seat with Nigel and Mack to the left of him, two strangers to the right, playing their phone games, and a family behind him with two, very unruly toddlers. Between the "beep, boop, bop" of the phones, the kids behind him crying and kicking his seat, not to mention his leg cramps; he wasn't sure he would be sane when he exited the plane. The only saving graces were he could watch movies the whole way and drink as much alcohol as he wanted.

When the plane finally reached the gate, almost everyone immediately started fighting for a spot in the aisle. Derek had to wonder, where in the hell did they think they were going?

At the same time, making her way to the back of the plane, fighting through the gauntlet of impatient passengers and ducking luggage being pulled out of overhead storage, was one of the flight attendants. When she arrived at their row, she looked down at Nigel.

"Mr. Shackelford?"

"Yes?"

Passing a piece of paper to him, "I was asked to give you this." Turning around, she headed back to the front of the plane.

Mack was also watching all this unfold. "Well, that was interesting. What does it say?"

"It only has a name on it and that he will meet us in the receiving area outside customs. Mack, before we get out there, I feel like I need to first thank you for coming along. I truly appreciate it. I know you'd rather not be a part of this mess. On top of that, I also need to ask a big favor; I know one of the biggest reasons you came was to help translate, but please be careful by speaking English as much as possible. No one must know you can speak Mandarin. If people here think you don't understand what they're saying, it could be invaluable for you to be able to eavesdrop."

"No problem, I understand. I'll be keeping my ears open and mouth shut unless, of course, we need directions, or I can help get Derek laid. Deal?"

"Deal"

Mack, Nigel, and Derek made it through immigration, luggage, and customs in less than an hour which, for Pudong International, was about as quick as it got. Outside in the receiving area was a mass of people with their signs waving. Most of them had a person's last name or business name on it. After some searching, Nigel saw the one with "Shackelford." As they walked in that direction, the sign holder could see they were coming his way.

Hand held out, "Mr. Shackelford, good to meet you. My name is Zhiban Wang. Everyone calls me Jack."

"Jack, good to meet you. This is my son Derek, and my associate, Mack. Please call me Nigel."

"Good to meet you guys; I will be your liaison and protection while you are here in China. Your friend Talia Levy requested my help. She is monitoring the situation and standing by in case we need her. Talia told me she filled you in on your cover stories. As a review, you are in China to make contacts with seafood importing companies about doing business with Serendipity, which we will do to legitimize the trip. You are also planning on vacationing a little bit just in case we have to travel around. I hope you studied the rest of the cover; you may need it. Your visas are good for thirty days. That should be plenty."

As they walked to the car, Jack filled them in on his remarkably fascinating background. He was born in rural Mongolia, which made sense when you saw him. He was taller than average, lean, and muscular. He also had a strong forehead, nose, and jawline, sporting a rough beard that was heavier at the chin and mustache areas. He was what you might expect to see in a National Geographic article on the Kazakh Eagle hunters in the Altai mountains of Mongolia. He did present himself as much more metropolitan though, with his custom suit and nicely coiffed hair.

Jack grew up as a miner's son. Their family didn't have much. He didn't even have proper shoes until his late teens. He was a smart kid, but a little bit of a troublemaker. In his early teens, the party authorities told him he would be going to the mines to work due to his lack of attention at school. Upon hearing that, Jack immediately apologized and begged for one last chance to do things right. He knew he had more to do in life than be a miner. Fortunately, for him, his request was granted. That unusual act of kindness from the village leaders changed his life forever. You could also say it sealed his fate.

Jack moved on to be the top student in his village. He was chosen to represent the village at Peking University in Beijing, where he excelled in international business and English. He bonded with an American English professor on loan from the North Carolina State University. They became good friends.

When he graduated his professor and friend recruited him to come to the States to get his Master's degree. After three tries and failures at a visa, the fourth was the charm but required the intercession of a US senator. China Immigration finally gave him the go-ahead. While in the US, Jack earned his Master's in finance and went into banking, working in North Carolina for one of America's largest banks. Within the next few years the CIA recruited him as an asset. They set him up in his own international trade business in the seafood industry and moved him back to Shanghai to start his business.

"I know you guys are probably hungry and beat. We'll grab some food on Láowái Lu (Foreigner Street), and I'll drop you off at the hotel, which is nearby. We can go over the details in the morning." The rest of the ride was pretty quiet for a couple of reasons. The biggest was that Mack, Nigel, and Derek were awestruck.

Jack decided to take them on the scenic route via the Pudong District, under the Huangpu River, and through the Bund.

In Pudong they were able to go past The Jin Mao Tower, which houses the world's highest hotel, the Shanghai World Financial Center, and the Shanghai Tower. The latter being the second tallest building in the world. Passing into the Bund, you could see architecture that depicted the Western influence of the late 19th and early 20th Centuries. Beyond, in all directions, were skyscrapers as far as you could see, all different shapes, sizes, and colors. It was like being in a futuristic science fiction movie. Mack thought to himself, "*This is why I wanted to come to China*."

Both Foreigner Street and the hotel were located in a part of the city on the other side of the Huang Pu River, called Hongqiaou (hōng chow). It is an area where many, mostly Western ex-pat, enclaves are located (thus, a place you would not be surprised to see a "Foreigner Street").

The street itself is located in a vibrant, fun area of town with an international blend of restaurants and bars, including a couple of very typical Chinese bars.

Jack warned the guys to try to stay away from those bars, if possible. As a warning, he gave them the skinny on how they operated. Once in the bar girls serve you as much as you can drink while playing dice games with you, mixed in with some flirting for tips. They drink soft drinks, making you think they are inebriated too, finally reeling you in by asking you to play pool when they know you are past your drinking limit. The final blow happens when they pool shark you out of the rest of your cash.

After a short walk, they took a seat at the Thai restaurant. Nigel couldn't hold himself back any longer, "What have you got so far, Jack? Anything relevant?"

"Not a lot. I'm hoping for more tonight so we can discuss it in the morning. We know Zhang is in Shanghai and has been spotted in this area more than once. We have seen some cryptic messages on the dark web indicating some especially important biomaterial will be auctioned off on Saturday, which is three days away. We also are fairly sure this is what we are looking for because whoever is running the ad is requesting some very concise information, including bank account numbers. They also require that a minimum of $100 million be deposited in those accounts. Your friend Talia's people are looking into it."

"Jesus, my wife was working on something worth $100 million?"

"Probably much more than that to the right people or, should I say, wrong people, considering a hundred million is the minimum. I hope to know more in the morning."

"OK"

Silence returned as they finished their pad thai, larb gai, and basil mu. Of course, several Singhas were enjoyed by each of them.

Jack picked up the bill and they headed back up the street towards the car, which was parked at a knockoff mall called Pearl City. Jack smiled and shook his head. He always did that when he was around Pearl City. It never ceased to amaze him how all the foreigners with money wanted cheap knockoffs and would negotiate over a dollar. Yet, relatively poor Chinese citizens would spend a fourth of their yearly salary on a real Gucci purse with no negotiation at all.

It also amused him China proclaimed they had eliminated these markets before the Olympics to appease America. In reality, they had only moved them from the outside to more legitimate looking indoor locations. They never intended to eliminate them. Too many citizens were making money off of the gullible Westerners.

As they walked past the Brazilian churrascaria near their car, unbeknownst to them and not more than a hundred feet away, another conversation was going on in the back of that restaurant. The topic was them.

"Yeah, cut me off some of that tenderloin, and a few of those chicken wings. Zhang, has anyone spotted those guys?"

"Gus, first let me tell you, I'm not here to discuss finding and killing your new best friends, I'm here to make sure you know you are being paid to keep eyes on them until this deal is done. Once I've sold the package and am safely off the mainland you can do what you want. Remember, whatever that might be, I don't know you if you get into any trouble. Do you understand?"

"I understand."

"We know an Asian met them when they arrived. We lost them in traffic after that. We'll have to start checking the hotels. That may take a while. There are thousands of just four and five star hotels here. We are not even guaranteed they are in one."

"Well, your guys better get on it. I can't protect you or take care of my business if we don't know where they are. By the way, that package better fetch what you think because your bill just went up a mil. I wasn't planning on coming to China."

CHAPTER 23

Thursday May 23, 2019 - Shanghai

The sun was just beginning to rise over Shanghai. Because of the city lights it is sometimes hard to tell exactly when the day was starting or ending, but today was a rare clear day in the city. You could see the sky. The hues of pink, orange, and purple were blending on the horizon and the metropolis was starting to wake up.

"Dad, would you go back to bed? It's only 6:00 AM."

"Sorry, Derek; my mind is racing. I can't shake this feeling we are missing something important. Why was the project so secretive? If it had the potential for so much good, as your mom said it had, why not go public and open up the study to more resources rather than having it go on secretly in a back lab?"

"Maybe it was the potential for something bad they were worried about, Dad. She did say their motives were to introduce it when the time was right, using it as a tool for political and power reasons."

"That makes sense on the face but there's still something missing. If the project had been made public, yes, the entire world would have known about it, but there would have been better security and data backup. More than likely there wouldn't have been a reason to steal it or kill people to get it. Also, the same political and power goals could have been achieved. The other thing that is bugging me is, why would the CIA be interested in stealing the information? Shouldn't they have been in on the secret and hanging around to protect it, not set your mom up to steal it for them? Right before Sam got shot, he was arguing with your mom about reporting the details to the FBI. I'm not sure why. Now I'm not so certain we were the main targets the second day Gus showed up. The bullets went to Sam first. I'm wondering if Gus used that opportunity to deal with Sam then handle us at the same time?"

"So, you think Sam may be the inside guy?"

"I'm not sure son, but the more I think about it, the more it makes sense."

Jack had told the guys to meet him at the breakfast buffet at 8:00 AM. Mack had been on the phone with Nick, so it was a little late.

They ordered coffee and went to fill their plates before talking.

After finally chasing off the waitress off because she kept coming back to top off their coffee, Jack started the conversation.

"We've determined it is Zhang holding the auction on Saturday. Your contact Talia and her crew have been turning over many stones but have not come up with anything significant. She said the only sure way we may be able to track down the location of where the auction is originating would be someone coming forward with information or joining the auction, both being longshots."

Taking a second to stop devouring the star and litchi fruit on his third plateful, Mack looked up, "So how would joining the auction help? Won't these guys be using multiple VPN's (Virtual Private Networks) and be monitoring bank accounts? Even if we somehow got through to their IP (Internet Protocol) Address they'll be protecting themselves with firewalls and other anti-virus software. I'm clearly not in the spy game, but know enough about this stuff to be concerned they'll see us coming long before we locate their IP."

"Right now Talia is convinced this may be the only option and worth the risk. If that box disappears, we won't hear about it, or its contents again, until it's too late.

The issue she's having is finding a $100 mil to set up a bank account. That must happen before we do anything. We need to put a plan together. We've set up shop in the New World area called Xintiandi (Shin-tin-dee). It is a place frequented by Westerners, so locals shouldn't notice your presence. It also has easy access to the elevated roads and city loops and has the added feature of having a perfect mix of restaurants, including the best dumpling restaurant in town."

That finally got Derek's attention, "What's a fucking dumpling?"

Nigel laughed so hard; milk came out of his nose. He gained his composure and glanced over at Mack and could see he was distracted. "Mack, how's Steph? Was Nick able to update you on anything? I haven't had a chance to talk with Elli."

CHAPTER 24

Jack's driver picked them up at the front entrance of the hotel. The vehicle was a Porsche Cayenne, definitely big enough for five. Derek yelled for "shotgun," but Jack wouldn't permit it. He joked locals liked to call it the "closed casket seat." When they hit the road for Xintiandi, everyone understood why.

The Greater Shanghai population is 24 million. It looked to Mack, Nigel, and Derek that every one of them was in a car that morning.

With eyes as wide as silver dollars, Derek couldn't believe what he was seeing. Cars, trucks, and every other transport vehicle were fighting for a spot on the road. There was no such thing as right of way, courtesy, or rules. Vehicles would come out of side streets without even slowing down. Horns were constantly honking either as a "courteous" warning, which was a quick "honk-honk," to a "get the fuck out of my way, ok;" one honk that lasted several seconds. There were also many others in-between. The horns had a language of their own.

"This a giant game of chicken. These people have to be the worst drivers in the world!"

Mack and Nigel stayed quiet for about ten minutes, fixated on what was going on.

Finally, Mack spoke up, "Derek, I think you are wrong. I believe these people may be the best drivers in the world. Through all of this chaos, I've probably seen twenty instances where vehicles missed each other by a couple of inches, and no accidents yet. I would have been in one in less than a minute."

"I believe you're right, Mack." Nigel chimed in. "This is all very chaotic and stressful, but somehow it works. Jack, how long to our location?"

Jack smiled and shook his head a little, knowing he had answered this question a million times. "Nigel, in Asia, there are two answers to that question. The first one is 'about ten minutes.' If someone gives you that answer, don't believe them. Ten minutes could mean ten minutes, or it could mean an hour. They are just trying to get you to quit asking. The second answer is, 'it depends on the traffic.' That is the truthful answer. In both cases, the answer gives you no useful information. About the only thing for sure is if you get in a car, it's going to take you at least an hour to get anywhere."

Mack couldn't help himself as he let out a loud belly laugh. "I should have come to China sooner."

Around an hour later they arrived at Xintiandi.

They parked the car and walked into a building directly across the street from the main entrance to the Xintiandi walking street and made their way up to the third floor.

The office was at the end of the hall. On the door was a sign which had both English and Chinese writing. The English version read "Corporate Offices - Crazy Zhiban's Fine Seafood Importing."

Like in any office you would expect, the main office area was a reception desk, a copier, a tea area, and about ten desks with computers where Customer Service Reps were taking orders. Around the outside of the room were several doors to the other departments. Jack took them into his office, promptly closed the door, walked over to his desk, and reached into the center drawer. At the same time, a panel on the wall opened up. Behind the panel was a room about 30' by 30', with soundproofing on the walls. There were also two people behind computers, many computer servers, communication equipment, and signal jamming equipment. Jack explained all of this stuff was running off of shielded cable in conduit they installed so the jamming devices were only blocking people from trying to hack or listen in on them. He explained they also used a combination of VPN's to keep anyone from tracking their IP address.

"This will be our home away from home for the next couple of days. We have all the equipment and personnel necessary for tracking, hacking, and, hopefully, bidding on that box full of danger. I'm going to let Andy here, who is our head tech, show you around and explain the operation. I've got to head over to Pudong for a short meeting. I should be back by 3:00.

Over on the table, you'll see three phones; each has a sticky note with your name on it. Take the phone with your name. I have programmed my number into each of them."

"You will also see belts and rings. Find one of each that fits and give Andy the tag off it so he can log which one is yours. The belt has a GPS built into it so we can track you around town if necessary. It could be especially useful if you spot Zhang and are able to follow him. The rings are backups. They are part of an active Radio Frequency Identification (RFID) system with a range of about 200 meters. It's a common technology that uses electronic tags placed on objects, people, or animals to relay identification to a reader. You might find it at an automatic toll booth where you place an RFID tag on your dashboard, and the reader notifies the DMV to charge you when you pass through.

Unfortunately, we can't fit a GPS into something as small as a ring due to the battery and antenna size requirements.

We have also hacked ourselves into the Chinese government's facial recognition cameras. If something goes wrong with the belt or you are in a place where GPS won't work, we hopefully can use the camera system to locate the area you are in, and then use the RFID to determine your exact position."

Derek was confused and curious. "So other than using the GPS for tracking Zhang if we find him, are there any other reasons you'd want to have our locations at all times? Aren't you over-reaching a little on our privacy?"

Jack couldn't keep from laughing. "Ha! My friend, as they say in the States, 'you aren't in Kansas anymore.' You lost your right to privacy the second you stepped into China. Don't be fooled by the ease in which you get around. The Chinese government is trying to watch every move you or any foreigner makes.

They currently have over two-hundred million cameras in place, most of them tied into a facial recognition system. They are primarily there to track Uighurs, a Muslim minority in this country. They are considered dangerous by the government, and are being watched very closely. Jaywalk as a Han, and you lose 10 points on your social score, or at a maximum, lose your driver's license. Jaywalk as a Uighur, get sentenced to a lifetime of hard labor in a concentration camp."

"No shit?" Derek was in shock.

"No shit Derek. If the government knows where you are, we need to know it too."

"When you guys finish here, you can head across the road to the walking street. There's about any type of food you would want. I'd suggest Paulaner for a good sandwich and German beer."

Jack left them in Andy's hands. "See you at around three."

Andy proceeded to show them around, explaining what each piece of equipment was and what it did. They understood about 20%. After about an hour, they had about enough.

Mack was the first to speak up. "I've got a headache, why don't we go grab a sandwich and a beer. We can come back to this when we finish eating."

Nigel was quick to answer, "I agree."

They all grabbed their new phones and headed to Paulaner, sitting down at an outdoor table and ordering a beer.

After the beers arrived they toasted the occasion and each took their first sip. Just as they were getting comfortable, the phone in Nigel's pocket started ringing. It was from Jack.

"Sorry to bother you, but I just got a call. One of my associates called and said he spotted Zhang in the garment district. I thought you guys might want to go down there to see if you can find him. Make sure you are as discreet as possible if you do. See if you can follow him a little to track where he is going. I'll meet up with you as quickly as I can. If you don't see him, you can always go shopping."

"How do we get there?"

"You'll have to take a taxi. Just tell the driver Lujiabang Lu. They'll know where you need to go. It is a very popular place."

"OK, we should be fine. Well guys, you better chug."

They all finished their beers hurriedly and headed for the main entrance, hailing a taxi. They jumped in.

Grabbing his collar, Mack looked at the taxi driver and said, "Lujiabang Lu." The driver shook his head in a yes motion and took off.

Mack couldn't help himself, "duōjiŭ dào shìchăng." (how long to the market?)

As serious as he could be, the driver looked at Mack and answered, "shí fēnzhōng." (ten minutes).

Mack gave the same look to Nigel and Derek, "We might be screwed."

CHAPTER 25

"Well, I guess we weren't as screwed as I thought. Ten minutes only meant thirty in this case."

Nigel paid the thirty RMB taxi fee and gave the driver an extra fifty, refusing to take back the change. He didn't realize he had made a new friend with that tip.

It was hard for the three of them not to stop and take it all in. They were in an older part of Shanghai with mixed business and residential properties. Much of what they had seen so far was superhighways or modern, more westernized areas. They could see the landscape changing as they made their way from Xintiandi but now were out of the car. They weren't observers through a windshield anymore, but right in the middle of the chaos.

The most significant sensory impact on Mack was the smell. It was a mixture of aromas coming from the street food vendors, car exhaust, fabric from the clothing shops, laundry hanging out of all the windows, drying in the sun, the leftover rain from an earlier shower, and a little garbage and sewage mixed in. It wasn't a good or a bad smell, just so different from what he had ever smelled in his past. If he had to put a word on it, it would probably be exotic.

Nigel was hit first by the sounds. It was a cacophony of sirens, car engines, horns honking, construction, and street vendors all addressing them in broken English; "DVD, watch, best price for you, high quality, do you need a suit, come in and look?"

Two things struck Derek. The first was the number of high-rise buildings being constructed. He had heard some westerners joke the night before that China's national bird was the crane. Now he knew why they were laughing. He could see the buildings were going up with astonishing speed. So much manpower was being thrown at the projects. Workers were hanging off the bamboo scaffolds like vines from a trellis.

The second thing Derek noticed was the women. He usually wasn't particularly attracted to Asian women but, for some reason, the more accustomed he became with their type of beauty the more he was taken by it. He wasn't sure though just yet if being away from home and in his late twenties weren't the major driving factors for his current overly reactive libido.

"Derek, Mack, we need to make ourselves small here. If Zhang is around and sees us, he'll surely get the hell out quickly. I'm sure he knows we are in Shanghai, but probably isn't aware we are this close. If we can spot and trail him, we may be able to find out where the research is, or at least be able to get info we don't have right now. We also need to watch for that big bastard Peralta who is probably traveling with him by now. He should be easy to see, even in this crowd."

"Just how are we going to make ourselves small, dad? There are people all over the place. We probably won't even see him or Peralta coming."

"We won't see them coming if we keep moving through the crowd. What we need to do is find a store and observe from there. We can move to a few different spots while we're here to cover all directions. Let's use the crowd to our advantage. The first thing I'm going to do is head over to that street vendor and buy myself one of those "Hard Rock Shanghai" baseball caps.

"Don't you think that's a little cheesy, dad?"

"Not if it hides part of my face."

Mack and Derek relented. Derek ended up with Harley Davidson skull cap, and Mack ended up with a Tottenham Hotspur baseball cap and added a fake Rolex to his bounty. He was so proud he had been able to bargain the vendor down from $100 to about $60 American. Little did he know he could have gotten it for half that, and the vendor still would have made a livable profit.

It didn't matter. Mack was able to buy a Hotspur cap, his favorite soccer team in the Premier League. He had already heard the Rolex knockoffs were cheap, so he didn't care if the vendor could do better. In his mind, it would have been a crime to negotiate any lower.

Being a Brit and fancying himself as a soccer connoisseur, Nigel had to speak up at that point, "You got be kidding, Tottenham?"

"Yeah, is that a problem?"

"Liverpool all the way, baby."

They laughed at the idea a Yank and Brit were trying to one-up each other on soccer while in China.

Three hours and five stores later, they decided to move to their last spot down on one of the main streets, a little coffee shop named T-One. They would be able to case the main intersection from there and get some much-needed caffeine. Jetlag was kicking in hard on all of them.

After thirty minutes and a couple of cups of coffee each, Derek spotted Zhang. He exited the Sunshine apartment building next to the coffee shop and started walking towards a silver Mercedes E-Class parked on the street. They couldn't make out the driver. Fortunately for them, they had already paid for the coffee and were quickly headed for the door.

It was later in the afternoon and rain had started falling again. There was a mass of humanity and no taxis in sight. Everyone wanted out of the storm. If a cab showed up, it would get surrounded. The person pushing the hardest would eventually get the taxi. This moment may possibly be the only chance they'd have to follow Zhang before the auction; it looked like they had lost their opportunity.

They weren't going to give up just yet. All three were out on the curb waving their taxi hands, hoping for a miracle, when Mack noticed a cab headed their way with its headlights flashing. It passed several crowds of similar hand wavers, and in a split second, it pulled over next to them. The front passenger-side door flew open, and a hand started motioning them in, while the driver yelled, "xùn!" (fast).

The hand belonged to the same driver Mack had tipped so generously earlier in the day. This opportunity was either a monumental coincidence or the driver had been on the lookout for them all afternoon. In any case, it didn't matter; karma had smiled on them.

In his best Mandarin Mack smiled at the driver, pointed at the Mercedes, and said, "quiche zhuīsuí!" (follow that car).

"It's after three; I'm going to call Jack and let him know what's going on."

"Hey Jack, it's Nigel; we spotted Zhang and are following his car. We're in a taxi."

"Hand your phone over to the driver. I don't have the GPS tracker with me."

The driver proceeded to talk to Jack. You could tell by how he was craning his neck and looking out the windows; he was looking for street signs.

"What's he doing, Mack?"

"The best I can tell is he is telling Jack where we are and which way we are headed."

The driver handed back the phone to Nigel.

"Nigel, he's going to use your phone to talk to me and keep me posted on your location. Give it back to him and I'll be right behind you guys when he finally stops."

"Will do."

For another 15 minutes, they stayed behind the Mercedes. They could see they were entering an even older part of town with very narrow streets, a large park, and what looked like a temple of some sort. The driver continued to talk to Jack.

"nǎli?" (where is this?)

Handing Nigel's phone back to him, the driver answered Mack's question. "Yuánlín Yuyuan." (Yuyuan Gardens), pointing to the park; "Chenhuang Miào" (Temple of the Town of God), pointing at the temple.

"Mack, I heard what he just told you. Hold tight. I'm no more than five minutes behind you. Give the phone back to the driver."

Mack noticed the Mercedes driver had been on the phone for some time. He also could tell they had pretty much been going around the block. At that point, they were directly behind the Mercedes.

"I think we've been made guys."

The Mercedes passed through the intersection just ahead of them and slammed on its BRAKES. The taxi driver followed suit. Zhang had hemmed them into the intersection. Zhang's door opened, and he started getting out.

That was the last thing they remembered until they came to their senses, about a minute later. The taxi driver was alive but out cold. They had been broadsided by a typical, K01 Chinese work truck. It was empty and its driver was gone.

"Mack, Derek, you guys OK?"

"I'm fine, just a little woozy."

"Derek, how about you?" No answer.

Nigel looked across the car to where Derek had been sitting against the other door, which now stood wide open. Derek was not in the seat. Nigel and Mack scrambled out of the car as quickly as their beat-up bodies would allow, screaming for Derek, who was not answering.

As they exited the car, they could see Derek was gone. He hadn't been thrown from the taxi but removed, and likely in the hands of Zhang.

"Oh my God, what am I going to tell Elli?" Nigel was in shock and had a concussion. The sounds that had aroused his ears earlier in the day were now just a roar. Somewhere out of that roar he could hear a faint voice which started getting clearer.

It was Jack. He was running down the street towards them. "Mack, Nigel, are you OK? Where's Derek?"

Part II

CHAPTER 26

August, 2018 – Bangkok

It was a typical, hot, clammy morning in Bangkok. Nick woke up to sheets drenched in sweat and the aroma of cheap perfume.

The sounds of a barking dog and shouting coming from the outside courtyard broke Nick's slumber. He couldn't recall what time he got back to his flat the night before, or much about the encounter with the woman he met. Nick did remember waking from his troubled sleep earlier that morning, with his brain racing over the day about to unfold. He was able to finally fall back into his slumber for a few hours only by listening to the hum and focusing on the rotating blades of his ceiling fan.

As Nick crawled out of bed and rubbed the sleep from his eyes, he walked to the window, squinting as the light from the harsh sun intruded into the room. Nick couldn't make out who was shouting so he turned back, looking to see if the girl was still there. There was no girl but his wallet laid open on the nightstand and his last few Baht were gone. Nick shrugged off the robbery, knowing he had planned on giving her the extra baht as a tip anyway.

It was a Saturday and Nick was thankful he didn't have to meet his contact until later in the morning. He had been told the contact would share a confidential report concerning research being carried out at Lerdell Labs in the United States. His recruiter, Talia, had insisted he pick the document up in person. She called it a favor but he knew it was a test to show his ability to obey instructions without understanding the "why" behind them. His life had changed significantly in the past three months. It had started as him being a nondescript Westerner teaching English to now preparing to go to Israel.

Nick plodded into the bathroom with his temples pounding each time his heart took a beat. He looked into the mirror at a face he would have hardly recognized when he arrived in Bangkok nearly three months ago. Opening his mouth wide, Nick examined each tooth, expecting to see one of them missing. His breath and sweat smelled of whiskey and the meal of pandan chicken he ate the previous evening. After turning on the shower he reached to the counter, found the mouthwash, proceeded to gargle, and spat into the sink. The dog started barking again.

Nick managed his way closer to the shower, placing his hand under the spray to test the water temperature before he stepped in. Sometimes, if he let it run for a while, the small water heating unit on the wall would bring up the water's temperature enough for him to enjoy his shower. Today it was steamy hot, so Nick stepped into the stall as quickly as his tired legs would let him. The massage of the spray and heat of the water on his back put Nick into a trance, sending his mind back to a day a month earlier when his life changed entirely by what he thought had been a chance meeting. The more he relaxed, the more rapid the memories flowed.

Sitting at his favorite coffee shop at the corner of Soi 9 and Sukhumvit Road, Nick noticed it was packed that morning, mostly with coffee-loving Thais, but interspersed in with a few Western businesspeople. Nick had been coming to this shop since moving to Bangkok. The charitable organization he was working for had set him up in a small flat off Sukhamvit Road, near the Nana overhead train station, close to the shop.

Nick would soon find out the Nana district was one of Bangkok's more notorious areas, known for its strip clubs and sex shows. At first, he hated the location. It felt dirty with the dancers, drunks, and the ladyboys, called Katoys, running around. After a while he got used to it. The people living and working there were fascinating. He loved hearing their personal stories. The stories ran the gamut of them being sold into the sex trade by their families, to picking that lifestyle on their own. Many were there to merely make a living while they were young and pretty.

In the end Nick came around, actually liking being a part of that circus and embracing its performers. The action had become fun even if he was only on the fringes. Easy access to many authentic street food stands and the overhead train and subway systems made it even better. Eventually Nick would adapt to eating spicy food and making his way around Bangkok better than most locals. He also learned to love his coffee strong and rich like the Thais drank it, which was also a reason for coming daily to this particular spot.

Nick recalled his first encounter with Talia, "Excuse me, would you mind if I sit here?"

He looked up at who was speaking with him and was caught a little off guard by a very well dressed, attractive middle-aged woman. He couldn't quite make out her accent. It sounded Eastern European, but that wasn't quite it.

"Sure. No problem."

"Thanks, I won't be long."

"Please have a seat. It's no problem. Stay as long as you'd like."

"I appreciate it. This is my first time in Bangkok, so I'm a little unsure of what's acceptable or not. All the traffic, pollution, and everyone bowing to me is a little overwhelming right now."

"Oh, you'll get used to it. Most Westerners that come to Thailand end up loving it, even with its obvious blemishes, and the people are genuinely friendly. Before you leave you will probably be bowing too. It's catchy."

Nick put the palms of his hands together at neck height, like he was getting ready to pray, did a slight bow, and said, "Sawasdi Krup." His new table mate reluctantly did the same back.

"Was that OK? What does it mean?"

"It was perfect, but because you are female, you say 'Ka' instead of 'Krup', as in 'Sawasdi Ka.' I know that sounds weird, but people speak in genders here. It is a general form of hello."

"Well, thank you for the lesson and for letting me sit down. I must be going soon. By the way, I'm Talia, what is your name?"

"Nick."

"Nick, nice to meet you. I'm feeling less stressed already. I'll be in town on business for a few weeks. Maybe we'll run into each other again. If not, take care."

"Same here. See you around." Nick was confident that would be the last time he'd run into Talia in this small town of ten million people.

CHAPTER 27

Nick finally came out of his trance when the water heater couldn't keep up any longer. Although he was chilled, he was managing to feel much better.

Nick quickly wiped down, shaved, and put on his jeans and a black t-shirt. As he headed for the door he had a hunch today was going to be significant. This feeling made him think about his grandfather and how great a mentor he had been. Gramps had taught Nick to trust his instincts and pay attention to his premonitions. Nick's father was just the opposite; he was a great dad and his go-to for any questions about his decisions or moral dilemmas, but was overly protective. Nick's father would never understand his choices and would be disappointed in him leaving Bangkok three months early. Nick was starting to run late. He hurriedly fumbled with his backpack while juggling his cup of coffee and pushing his way out the front door, managing the stairs without spilling a drop. He was so proud of himself.

"Mr. Nick, Mr. Nick, I know you hear me." A woman shouted in broken English.

"Dammit!" wiping the hot coffee from his shirt. "Yes, Miss Kwang?"

"Your dog got into my garden again and dug up my carrots."

"Miss Kwang, how many times do I have to tell you I don't have a dog."

The dog she spoke of was a homely little mutt that started hanging around the rundown apartments about the same time Nick arrived. It looked similar to a dog Steven and he had when they were little. The locals would tell their Western friends, they lovingly called "farangs," these types of dogs were known as "mid-roads." The Thais gave them that name because the poor animals were born, lived, and died in the middle of the road.

Sometimes Nick wasn't sure about Thai humor but liked this attempt to name street dogs. The dog could have been handsome if adequately cared for. Nick felt sorry for the mangy thing so he would set out some water and a bowl of dry dog food for it now and then. Nick had always had a soft spot for strays like the dog and other living things which couldn't seem to beat the odds, like his brother Steven. For some reason, Nick had taken an extra special liking to this particular dog, maybe because it reminded him of his childhood with Steven. In any case, Nick resisted getting too close to it.

Other than the barking now and then, the dog never bothered him or anyone other than Miss Kwang. For some reason, it would only crap in her garden and usually did that while it dug up her vegetables. Nick figured one day, in the not so distant future, the ticks or a vehicle would kill the poor thing, so why not make its life more comfortable for now.

The taxi driver picked Nick up, and he got into the back seat. As they drove away the driver looked up at his rear-view mirror and started to laugh. Nick thought, *oh God, what now*. As he turned in his seat he looked out the back window. He could see why the driver was laughing. Miss Kwang was standing in her garden, flipping him off as the car drove away.

"Take me to the Chatuchak Market."

Chatuchak Weekend Market is possibly the largest street market in the world. You can find anything there. Nick knew it was perhaps the best place in the world to get lost if someone was watching him. More than 100,000 people running around in tight aisles would hide anyone. However, what Nick was after today wasn't an exotic snake or authentic Nepalese fighting knife, but a report hidden in a book. The report supposedly contained vital information about a new treatment showing great promise for treating cancer and fighting viruses but was currently being held from the public by its researchers until they were confident it would be successful.

The drive would be exceedingly long this morning due to a protest blocking the street. The extra time gave Nick plenty of opportunity to think, which he preferred at the moment. Instead of getting out at a train station to make his way to the Market he returned to reminiscing, particularly about the next encounters with Talia and his journey to this day.

Nick had been very wrong that day two months ago when, after their first meeting, he thought he'd never see Talia again. He should have known something was up when he continued to run into her at the coffee shop almost daily.

He intently wondered if their first meeting was a ploy in a predetermined scheme or the beginning of a fateful journey leading him to his destiny. He knew he would eventually find out but, in either case, Talia had been the maestro of a well-played symphony. Nick knew he was all in, whether or not he was being played. He had made that decision even before Talia asked him to retrieve the book.

Nick recalled with a smile those first coffee shop meetings when Talia was flirtatious. Although he was relatively naïve, he knew he wasn't comfortable with her actions and reacted negatively to them. He remembered brushing her off and sometimes going to a different shop for his morning coffee. Nick also recalled how quickly she understood his uneasiness and stopped her flirting. Her entire personality changed to that of a concerned mother. The immediate change concerned Nick. He wondered if Talia was somehow manipulating him but let it go as their relationship became more comfortable.

Eventually Talia talked with Nick about life in Israel and her job as a CPA in the pharmaceutical industry. She was in Bangkok to review the financials of a company her company was considering purchasing.

She let on later how little she liked working in pharmaceuticals. She was disgusted by their strategies of bringing doctors to the table using questionable financial practices or creating physical and mental addictions in patients to maintain their sales. She couldn't wait to get out. She wanted to advocate against them eventually. Nick recalled being impressed with her character for the first time when she confided with him concerning this aspect of her life.

Talia confided even more when she mentioned her late husband had died of Multiple Myeloma; a rare blood cancer diagnosed too slowly. The wrong course of treatment was given by his oncologist who knew little about the genetic role in the disease. He used a standard treatment not meant for her husband's particular genetic make-up. He quickly died of kidney and liver failure that never should have happened. Nick remembered the authentic grief in her eyes. It reminded him of the grief he continued to carry when he thought about his brother.

Nick had been reluctant to share any intimate details of his life with Talia until he heard the story about her husband's illness. He proceeded to tell her all the details of Steve's life and death, including his own enraged, post-death social media tirades against the medical and pharmaceutical institutions. He felt more connected to someone now than he had in a long time.

Near the end of that meeting Talia told Nick she had some personal things to take care of in Israel and would be gone for a few weeks. She mentioned she would like to finish their conversation when she returned. Nick recalled not being sure what she meant by "finish their conversation," but figured he would find out soon enough.

CHAPTER 28

"Mister, Mister," the cab driver was yelling at Nick, who was still lost in the memory of that day in the coffee shop before Talia left for the first time. "We are here. Time to get out." Nick regained his sense of today, paid the driver, and exited the taxi.

He made his way across the bridge, dodging other shoppers while stepping over the deformed beggars on mats. The money naïve passers-by would drop in their baskets would be picked up after closing time by the criminals who had placed them there. The criminals would take the money and give their "accomplice" just enough food and water to stay alive for another day of collecting.

Nick's destination in the Market was called the "Dream Section." His contact was the owner of Ex's Rare Books and Novelties.

Walking in the main entrance, Nick had a thought that made him smile. Wasn't it ironic the train station's name Mochit sounded like "More Shit?" This place probably had more shit in it to buy than other Market in the world. Nick was sure he wasn't the first Westerner to recognize the irony but had to smile anyway. He made his way to the Dream Section.

The sign outside the shop was handmade but very well lettered and conspicuous enough you couldn't walk by without seeing it. It read "Ex's Book Store and Novelties." The shop was small and enclosed. There was even a door on it, which was unusual for this Market. Nick could smell dampness, which he associated with wet newspaper, turned the handle, and entered.

A slightly built, older gentleman greeted him. "Sawasdi Krup."

"Sawasdi Krup. I am looking for Mr. Ex. Is he available?"

"Can I say who is interested in speaking with him?"

"Please tell him it is Mr. Nick, the English teacher."

"Mr. Nick, I'm Ex. Good to meet you. I've been expecting you. Would you be interested in a book or a novelty today?"

"I guess you'd say it's a combination of both."

"I think I have exactly the item you need. I'll be right back."

Mr. Ex walked into the back room of the shop, returning about ten minutes later. He handed Nick a loosely bound copy of "Cat's Cradle" by Kurt Vonnegut, who oddly happened to be one of Nick's favorite authors.

"I'm sorry I took so long; I received a phone call. It was Talia; she is in Bangkok. She said to meet her at the coffee shop at 8:00 AM tomorrow and not do anything with the book until she speaks with you."

Nick wasn't expecting a personal visit from Talia. It didn't surprise him, but made him a little nervous all the same. Things would be getting interesting soon, and his time in Bangkok was getting ready to end.

CHAPTER 29

The book retrieval had taken less time than Nick expected, so he headed over to the food court. When he got there, he grabbed himself some chicken satay and a couple of Singha beers. For some reason, Nick had expected more trouble retrieving the book, mostly based on the feeling he got whenever he talked to Talia. She could be intimidating and always seemed vigilant and cautious. Nick continued to be a bit nervous about meeting Talia the next morning, wondering if she was here to tell him there had been a change in plans. As he was sipping on his beer he withdrew back to the memory of the day Talia had returned to Bangkok after her two-week hiatus.

Nick's phone rang. It had been exactly two weeks since Talia had left. She asked him to meet her for coffee the next morning.

When Nick arrived at the coffee shop, he saw Talia was already seated; she waved him over and had his coffee sitting on the table waiting for him.

After a few pleasantries, Talia got straight to business. "Have you decided what you are going to do when your tour is up?"

"Probably stay here. The organization I work for needs a Program Manager up in Chiangmai and offered me the position. It pays a little extra, and that part of Thailand is magnificent."

Nick recalled Talia seemed especially on edge. She seemed like she was thinking deeply about what to say next. "That sounds great, Nick. Congratulations."

Talia was guarded with Nick, so he felt like he needed to respond. "You don't seem happy about it. Is something wrong?"

"Oh, no...no, I just thought after the last time we talked, you seemed ready to do something bigger than being a low paid English Tutor."

"Yeah, I know what I said. It was wishful thinking. This job is my reality right now."

Talia jumped on Nick's response. "Nick, what if I told you there is something more?"

Nick remembered Talia explaining that after she finished this job she was joining a worldwide lobbying organization created to develop global standards to control the research, manufacturing, and distribution of pharmaceuticals. It would not be a clone of the World Health Organization, but an independent organization also monitoring

WHO. She would be in charge of evaluating new technologies like CAR-T and CRISPR, both of which could significantly impact the treatment and cure for cancer. These same technologies would also be used to stop new types of viruses that could become pandemic and deadly.

Talia further explained secret research was being executed by all major countries, including America, Russia, China, Iran, North Korea, and Israel. The organization's initial focus would be to determine where the research was proceeding, who was funding it, and what intent there may be by keeping it secret.

Nick couldn't help reacting in what he believed now, was complete speechlessness; his brain was trying to absorb everything Talia was saying. "Why me? I mean, I'm a young kid without much experience at anything. What on earth could I do to be productive in an organization like that?"

Her next response stuck with him to this day. "Nick, don't sell yourself short. You have the kind of passion that only comes with your type of life experiences. I read your blogs and Facebook posts. This stuff is personal to you. We can train you on all the other stuff."

His recollection of the conversation continued.

"Like what other stuff?"

"Medical terminology, data mining, computer code, certain forms of espionage, self-protection, language arts, and...."

"Whoa, hold on a second, self-protection?"

"Yeah, Nick. Things like hand-to-hand combat. In fact, a special Israeli form called Krav Maga."

"So, this could be dangerous? What about things like guns?"

Nick wasn't scared. He was hungry like something wild inside him had been let loose. Talia continued, "It's probable. We know you can handle a gun because of our background and the importance of security, yours, and ours. The check also indicates you spent a lot of time with your grandfather hunting and learning about firearms. Based on what our files say about your grandfather, you probably learned a lot more than using a gun. I'm sure he would be immensely proud of you."

Nick recalled being shocked by Talia's comment. "You obviously know a lot more about my life than I would have thought. I don't know if I should be impressed or scared."

"Nick, we are thorough. There's not much out there that can't be found with a comprehensive internet search by a professional. We just have better resources. That should impress you, not scare you."

Nick remembered smiling then, and was smiling now.

"I think I'd like to give it a try but no promises. I'd like a thirty-day, money-back guarantee, if that works for you."

Talia smiled, "of course."

Nick recalled being ready to go. "When do I start?"

"Soon. I'll be heading back to Israel tomorrow. It may be a few weeks to get everything set up. In the meantime, I'm going to need you to do me a favor. I need someone nondescript like you to take care of a pickup for me. I have no idea if anyone is watching me, and would rather be safe. The probability of someone watching you is much smaller."

"Is this assignment going to be dangerous or illegal? I don't want to end up in a Thai prison."

"Don't worry, Nick. It will be neither. You will be picking up a critical report hidden in a book, but we have everything handled. I'll fill you in on a need to know basis as the day for pickup gets closer."

For some reason, Nick didn't believe her, but said he'd do it. He wanted to show her he was a team player, but he was still fearful.

Nick came out of his thoughts, staring down at his satay, only half-eaten. He gulped down his beer and headed for the train station to take him home.

Nick was undoubtedly having a day of reflection. The memories he had been recounting today had been just as relentless for the past week. Nick wondered if they were trying to tell him something, or warn him? Maybe they were simply giving him one last chance to take them in before fading to make room for others? He wasn't sure. In any case, he was going to take a catnap on the way back to Nana.

Nick awoke when he heard the announcement for Asok station, which was a stop past Nana, and quickly exited. He decided to take the fifteen-minute walk back to Nana.

CHAPTER 30

Nick was running late that morning. He was so excited the night before he had trouble falling asleep. He went down to the district to walk around, have a few beers, and say hi to the friends made during his time living there. Nick was reasonably sure these conversations were actually goodbyes. However, he didn't let on to anyone he may not see them again.

Nick arrived at the coffee shop at 8:10. Talia had a perturbed look on her face as he entered, but was ready with a smile and a hug when she saw Nick.

"Mr. Ex told me you had no trouble finding his shop. He followed you to the train station to see if anyone else was following you, and was certain no one was there. So, it looks like the retrieval was a success. Congratulations. Can I please see it?"

Nick reached into his backpack, pulling out the book. He hadn't noticed the night before; the book was sealed shut by a tiny dab of wax.

Talia broke the seal peering into the hollowed-out pages, and pulled out an envelope that contained the report. "I'm glad you didn't look, Nick."

Nick, feeling mistrusted, asked, "Why would you think I would look? You asked me not to. I had to assume there was something in there I shouldn't see."

"Not really, Nick. It's an important report written by an Israeli operative who has been monitoring the lab in Maine I mentioned to you. Much of it is in code and technical jargon, so you would not have understood much. Suffice it to say; it verifies critical undercover genetic studies are being carried out at the lab. It also leads us to believe we need to quickly get you back to Israel for training to insert you as swiftly as possible."

"If I wouldn't understand most of what was in there, why did you tell me not to look? Why did you come all the way here to open the book?"

"I'll answer the second question first. I don't trust anyone but me with the book. I was concerned about you having it for a night, which should answer your first question. Telling you not to look was a simple test of trust, Nick. You passed. Assuming you are ready, we have a plane to take you to Israel this evening. We have already had your visa issued, so you are fine there. We have also worked with your current employer to give you a six-month sabbatical and pre-payed your rent in case you have to return after training. You'll need to gather enough belongings to fit in a carry-on, and we'll have a car waiting outside your complex at 6:00 PM."

"I'm good with that, Talia. I hope this trust issue is over; I'll see you at the airport.

Nick strolled to his flat, taking in all the sights one last time. As he walked into the courtyard, he saw Miss Kwang walking up to him with her head down. Nick wondered what she was going to complain about this time.

When Miss Kwang finally got to him, she looked up sadly, "I'm sorry, Mr. Nick, your dog was hit by a car and killed."

Nick thanked Miss Kwang for letting him know and walked into his flat, relieved he hadn't gotten too close. He knew getting too close to anything could break your heart.

CHAPTER 31

October, 2014 – Texas

Nick's aim was steady and his eye sharp on the prize.

Gramps knelt at Nick's side and placed his hand gently on his shoulder. They were both covered in camouflage from head to toe and lay flat on the wet ground to hide from their prey. Sixty feet away they could see the wild beast devouring the carcass of an abandoned kill from another predator. Little did it know it was now the prey, and its fate rested upon the hunter's skill. The wild boar was an adult, large for this part of the area. The male looked to be about 180 pounds with dark, bloody tusks that matched its enormous size.

"Easy son, readjust your body to make sure your hash marks are fixed on the kill zone. Only a direct shot in the heart will take that beast down. Wounding the animal would only piss it off. When you're ready, gently squeeze the trigger, but only when you have a shot."

Nick's eye was steady; the beast moved just to the right spot where his aim would be true. His finger gently was squeezing down on the trigger, ready to take the shot. At that moment, Steve burst through the bush, shouting, "Hey guys, any luck?

BOOM, Nick's rifle went off, striking the wild boar in the shoulder, missing the kill zone due to his brothers' interruption. The boar was hurt, not dead, but angry.

As the boar came charging towards them, Steve shouted, "Oh shit," and ran the other direction expecting his brother and Gramps to be close behind.

Nick never flinched, and neither did Gramps.

His eye remained on the target as the boar charged towards them. Gramps, with his hand still on Nick's shoulder, whispered, "easy… easy… easy, take the shot!"

BOOM, the wild boar dropped just within ten feet from both of them.

Gramps had taught him well, and he knew he was prepared to take on other challenges in life. Nick could only chuckle when Steve made his way back to the spot where the animal lay. Nick always admired his older brother, but now he had something over on him, and Steve knew it as well from that day forward. Gramps handed Nick his hunting knife and motioned to him without saying 'your kill, your responsibility.' Nick knew what Gramps was getting at, only kill to survive and respect what you kill by giving thanks and honoring its spirit. Steve did join and helped Nick hang the beast and field dress the meat.

After his grandfather's death, Nick never picked up a gun again, not yet anyway. However, he and Steve continued to go camping together, enjoying sleeping under the stars and telling tall stories. Although Gramps left Nick and Steve all his guns they never brought them along. It didn't seem right to hunt without Gramps being there. When at home, Steve hung out with his older friends, racing cars, and chasing girls. These camping trips at least allowed Nick to have his brother all to himself until his brother got sick.

February, 2019 – Israel

Nick lay flat on the sandy ground. As he carefully sought out his target, he could still feel Gramps' hand on his shoulder quietly whispering to him; "easy… easy… easy, take the shot!"

This time it was no wild boar or any animal. It was wooden targets of men, women, and children.

The instructor yelled out commands, "One of these targets is carrying a bomb; you have a fraction of a second to take the shot. The wrong shot will kill us all, including those innocent children."

Nick knew at that moment; it was a child carrying the bomb, but which one? He quickly scanned each child and noticed one carrying a backpack slung over his shoulder and dragging a doll. He took the shot and neutralized the target.

The instructor acknowledged the shot with "damn good job."

"How did you know it was the little girl?" asked another trainee who was observing the drill.

"She was carrying a doll but dragging it on the ground. Any little girl, especially in these poor conditions, would hold her doll tight in her arms to protect it." After Nick spoke he realized what he had done and was sickened by the thought of shooting a little girl. He hadn't expected the Israelis would train him for something like this, but let it go.

Nick secured his rifle and walked back towards his barracks; he needed a break.

"I did not excuse you," the instructor shouted.

Nick continued to walk away, flipping the bird over his shoulder to the instructor as he entered the building.

The instructor attempted to follow Nick. However, she left him alone after her Commander called her off.

Nick put his gear away, laid on his bunk, placed his arms behind his neck, and looked up at the ceiling. He thought about the exercise he just went through and the reality of the situation he placed himself in. He thought about the words his Grandfather said to him every time they were on the hunt, *kill to survive, and respect what you kill by giving thanks and honoring its spirit.* How can you honor the soul of a terrorist or anybody else who does harm? A boar or deer gave up their life for others to survive. Surely Gramps never honored the spirits of the enemy he killed while in the service.

Nick could hear gunshots and the shouting of commands outside his barrack as other trainees were going through their drills. He was taught never to walk away from a fight. However, he didn't regret going back to his bunk. The flipping off the instructor was something he wanted to do that from day one. He decided to go back and got up, grabbed his gear, and joined the others. He could sense the female instructor was giving him the stink eye, but ignored her glances.

Nick finished his drills for the rest of the day, had a quick bite in the mess hall. He wasn't in the mood to hang out with the other trainees so he took a shower and then went straight to his bunk. He felt alone. His Commander gave them strict instructions on communicating with the outside which isolated them even further. He missed his mom and dad the most.

The separation from those he loved was heartbreaking.

"You made a good friend today," a voice came from another bunk.

"Excuse me?" asked Nick.

"Today I overheard the Commander ask our instructor if anybody else had ever shot the little girl first at this exercise. She said no, never."

"So, who is my new friend?"

"The Commander, he is never impressed by recruits."

"My name is Tamar. Your American, right?"

"No, Canadian."

"Bullshit, you're American. We all know it."

"OK, I'm American, what does it matter anyway."

"It doesn't; you're not the first American who has been trained by the Israelites."

"I wouldn't think so," Nick stated as he was getting a little annoyed.

"Your name, or is it an American secret?

"Well, since you know I'm American, doesn't look much like secrets are kept here. I'm Nick."

"Well, Nick, welcome to my country, yasher koach, may you have strength."

"Tamar, thank you, I guess. If you don't mind, I'm going to turn in. It's going to be another tough day tomorrow."

"Goodnight, my friend."

Nick turned off the light to his bunk, rolled over, and within minutes fell asleep.

He dreamed about his Grandfather and those summers in the woods, hunting with his brother. The ground was soft, the air was fresh, and no sand to be found. It was restful and peaceful until the explosion woke him up from his sleep.

CHAPTER 32

"Chaos" was the only thought Nick could wrap his brain around. A mortar had hit the front side of his barracks. More were falling throughout the compound.

Nick's ears were ringing; he couldn't hear anything other than the sound of a lone drone against the muffled screams. A large cloud of smoke wafted past him, eerily taking the shape of the Grim Reaper as it passed him, smiling as if he had done Nick a favor. Nick was confounded. Eyes and throat burning, he willed himself to grab onto reality again. He needed to get the hell out of there. After wiping his eyes with the bedsheet, his vision improved enough to see several recruits were dead, and the barracks was burning. He quickly threw on his pants and boots.

Immediately Nick started looking around for his new bunkmate, Tamar. He didn't have to look long. Lying in a growing pool of blood at the foot of Nick's bed, laid Tamar. Nick didn't have to check his pulse. The fog of death could be seen in his wide-open, hollow eyes. This time he heard the Reaper laugh as he sped away with the souls of those around him.

"Well done, Tamar. I'm sorry we didn't get to know each other"

Nick slowly made his way through the barracks, looking for survivors on his way out. He found one and dragged him to safety by his arm. It looked like most of the group had either been killed or already made it out.

As the sun came up the following morning, the encampment was being cleaned up by the soldiers stationed there. Nick and the remaining "recruits" had already been moved to another section of the camp. The Commander told them the compound had been attacked, and speculated it was the Palestinians or another terrorist organization funded by Iran. Nick wasn't sure it was either of those two but kept his mouth shut. His opinion probably wouldn't matter anyway; it was near the end of his training and only a couple of weeks before going back home for a visit, and then back to Thailand until needed.

Nick reflected on his training amid the rubble and destruction. *In the past months a lot had changed. When Nick arrived in Israel with Talia he thought he was walking into the situation with eyes wide open. His mindset didn't change much during the first few months. It was exactly as Talia had explained when she sold him on coming with her. The only odd thing to him was his training was at an Army base. If this was training for a Non-Government Organization (NGO), it was indeed a strange place to do it.*

Training started with a lot of introductory courses on virology, oncology, and baseline treatment options. These courses became more technical and intense as time went on. The most promising immunotherapy and gene editing techniques were studied in detail, including the moral and social issues of how they could be used. Nick enjoyed learning about treatments that would help people like his brother Steven. Still, he didn't care much for studying the politics of moralism, but knew it was part of the package. He was especially enthused this knowledge would make him an integral part of a watchdog group, monitoring illegal or unethical use of these technologies.

Training got even more intense when computer hardware and software courses kicked in. Instruction on the use and manipulation of the dark web came first; then, Nick immersed himself in code writing over the next month. The training began with primary languages like C++ and SQL. Then, it moved into the more high-powered software like Python and PHP. Although all these programming languages were used internationally for upstanding purposes, the trainers told them they were learning these for computer hacking purposes. As training went on, Nick became very proficient.

He was then trained in general subjects like language arts, business. Other skills like negotiating, psychology, and crisis management were also sprinkled into the mix.

The part of the training that got most of Nick's attention was the physical, self-protection, and combat training. He understood he was on an Army base and needed to be treated like the soldiers there. Still, his training and the rest of the group's training was even more intense and specialized than the soldier training going on in the boot camp. A more significant difference was the patience given to his group; no loud, obnoxious drill sergeant, no name-calling or physical punishment, just patient teaching.

It started with the standard physical training you'd expect in that setting. The group performed tasks like calisthenics, cardio, and weightlifting, then quickly moved on to activities like land and water survival, rock climbing, and martial arts.

Towards the end, the Commander split the group into smaller specialized training groups, mostly done individually. Nick's group spent much of their time on special weapons, anti-terrorism, and advanced security techniques.

Nick was also sent out on a boat onto the Mediterranean Sea near the West Bank to learn lobstering techniques. He thought about asking why but figured he'd find out.

Although Nick thoroughly enjoyed the special training, the move in intensity concerned him. It certainly wasn't "hand-to-hand combat with little gun training" like Talia had let on during their conversation in Bangkok. The things they were teaching him were not just about protecting yourself and the world from bad guys creating dangerous diseases but also about much more. Nick was sure his mom and dad would be outraged and unsure whether Gramps would be proud or disappointed.

In any case, he knew he had a moral compass that would come in handy when needed. Both Gramps and his mom and dad had raised him to respect life and understand there were evil people in the world that sometimes could push you to do things opposite of your North if needed. Even in his discomfort, his focus continued to be on stopping the bad guys, whoever they may be. The problem was the line between good and bad guys had become somewhat blurry during his training.

What happened the previous night hadn't scared him about what he had gotten into, but made him much more aware of that blurred line. Whoever fired the mortars did it for a reason. Was it because they were bad guys or because he was with the bad guys?

All he understood at that point was good people had died. He also felt a little sad that even if he succeeded in his quest for medical altruism, people worldwide might be saved from death due to a disease. However, many more would still die from bombs, mortars, guns, religious zealousness, and conflicting ideologies, killed by people who would consider themselves altruistic.

Talia would be there in several days to fill him in on his future. Tomorrow wouldn't be soon enough.

CHAPTER 33

The day finally arrived for Nick to hear about his future. The Commander had contacted him to let him know Talia was waiting in her office. "Nick, I guess it's been an intense six months. I must say everyone has been extremely impressed with your skills, but even more impressed with your focus. Please don't take this wrong, but you have done much better than I thought you would."

"Yeah, thanks."

"After everything you've been through and all the new skills you have, all you have to say is yeah, thanks. You're kidding, right?"

Nick could feel the blood rushing to his face. He knew he was about to lose his cool, but he had to keep it. *Practice what you learned in those meditation classes.* He was in a position where he needed to die on the right hill if he was going to die fighting.

He didn't have all the information he needed for a straight-on attack. He needed to flank Talia if possible. Getting her pissed off would ruin any chance of him getting him answers. "Sorry, I am very thankful for everything I've learned, but with all due respect, you lied to me."

Talia was the one keeping her cool. It was going to be her doing the flanking. "Perhaps you misunderstood something. What lies did I tell you? You certainly didn't have any objections six months ago in Thailand, and I don't recall you asking for a conversation with me since then. Is this a new revelation for you?"

"I wasn't shooting at cardboard cut-outs of children dragging dolls, learning kill techniques with knives, or dodging mortar rounds until recently. I was learning about biology and computer programming, which was in line with what you told me in Bangkok. Still, when I asked about things like fighting and weapons in Bangkok, you told me I'd be learning some hand-to-hand techniques and probably get some gun training. What I've been training for in the last couple of months is much more than that."

"Look Nick, I may have been withholding some detail, but I didn't lie. Our intentions were not to get you as far into weapons as we did, but you were a natural at almost everything we presented to you. When we did start pushing you, not a word came out of your mouth about any dissatisfaction on your part. You went along and even pushed yourself to excel. I saw that look in your eyes when you were asking about danger back in Bangkok. Deep down in your heart, you were hoping for more. Whether you like it or not, your actions here prove that."

"So, you don't think fear had something to do with me not saying anything?"

"C'mon Nick; you came into this on your own; no one has forced you to do anything. When we first met, you were a very moral, naïve young man, teaching young kids how to speak English. You can go back to that safe place if you want. We won't stop you. You must remember the feelings you had when we talked about all the fixing needed in the world. We talked about saving lives, protecting those who worked on cures, or stopping those who would misuse medical technologies to hurt and even kill people. That hasn't changed. We hope the extra weapons training you got will never need to be used but we will sometimes deal with despicable people. You may thank us for this training sometime in the future. You saw what they are capable of when they rained mortar on the compound the other day. The deaths of innocents don't matter to them. Do you think they would play nice if they were allowed to infect the world with something deadly, especially if it couldn't ultimately be traced back to them?"

"So, you say I'll be dealing with evil people sometimes; does that make me one of the good guys?"

"I hate to tell you this darling, but good and bad are relative. The quicker you learn that lesson, the better off you'll be. All you can do is decide where your morals lay and act accordingly. There will be times you will do things considered bad by other people but if you act with respect to your moral compass, you won't need to question yourself. You are a fine young man Nick, and talented. You have the potential to do a lot of good things. It's your decision now that you have graduated to this part of your life."

Nick knew what his answer was. Talia was right. The line is blurred, and there was no absolute good or bad. He was pissed off she wasn't forthcoming with details of his training, not because he was having some sort of moral breakdown. He wasn't going to let his ego ruin this opportunity. "I need you to agree to three things before I answer. A no answer to any of them will be a deal-breaker."

"Go ahead; I'll do what I can."

"First, you will never ask me to do anything that will hurt my family, friends, or my country. I am not a spy for Israel or whatever your organization is, and I'm not a traitor. If that ever happens, I'm gone. Second, I will never be asked or ordered to kill anyone. If I have to do something like that, it will be my decision. I didn't agree to come here to train as an assassin."

"And third?"

"You said I graduated. That means I'm a professional now, and professionals are paid for their services. I'm going to need to get paid well if I am to be on call to you."

"My, you have come a long way. You've really grown a set. I can promise you we will never knowingly ask you to harm anyone or do anything that will put your family in danger. As far as your last request is concerned, let's put it this way; you'll probably never have to worry about money again for a long while.

We have already set up an account for you and deposited a quarter of a million dollars in it. An additional quarter mil will go in when your first assignment is complete. From then on, we will have you on retainer at a quarter a million per year. I assume that's satisfactory. Are you ready to hear a little about what your first assignment will be before you catch a plane back to Massachusetts to see your family? Or are you prepared to go back to Thailand to teach grammar?"

Nick couldn't believe what he just heard. In six months, he went from being a guy living above a strip joint in Bangkok, eating cheap street food, to making more money than he could have ever imagined.

What was it his Gramps and dad had always said about things being too good to be true? Forget about that. "Yes, Ma'am, I'm ready."

CHAPTER 34

"Glad to hear that, Nick. I believe you'll find you made the right decision."

Nick still wasn't sure he was doing the right thing but knew the decision was made, especially after being given mission details. There was no walking it back after that. "I hope so, Talia. Go on."

"This is a long story, Nick. After hearing it, you'll probably be like most of my colleagues who believe the story is fraught with coincidences. I choose to believe those coincidences are part of a much larger plan not controlled by me, but I've chosen to carry it forward."

"You mean part of God's plan?" Nick was bemused. His question was not one of sarcasm but sincere interest. He hadn't been raised with religion being the cornerstone of his morality system. His parents weren't "non-believers." They simply raised him and Steven to respect what they considered were proper morals. They eventually let their boys decide what role spirituality, religion, God, or Jesus would play in their lives. Since Steven's death, he leaned more towards agnosticism, although he frequently caught himself praying for some reason.

While in Thailand, Nick also had spent the first three months of his post-high school journey in a Buddhism centered culture. It was a place where people became monks, meditated, had little shrines in their houses to commemorate their ancestors, and believed profoundly in karma. These beliefs required them to live in a peaceful, serving way, not so unlike many tenets of Christianity.

Nick was amused at the Buddhist karmic belief of "what goes around comes around" was similar to what Christians believed in their Golden Rule. The Buddhist view was on an entirely different level and could span this lifetime and many lifetimes to come.

The Christians he knew believed there was only one chance, and God would judge you (ultimate karma) at the end. Good guys to the right, bad guys to the left unless you were "born again." In that case, you were automatically on the right.

His last six months had him in Israel, the land of God's chosen people. Like the Doobie Brothers, Jesus was JUST ALRIGHT with them, but not the savior they were looking for. Their moral code was based a lot more on their history with the Yahweh of the Old Testament. Nick was influenced by those beliefs but confused about how it was different from the Muslims, who based their dogma on the same Old Testament and the same God.

In any case, the past nine months had indeed impacted his spirituality and associated morality. Nick just wasn't sure what that impact was yet.

Talia continued to explain her conviction. "Next time you get your hands on a Bible, read the story of Joseph in Exodus, he was the youngest of 12 brothers and just a sheepherder, but his brothers were jealous of him. They decided to get rid of him by beating him up and throwing him in a hole, thinking he was dead. Slave traders found Joseph and sold him as a slave in Egypt. Long story short, he used his guile, intelligence, and personality to befriend Egypt's king and eventually become the second most important person in Egypt, and greatly trusted. A major years-long drought hit that part of the world, but Joseph had stored grain for the Egyptians and was now getting them through it. Joseph's father and brothers were on the verge of death, so decided they needed to go to Egypt and beg for their lives. When Joseph found out they were in Egypt, he went to reveal himself to them. When they saw him, his father rejoiced, and brothers thought Joseph would put them to death for what they had done to him. Joseph forgave them and told them to go back home and bring all the Jewish people to Egypt to be taken care of."

"You can call your place in the world anything you want, Nick; God's plan, destiny, fate, karma, or luck. I just know it is more than coincidence, and God, or whatever you want to call it, chooses ordinary people to do great things."

"OK, let's hear it. You have me very intrigued now."

"Here goes; first things first. You won't be going back to Thailand. We need you home; Your employer has been contacted and will not be expecting your return. Any belongings you left in Bangkok, which I doubt was much, will be shipped back. They thanked you and wished you well."

Nick, a little shocked, nodded his head up and down, "OK?"

"Now, some background. Almost forty years ago, when I was just starting with Mossad, I was teamed up with an MI6 agent named Nigel Shackelford. We were working together on Middle East information data networks, otherwise called "intercepting enemy communications." Nigel was good at just about everything he did; he came up with quite a communication record database. Unfortunately, other, more important things came up. We were both called to new duties in late 1981. Mossad sent me to Moscow, and he became involved in the Falklands War."

"Falklands War? Never heard of it."

"I suggest you look it up on Wikipedia or something. It plays a significant role here, but too much to go into right now. Let's continue. At around the time Nigel was mucking around in Argentina, we found some significant inconsistencies and changes in the project files Nigel and I worked on. Of course, both of us became prime suspects. I was able to clear myself, but Nigel was neck-deep in gathering intel on the Argentinians. We couldn't get to him.

Nigel played a significant role in helping the Brits end the war quickly, using an informant named Eliza Fernandez. She supplied him with the critical information needed to finish a fledgling love affair between Argentina and Russia. When the Argentinians and Russians found out what Miss Fernandez had done, the Argentines ordered a hit on her.

Knowing that would be the case, Nigel risked his life to save her, getting her out of the country and set up in Maine under the fake identity of Elli Brunetta. As a side note, they fell in love. Nigel eventually left MI6, came into some money, moved into Bar Harbor, Maine, not far from where Eliza was, and started running a lobster boat."

"So, he and Eliza, or Elli, or whatever, became an item?"

"I guess you could say that. Eliza had to protect her new identity. They did get together but had to do it mostly in the shadows. Because we still didn't know if Nigel was responsible for switching out the project information. My superiors sent me to Maine undercover as a magazine photographer. I set myself up to get acquainted with Elli to try to get additional info on Nigel. We became close over that period, which seems impossible to me now. About six months into the project, the Mossad investigators found out an administrator on my and Nigel's project team had figured out a way of getting to the secured info. She had made the changes Mossad discovered, at the behest of the Iranians and a $10,000 payment. Such a small sum to risk spending the rest of your life in prison, wouldn't you agree? I was then called back to Israel."

"OK, great story, but what does that have to do with 2019 and what you and I are doing?"

"That's where the hand of God comes in. I kept tabs from a distance on Nigel and Elli. They ran a successful commercial fishing operation and started another behind the scenes, mostly small-time smuggling operation. I even gave them some Mossad business every once in a while, to help keep tabs. They eventually had and raised a son. More importantly, Ellie went back to school and became a well-respected biochemist, working for Lerdell Labs. We found out she was eventually put over a project dealing with some potentially important medical breakthroughs that could be used for great good, but if they landed in the wrong hands, immense evil."

Much of the basis of that research was contained in the package you picked up in Thailand.

"So, you kept tabs for what, like thirty years or more, because you had grown fond of Elli? That doesn't make a lot of sense. For all you knew, she could've become a mail carrier. What else was going on for you to do that? Were you and Nigel doing the nasty while you were working with each other? Like this was an ex-lover's infatuation, similar to your first high school crush. That's all I can come up with."

"I've decided you're sort of a smart-ass Nick, but in a likable way. Yes, I had grown very fond of Elli. We kept in touch for a while after I left. She was attending college at Harvard, excelling in her field, and was sharing a lot of hopes and dreams with me. She was extremely bright and motivated. In my business, keeping tabs on people like that may never lead to anything, but on the other hand, can lead to great things. When it came to Elli, those were the two reasons. As far as Nigel was concerned, he was an ex-spy. Ex-spies are always being watched. They normally carry a lot of good information they are willing to give up if needed, and are always observing things around them to get new information. Nigel was good at what he did and had a smuggling operation that was useful to us. Those are the reasons I kept tabs on him."

"So, you weren't doing the nasty with him back in 81'?"

"Jesus, Nick, you're a brazen little shit. If it's that damn important for you to know, yes, we were doing the nasty, if that's what you want to refer to it as, but that was way down on the list for reasons to watch him."

"Ha, I knew it! Things are making a little more sense now. The question that is now foremost on my mind is, what is my role? You are going to pay me a lot of money to do what eventually? You remember the deal we made?"

"I remember. There are more countries than ours that know what is going on or at least have an idea. They will want to get their hands on the research and will do anything they need to. Most of them know they can't let the States control something that might be more valuable than the atomic bomb in WWII. Quite frankly, we are not sure how we feel about the Yanks having total control. We do know if the US loses control of it, we at least want to be the ones that get it. In either case, we will protect each other. If an enemy of the state, ours, or theirs, gets control, we can't predict how it will be used. We need to put ourselves in a position to have it should something go wrong.

The other issue that should be near and dear to your heart is no matter who has the technology, it is doubtful it will initially be made accessible to those who need it, like your brother. That is where you come in."

"How do you think I'm going to get accepted into Dr. Brunetta's circle of influence? I'm just a kid coming back from tutoring English in Thailand and backpacking around Asia. Those aren't exactly exemplary achievements for my resume."

"You won't be rubbing elbows with Elli or her circle of contemporaries. You'll be rubbing elbows with her lobsterman husband. Why do you think we sent you out on a lobster boat for a week? You'll need to look like a quick study when you get on his boat. We've already arranged a three-month trip with him when you get back. I'm sure your parents will want you to head straight to school, but you need to convince them otherwise. Something is going to come down in the next three to six months. We need an inside person not only to feed us information but be there if, or when, needed."

"How long have you all been planning this?"

"Several years Nick. Things just started to align perfectly. Some might surmise the hand of God made its entrance when you started heavily advocating for changes in how medicine and drugs are developed and administered. Your advocacy was happening at about the same time we realized Elli was coming up with maybe the most important medical discovery since antibiotics. We are playing a risk/reward game all the time. Elli was developing her product; you were advocating with a strong voice and conviction. There was a risk but, potentially a big reward. We decided we needed to get you into the fold somehow. We were monitoring your social media and your email. I guess you can find it believable that it was us who led you to find the job in Thailand when you were doing your searches, and if you didn't end up there, we would have led you somewhere else. I can tell you; we never thought your involvement would be at this level. Hand of God, maybe?"

"Wow, I am blown away. I couldn't have ever imagined this scenario. It's like I'm a character in a book. How will we communicate while I am in Maine?"

"Don't worry, we can communicate from anywhere in the world using a technology called Voice over Internet Protocol or VoIP and a technology called Direct Inward Dialing. Both have been around for several years. I'll set it up on your phone. When things get closer to day zero, I'll make my way to Bar Harbor."

Nick, still amazed, could not hold back, "I know God is good, but you people are amazing!"

CHAPTER 35

February, 2019 - Boston

Nick's plane landed at precisely 3:47 PM in Boston. His parents agreed to meet him at the passenger pickup outside at the arrival exit. He went into the bathroom to splash some water on his face to wake him up from the long trip. Looking into the mirror, he didn't look like the young man who left nine months ago to teach English to kids. He looked like a much more mature man who had been trained to sense danger and inflict harm to his enemies by any means necessary. His eyes were deeper now and, if you looked into them long enough, you would know there were secrets hidden behind them.

He reached into his backpack and pulled out a t-shirt that read - *All the Cool Kids are Reading*. He replaced his blue button-down with the t-shirt, and, although his hair was longer, he messed with it, then combed it into a similar style he had before he left. OK, time to be a kid again, he thought to himself as he prepared to meet with his parents.

Although cars and buses produced the chaotic sound of Thailand, walking out into the American air was sweet, unlike the dusty, stale air he had to breathe for the last nine months. It was February, and there was a distinct Boston chill in the air. The Pats had just won another Superbowl. Golden Boy, Tom Brady, had just won his sixth Superbowl, and the rest of the NFL and their fans hated the Pats even more. Brady's contract was ending, and rumors were rampant the Pats were trading him away. Nick thought, *it figures, I have enough money to go to the Superbowl and I may not be able to see my Pats there for a while, especially if they trade Brady.*

He took another deep breath and held it in for a moment, so happy to be home.

He watched the traffic drive by, searching for his parent's car. Nick looked at his cell phone to see if they had called or texted. "WE'RE HERE AT GATE A 10 WHERE ARE YOU?" was typed across his screen. Nick typed back "GATE A 14 ARRIVALS", waiting for a response. What he got was a big hug from his mother sneaking up from behind.

"Mom, I thought you were at the wrong gate."

"That was your dad trying to be funny. My God, Nick, you look so grown-up; look at you."

"Where's dad?"

"He is driving around in circles. I couldn't wait, so I told him to drop me off at your gate. He should be coming around shortly. Sweetie, we missed you so much. We can't wait to hear about your trip and all your adventures."

Nick thought to himself, *they don't want to know, and* he didn't want to tell them. "Mom, we will catch up; I just want to get home and rest. It's been a long flight."

Nick's dad pulled up and was honking, the same honk he did when he would pick up him and Steve at school. It was the same tune as Mr. Roger's Neighborhood. The memory brought a smile to his face, good memories, peaceful memories.

"There's your dad, sweetie. Hurry before he continues blasting the horn."

Nick slung his backpack to the rear of the car and proceeded to get into the back.

"Whoa son, let your mom sit in the back. Come up front with me," Nick's dad beckoned.

Nick held the door open for his mom and then jumped in the front seat where his dad greeted him.

"You look great; nine months away did you some good. You even have stubble on your face."

"You look like an action hero, so rugged and handsome," Nick's mother jumped in.

"Thanks, mom and dad. You guys look great too."

The drive home was filled with his parents chitter chatting, updating Nick on the last nine months. All he could do is listen and occasionally stare out the car's window. The drive seemed long, probably because of his long flight. Nick found himself dozing off, trying to sleep only to be awakened by his parent's voices asking him about his experience. Nick had forgotten how cold it could get in Boston this time of year. Snow started falling.

By the time they got home, Nick had been caught up on everything. Nothing too alarming; the Allen's across the street were getting a divorce. No surprise there; she has been cheating on Mr. Allen for years. As Nick got out of the car, he looked up at his bedroom window. His parents had turned on the lights, which he figured was a symbol of welcoming him home.

"Hungry?" his mom asked.

"Yeah, a little bit. Let me get settled, take a shower, and I will be down afterward," Nick responded.

"Should we tell him now?"

"Steph, let him clean up and rest awhile. We can discuss this at dinner."

Nick was curious, "Discuss what?"

Before Nick's dad could answer, his mom jumped in, "The University of Massachusetts has accepted you. We enrolled you in summer classes. We know you had planned to wait for fall, but we took the opportunity when we found out you were getting back early.

Isn't that great news? You can catch up for the last nine months and graduate on the same schedule as if you never left."

Nick knew he would not step into any classroom, not for a while, anyway. He was expecting to hear from Talia soon to start his first assignment. Nick had to go along with his parents for now. They were so happy and excited for him, but he knew he might be gone in a week.

Nick took a long hot shower, washing Israel off him. Nick's cell phone dinged, indicating he had a new message. It was Talia asking him if he could talk, knowing he was home with his parents. Nick typed back, "SURE, GIVE ME A MINUTE."

Nick got dressed and made is way to the backyard to avoid his parents to take Talia's call.

"So, I can see you made it home safely. How are your parents?"

"I don't think you called to inquire about my parents. What do you have for me?"

"It's time for you to go fishing."

Part III

Redemption

CHAPTER 36

Saturday May 25, 2019 - Shanghai

Derek was woozy and disoriented. He reached for his left arm and could feel a cast in a sling. The cast's texture reminded him a lot of the papier-mache' volcano he made for his fourth-grade science project. His arm must have gotten broken during the accident.

How long had he been here? Were the other guys looking for him? Were they OK? He remembered coming to a couple of times but had lost track of time. He looked down to his right wrist to see what his I-Watch said and realized it was gone. Shit, he thought, what else did they take? He reached for his belt with his left hand, the one in the sling. "Aargh," he screamed in unison to the scream of pain in his shoulder.

Reaching down with his right hand, all he could feel was the woven denim's roughness as he fingered the loop where his belt should have been. He wrongly figured they had taken that to protect him from himself. Hopefully it's nearby, he thought.

He looked at his left hand. The cast extended down to the middle knuckle of his fingers. They had removed his ring to put the cast on. "Fuck". He knew he was in big trouble. Banging his right fist on the pillow, he noticed something he had missed up to this act of frustration... a ring! They had moved it from his left hand to his right, evidently thinking it was his wedding band. Killers with a heart, he thought. He knew he at least had a fighting chance now.

As his vision started to clear, Derek took a survey of the room. It was obviously in an old building. The walls were cinder block, painted a pale white color, cracked in every corner, and covered with water stains the color of rust. It was only about 10' by 10', with no windows and a door directly across from the mattress he was laying on with a single, loosely woven blanket. Next to the mattress was a small rosewood end table, intricately carved, but old from wear. On the tabletop were two bottles of water and a box of crackers with Chinese writing on the packaging. There was a chair in the corner to the left of him. In the other corner was a hole for pissing and shitting. The floor was made of tile, an ugly green color that reminded him of those awful lime jello and cottage cheese salads his next-door neighbor Katie would make at Easter or neighborhood potlucks.

"Can anybody hear me?" He yelled.

The door was immediately unlocked from the outside, swinging open and rattling as it hit the wall. Gus leaned into the doorway, "Only me shithead. If you yell again, I'll have to come in and shut you up".

Derek wasn't sure what he meant but wasn't going to push him too far. "What day is it?"

"Why does that matter to you?"

"I just want to know how long I've been here."

"It's Friday night, now shut up."

The auction is tomorrow, he thought. I wonder if Jack's people have figured out a way to participate.

"We tracked Derek's belt to a side street near Yu Gardens. It had been at that location since right after the accident. We also found his shoes, so we don't think he was made, just getting some of his clothes tossed off to keep him from considering escape." Andy said.

Nigel had been visibly upset since the kidnapping two days earlier. Now, he was getting exasperated. It was Friday evening, less than twenty-four hours away from the auction. "Do we have any damn info that helps us locate Derek?"

"We went to the belt location with the RFID trackers, walked a kilometer in every direction, and got no signal. That doesn't mean he's not near there. He could have had the ring taken away. I do have a bit of good news; we got a camera hit for Zhang today. He was headed into a noodle shop about a kilometer from where we found the belt. It was back towards the Garment District. He had a baseball cap and sunglasses on. Fortunately, he took the glasses off to read the menu on the outside door. That's when we got him. We are looking at camera records near there to see if we can figure out where he's going or where he came from."

Mack made himself part of the conversation, "Are we positive we can't set up the fake bank account to get into the bidding? That may be our only chance of tracking Derek's location; we may lose the package and Derek if we don't get in."

"Zhang made it very clear in the message we received from him right after the kidnapping, that if he caught us even attempting to infiltrate the auction or track his IP, we would never see Derek again. I know how important this package is, but I'm not willing to lose my son for it. I believe Zhang will have him killed if he sees us coming."

"We won't get caught, Nigel. We've backed off actively pursuing getting into the auction. Quite truthfully, it probably wasn't going to happen anyway. Everything would've had to come together perfectly, and since we aren't certain of Zhang's security software or firewall, he would have fleshed out a fake bank account or an attempt to find his IP location. Andy, what else do we have? We've been looking for two days; there should be something."

"Not much. We have the entire office pouring through camera records from the past few days. We're certain something is out there. Once we have a few camera identifications, we should be able to get a track on Zhang. If we can get an RFID signal, we'll see his and Derek's locations. The system is accurate to within a few centimeters. Getting Derek back is our top and only priority right now. Hopefully, we'll also lock down the location of the package at the same time."

Getting up from the table, Nigel started walking towards the exit. "I've had it with shoulda's, mighta's, hopefully, and ifs. I'm going out to get something to drink."

"Nigel, you may want to hold on."

"Why?"

"First, we have a big day tomorrow and need to be on our toes. Second, I think I need to show you something I hope will convince you that you need to stay here."

Nigel followed Jack into the computer area. Bending down, Jack reached under a desk and grabbed a latch. At the same time, Andy entered a code into his laptop. The wall to their right proceeded to open up, showing a two-foot-deep room housing many long arms, pistols, and knives.

"Nigel, we will find Derek."

Derek was feeling better. His fatigue level was still high but manageable, with the past few days being a blur. Each time he tried to recall something, he felt like he was peering into a cloud, where shadows were moving in and out, occasionally showing a face, and where muffled conversations were taking place, with words sometimes revealing themselves. The one memory that kept coming back was of a rat coming into his room during the night. He thought it was the pain drugs causing him to hallucinate.

The thought of the rat somehow made him smile. There were no feelings of fear, only of comfort.

Derek knew he needed to get some sleep. He would need energy in the morning. If something were going to happen, it would be tomorrow. It didn't take but minutes to fall into a deep sleep and dream of a rat. In the dream, he named the rat Socrates after a rat he remembered from a horror flick when he was a kid. There was also a distant sound of crackling like someone was crumpling cellophane, or a fire was popping because of wet wood.

When Derek finally awoke the next morning, he felt invigorated from a good night's sleep and pleasant dreams. Attempting to swing his legs onto the floor, he felt an odd weight on the blanket, making it difficult to do. Looking towards the bottom of his bed, he saw something lumped on at the crook of his knees and lower legs. Trying to pull his feet away, Derek could have sworn he saw the lump move. Rubbing the sleep from his eyes, he pulled his feet up and sat up on the mattress. Looking over to his side table, he saw the open half pack of crackers he had left there the night before, were gone. Only cellophane wrapping and a few random crumbs were left.

He looked back towards his bed; the lump uncurled itself into the shape of a rat. "Well, I'll be damned." Reaching to his table, he grabbed the other pack of crackers, opened it up, placed one in the palm of his hand, and stretched it out towards the rat. Slowly, but unafraid, the rat walked up to his palm and started nibbling on the cracker.

"Nice to meet you, Socrates."

The sound of his door unlocking disturbed the moment. Socrates jumped off the bed and disappeared into a hole in the wall.

"Jack, take a look at this. It looks like Zhang went past the noodle shop again last night. There was another sighting of him entering an old fabric warehouse less than a click away from the noodle shop. We have sent a tracker over to watch the building entrance and are going over the last few hours of camera footage to see if he ever left the building."

Andy, get us the RFID trackers. We need to get over there right now! Mack and Nigel go to the back and grab your weapon and choice of ammunition. There are also holsters and company jackets you can put on to conceal the weapons. The last thing you need is for someone to spot a gun on you."

Nigel and Mack hustled back with Andy. As Mack grabbed the latch, Andy entered the code. Nigel couldn't resist, "Open Sesame."

The long arms were all mounted on the wall of the room. Although Mack and Nigel knew they weren't going to use them, they couldn't help but admire them. Everything from Mossberg Patriot shotguns to AR Bushmasters. The best of everything, depending on the situation.

Nigel pulled out the drawer housing the handguns, silencers, and ammo. Mack immediately reached for the Glock G19. "That looked easy," Mack said as he stood to examine the contents of the drawer. "Why did you go for that one so quickly?"

"It looks like the one my dad carried around when I was younger. He used to tell me it was the best of the best."

"Have you ever shot one?"

"No, not the Glock, but at the time I wanted to. I hunted with my dad a little when I was younger, so I can handle rifles and shotguns pretty well. I also went to the range with him for target practice. He did give me a Wesson 10mm, but he never allowed me to touch his Glock. As I got older, I didn't see much of a use for guns, but kept the Wesson for sentimental purposes."

"You picked a good one. It will have a little more kick than a .22, though."

"I suppose so. I'm sure I can handle it."

Nigel felt like a kid in a candy store but eventually went for the same gun he carried on his boat. Why get a twinkie when you can have a birthday cake?

"There it is." Nigel reached for the Ruger MK. "I think I may take this switch-blade with me too."

The others followed suit, and all grabbed daggers.

Gus was in his early sixties now but still an imposing figure. He had gained some weight over the years but it made him look hardier than he had forty years earlier. The six-pack was gone but the circumference of his torso and arms had increased substantially over the years. Back in the "Nigel days" he was known to be quick as a cat and extremely dangerous if he got ahold of you. These days he could be best described as a mountain. He didn't have to be quick as a cat any longer; he only had to get in your way. You still wouldn't want to go hand-to-hand with him. Derek couldn't help thinking about his numbered days. Maybe they should have gotten the law more involved.

"So, Mr. Derek, I see you are getting stronger. I hope that is not giving any thoughts of trying to leave these beautiful five star accommodations."

"Do I have a choice?"

"Actually, no. About the only choice you might have to make today is whether you will live or die. Your father and his friends are out searching for you. It has been fun watching them run around town, but they haven't even gotten warm yet. I have also warned them, if they try to interfere, they will never see you again."

Gus threw Derek the flip-phone they had taken from him. Again, he went for it with his left hand as would any right-handed kid who had spent any time in Little League. Pain…

"I see there is only one number saved. I'll have to assume it's Wang's phone. I'd like you to call that number and ask for your dad. When he gets on, I need you to let him know I will be with you all day. Remind him that if they are caught messing with the auction or interfering in any other way, I will personally kill you."

Derek pushed the auto-call.

Jack was startled when he heard his Trak-phone ring. The call was from Derek's number.

"Hello? Derek, is that you? Are you...?"

"Yeah, it's me. Overall, I'm fine, but I do have an injured shoulder and broken arm. My fingers are OK too. I need to speak to my dad."

As Jack handed the phone to Nigel, he knew Derek had just given him a signal he was still wearing the ring. He got Nigel's attention and pointed to his ring finger, then gave the thumbs-up sign.

Nigel knew what that meant and not to ask about the ring. "Derek, where are you?"

"I don't know, dad. I was drugged when they brought me here. I'm starting to come out of it now. This Gus character has been outside my door most of the time. He's a real charmer."

Gus pointed to his watch, then twirled his finger in the air. Derek knew Gus was telling him to move on and end the conversation.

"Dad, I gotta go, but I need to pass on a message from Gus. He told me to remind you he has orders to kill me immediately if you interfere with the auction."

"Derek, we have no plans on interfering with the auction. You can give that message to Gus. Please hand the phone back to that cocksucker. I love you."

"Love you." Derek handed the phone back.

"Do you have something to say to me, Nigel?"

"You son-of-a-bitch, if you do anything to him…"

"Cool down Nigel. You are in no position to make threats or demands. You and your friends need to behave yourselves; then maybe everything will turn out good for your son."

The line went silent.

CHAPTER 37

Wednesday May 22, 3:00 AM – Shanghai

Tuesday May 21, 3:00 PM - Bar Harbor

Agent Johnson's cell phone rang as they all left the room. Nick and Elli continued down the hall back towards the cafeteria as he took his call.

Nick kept his eyes open, hoping to see Gen, but she was nowhere to be found. They took their seats at the same table sitting in silence, waiting for Agent Johnson to return.

Nick broke the silence and spoke first, "The men at the restaurant; not only did I see them, but I also heard them."

"What do you mean, Nick?" asked Elli.

Just as Nick was ready to respond, Agent Johnson walked up, overhearing Elli's question and said, "He means he overheard that Sam Wilder knew them too."

"What is this?" asked Elli.

Agent Johnson continued, "I just received a call from our office in Portland; apparently, Sam was working with the Chinese."

"How did you discover this?"

"Bar Harbor is a small town. I did some checking with some bars and restaurants that have video cameras. In Portland my team reviewed hours of tape and found Sam sitting at a bar with that dead man who we learned was Gen's brother. Nick, can you confirm this? What did you hear?"

Elli was getting stressed. "Why are you interrogating Nick like that?"

Nick finally responded to the questions. "Because he saw me in the same video with Sam and Gen's brother. I heard him tell one of his buddies he was meeting Sam later that evening at some bar called the Thirsty Whale, so I followed him there. Not only did Sam meet with the dead Chinese guy; Gus Peralta was there as well."

Agent Johnson asked Nick about Peralta, "Who is this Peralta character?

Elli jumped in, "Nick, why would you put yourself in the same room with Gus? Do you know how dangerous he is?

"I know now. I didn't then."

Agent Johnson looked frustrated and scolded Elli, "OK, hold on, you asked for my help at the lab and now you're holding back information that could help my investigation. I think we would all be better off to combine what we know and figure this thing out. I need to go back to your place; the Sheriff and his deputies are investigating it being shot up. Now is there anything else I need to know before I get there?"

Elli looked over at Nick and then to J, "You already know about Sam; you will find his body in the living room and lots of bullet holes."

"Jesus Christ, with Sam being killed and all the booby traps, this has become a clusterfuck. Let's catch up in the next few days while I clean up the mess at your place and figure this thing out. Where will you be staying in town?"

"We will be on Nigel's boat, the Serendipity; there's a cabin there big enough for us to stay."

"Good, it would have been helpful if Nigel hadn't left. I have questions for him."

"J, you're just going to have to wait for Nigel to return," Elli responded.

"And when is that?" Nick and Elli gave each other the OH SHIT look. They hoped soon.

Nick checked in on his mother at the hospital before heading back to Bar Harbor. He had arranged for Stephanie's sister to pick her up when she was released and take her back to Amherst; mom would be safer there. The doctor assured him his mom would make a full recovery, and they would watch after her until his aunt arrived to pick her up.

He and Elli drove back to Bar Harbor that night and settled in on the Serendipity. The boat seemed empty without the Skipper on board, and Nick hoped Nigel was taking care of his dad in China.

The next few days were quiet; Nick cooked most of the meals as Elli made calls and worked on her laptop. Agent Johnson made arrangements with the local Sheriff not to bother them and informed him this was now an FBI investigation. He was planning to meet with the authorities on Thursday to discuss the investigation.

"Elli, do you trust Agent Johnson?"

"Nick, I don't know who to trust. The only person I do trust is a million miles away with your dad and my son. Why didn't you tell me about Sam's meeting with Gus, and why did you place yourself in danger in doing so?"

"Elli, you are going have to trust me," Nick responded.

Elli just looked at Nick and then stared down at her laptop. Nick wanted to tell her about his mission, but wanted to be sure he could trust her. He was convinced she had nothing to do with the Chinese and Gus coming to the house, but how did they turn Sam? Was it the money, or had he sold out to the Chinese?

Talia told him things would happen within three to six months, but things moved much faster. It was difficult trying to be discreet during his limited free time to poke around. He was lucky to have been at the Chinese restaurant and overhear the planned meeting. Nick put it all together after he saw Sam at the Thirsty Whale with the Chinese. Sam was the rat inside the lab; he was the only one, besides Elli, who knew where the formula was kept. Sam's failed attempt at rummaging through Elli's office to make it look amateur was blatant, trying to throw the FBI off. When Sam showed up at Nigel's house that night, he knew his family's lives would be in danger. Once the shooting started, he had to kill Sam before Sam killed them all. Gus shooting up the place may have been a distraction to get Sam in the house. Nick had never shot a man before; he had to do it; he had to shoot Sam. Nick wanted to tell Elli everything he knew, but honored Talia's instructions to only report to her. Now that the FBI was aware of Sam's meeting with the Chinese, and now tailing him, it would be difficult to talk to Talia, but he needed to as soon as possible.

Wednesday May 22, 11:00 PM - Shanghai

Wednesday May 22, 11:00 AM - Bar Harbor

The next day, Nick left the Serendipity to call Talia to let her know what time to meet. Talia did not answer at first, but soon after Nick's cell phone began to ring. She told Nick to meet her at the Side Street Cafe in Bar Harbor at 11:00 AM. and to go ahead and order if she was not there.

After arriving, Nick sat down and waited before waving the waitress over. After fifteen minutes or so, he could see the waitress with thick eye makeup, nose ring, and arms covered in tattoos was getting impatient and approached him. "Hi, can

I take your order?" "Maddy," reading the waitresses' name tag, "I will try the Adam Bomb Burger and an ice tea.

"The Bar Island Rum Cocktail will get your day going faster than that ice tea," she replied.

"No thanks, just the ice tea."

She scribbled the order on her pad, gave a flirtatious smile, and walked away.

Just as Nick's lunch arrived, Talia showed up.

"Hello Nick, you didn't order me a cocktail?

"It's ice tea, and you're welcome to have mine."

"No thanks, I'm not that thirsty. So Nick, you have been a busy man. Hate to get straight to the point. Tell me what you learned about the break-in at the lab, Sam, Elli, and the Chinese."

Nick didn't know where to start, the shooting at the cliffs, the break-in, killing Sam. He began by telling Talia the series of events that led to his call, and more importantly, that the FBI was starting to ask questions. Talia wasn't too concerned about the FBI, not just yet. She had tracked Nick's activities and, no far, so surprises. Nick asked her what was going on in China and how Nigel and his Dad were doing. Although Nick's life had taken a big turn and now that he had the skills and insight to handle the current situation, he couldn't imagine his dad being in China taking the risk with dangerous people to recover the stolen package.

With his mother almost killed Nick wanted this to be over, bring everybody back home safe, go back to school, get his education, and then pursue his career as a covert operative for the US or any other friendlies.

He also planned to give some of the money he would receive from Talia to his parents to help them make things better for their lives.

Talia interrupted his thoughts, "Nick, first do not trust the FBI, I'm not sure you should even trust Elli. Now that we know Sam was the inside man working with the Chinese, we need to learn more about what is in Sam's office."

"Sam's office, why is that so important? The package is no longer at the lab, and Dad and Nigel are trying to recover it."

Talia responded, "Well, that is not entirely true."

"Why do you say that?

"You need to convince Elli to go back to the lab; Sam hid something in his office. We intercepted a call from Sam telling an unknown person he had insurance to assure his safety and demand more money".

Nick never got a chance to finish his lunch. They both got up and walked to the cashier. Elli was out collecting food supplies for the boat and happened to walk past the diner. Looking inside, she thought she saw her friend Talia standing in line in front of Nick. She and Talia had spoken to each other on the phone but she never said anything about coming to town. Elli couldn't tell if Nick and the Talia doppelganger were even together.

Elli was busy, thinking she must be confused, didn't want to embarrass herself, or cause a scene by confronting Talia if it was her. She would see Nick later to ask, so she kept walking. For some reason she had an unusual feeling in the pit of her stomach.

CHAPTER 38

Thursday May 23, 2:00 AM - Shanghai,

Wednesday May 22, 2:00 PM - Bar Harbor

It was Wednesday afternoon when Nick saw Agent Johnson walking down the dock approaching the Serendipity. From what Talia told him, he needed to divert Agent Johnson down another path. To do this, he required Elli's help.

"Permission to come on board?" J shouted.

"You only say that when the Captain is on the boat," Nick responded.

"Sorry, I forgot."

"I call him the Skipper anyway."

"It would have been good to talk to him before he left."

"Well J, you are just going to have to wait."

Frustrated, J responded, "I guess so."

"J, what did you find out at our place? Who is trying to kill us?"

"Elli, we found Sam's body, your booby traps, and a lot of bullet holes. The forensic team has completed their work there. Funny thing they told me from what they can tell so far the bullet wound in Sam was a smaller caliber compared to the twenty holes we found at your place."

Nick joined in the conversation, "So there was another shooter?"

"Yes, I would say there was. What is puzzling me is the one-shot that killed Sam. It doesn't make sense. Tell me, if this Peralta guy was shooting up your place with automatic weapons, why did his accomplice only take one shot and was so accurate?"

"Who said it was Peralta shooting up the place?"

"Nick, I believe you did."

"Well, you're wrong; I did not."

"Anyway, Nick, the questions for you are, why were you following Sam last week, and who is Peralta?"

"I heard three men talking at the Chinese restaurant. They mentioned Elli and seemed angry. Nigel's my boss, I was curious and wanted to make sure neither he nor Elli were not in danger, so I decided to follow them that night." One stayed at the restaurant, so I followed the two who left.

"Isn't that kind of dangerous for a young fisherman like you? How did you know you were not followed?

"I was careful they went to a placed called the Thirsty Whale, so I went in the back door and entered through the kitchen. The place is small and dark, and I was sure I could blend in with the rest of the crowd."

"When you got there, what did you hear?"

"The two Chinese guys sat down with two other guys in a booth. I sat at the bar outside their line of sight. I heard bits and pieces of a conversation, something about Lerdell Labs and Elli's work there.

"Who was there, Nick?" Agent Johnson persisted.

"The two Asian men from the Chinese restaurant, one white guy, and the other looked Hispanic. I did not know who Sam was until I got to the Thirsty Whale, or anyone else other than the dead man at the hospital."

"How did you know the white man was Sam?'

"Because the Hispanic dude yelled at him, 'Sam, you're going with me.' After that, I left and told Nigel what I heard." (which was a lie)

"Is that why all the bobby traps at the house?" asked J.

"Yes, that is correct." (another lie)

"Elli, anything else to add?"

"No, I think Nick pretty well said what took place."

"Do you think they had something to do with the stolen package?"

"Why Agent Johnson, you are smarter than I thought. Yes, of course, why else would they be trying to kill us?" Elli said in a very sarcastic voice.

Agent Johnson looked at both Nick and Elli and knew there was much more. He decided to end the conversation until he could talk to Nigel.

"Well, Sam's body is out of your house, and you can go back if you choose to; the bomb squad removed all the devices, but you have a mess there to clean up. Oh, by the way, don't leave town."

After Agent Johnson left, Elli turned to Nick, "OK, tell me more. I know you heard more of the conversation."

"Yes, I did. The other Asian guy was Zhang Wei, and the Hispanic guy was Gus Peralta. I figured he was Peralta at the time, but wasn't sure. Unfortunately, we now all know who Peralta is."

"How did you know it might be Peralta?"

"Nigel would tell us stories on the Serendipity to pass the time. He told me some crazy story about being in the British Intelligence and his nemeses was this Peralta guy. I never thought this would all be true, but considering the last few days, I guess Nigel is not that crazy after all. Elli, I need your help getting into the lab."

"The lab, why would you want to go back there?"

"I learned something else from that conversation at the Thirsty Whale."

"What?"

"I learned Sam made copies of some files or formulas. Some or all of those may not have been included in the package that was taken from the lab."

Of course, Nick did not learn this information from Sam or anybody else at the bar. This new information was provided to him by Talia. After the auction, she told him Zhang and Gus were returning to get the rest of the formula and tie loose ends, which meant coming back for us. He couldn't tell Elli he learned this from another source and had to tell her he heard it that day.

"Sam, that son of a bitch, how did he get into my files?"

"I'm sure as the Security Expert; he has been monitoring your office and computer. We need to go tonight and try to find that file."

"How do you know it's still there? If Sam was involved with the break-in, surely he would have grabbed that too."

"We don't know that for sure, Elli, but this is a detail we really shouldn't blow off with an assumption."

Again, Nick knew better. Talia told him they never retrieved it. Sam must have left it on purpose as some insurance with Zhang. Nevertheless, they needed to get back into the lab and search for it. Talia wasn't certain what was in Sam's file or whether it was the entire formula or a vital portion needed to complete the project. Whatever it was, Talia made it clear he had to retrieve it no matter what it took.

Elli wasn't too happy about going back to the lab and questioned Nick's information. All he could do is tell her where they were now; people are dead, Nigel, Derek, and his dad are risking everything to retrieve the package. If they didn't go back to the lab, it would make everybody's sacrifice worthless.

Elli finally agreed. However, she told him tonight would not be good because additional staff is brought in to do a thorough search of the entire building for bugs and other security risks. Thursday night would be better; Elli could get Nick in under his pretense as an intern. They would have all night to search for the file.

They decided to stay on the Serendipity. Neither wanted to go back to the house. Cleaning up the blood where Nick's mom was shot, and patching bullet holes didn't sound too fun.

Nick told Elli he would make them dinner tonight and discuss the plan to go into the lab. He could see she was exhausted and needed a break.

All Elli could muster was, "What are you going to make for dinner?"

Nick, proud of himself, "You haven't heard of my famous hamburger surprise?"

CHAPTER 39

After dinner Nick and Elli discussed how they would approach the lab. Elli had access to her office and going there would not draw any suspicion, except for Nick being with her. The more significant challenge was gaining access to Sam's office and searching it. They both agreed going to the lab after 9:00 PM would be best. Most of the staff would be gone, and her working late would not be unusual. They would stay in Elli's office until after midnight and then make their way to Sam's office. Nick assured her he knew a little about locks and could get her in. Searching all the drawers, bookcases, and file cabinets would take some time. There is no guarantee they would find something, but they would have to try.

Elli wanted to know what was on the file and its impact on the formula and Nigel's effort in China.

They spent the next day going over their plan, looking over the facility, and who may be there tonight. They left for the lab that evening and eventually made it to the security gate. The guard on duty recognized Elli, but still looked carefully viewed her ID and credentials.

"Evening Dr. Brunetta, putting in some late hours, and who do you have with you?"

"Yes, Security Officer Hortin, I need to finish some reports, work on some projects, yadda, yadda."

"Sounds like you have a long night ahead of you. Young man, can I see some identification?"

"He is an intern from Brunswick."

"Really, where are you going to school?"

Before Elli could answer, Nick, with confidence, replied, "Bowdoin College."

"Great, I still need to see your ID to check you in."

The security guard carefully checked Nick's ID and saw Nick was from Massachusetts. "Mr. Griego, do you have your college ID?

Elli was getting upset with the guard, "He is with me and we have a lot of work ahead of us. Sam cleared him weeks ago, and I don't need your bullshit."

"Sorry, Dr. Brunetta, with the break-in and Sam's murder, I'm just doing my job. If Sam cleared him, it's not on my tablet; I could lose my job."

"I would say you're close to losing it anyway."

Elli picked her phone and started scrolling through her contacts and pressed call. After a few moments, "Hello Dr. Bagchi, it's Dr. Brunetta here at the gate.

Security Officer Hortin won't let me in to complete the work you instructed me to do. I have my intern Nick with me who you met last month. If I remember correctly, not getting this to you can cost the lab millions!"

"There must be an error in my tablet. If Dr. Bagchi cleared him, that is good enough for me," the nervous guard replied.

Elli flipped the Officer off as she drove through the gate.

"Who is Dr. Bagchi?" asked Nick.

"He is the CEO of the lab; I faked the call. My question is, how did you know Bowdoin College was in Brunswick?"

Nick smiled and, lying through his teeth, said, "Bowdoin College, a good friend goes there."

He knew the call Elli made to Dr. Bagchi wasn't real, but enjoyed the performance. Luckily, Security Officer Hortin bought it.

They entered the lab with no resistance. The security detail in the building wished Elli a good evening with no questions about Nick being there. Elli and Nick stepped into the elevator and she pushed the button for the 2nd floor. They made their way to Elli's office. Once in, she locked her door and took a seat at her desk.

"What do we do now, Elli?"

"We wait, I want them thinking I'm working in my office. I would say it would be safe going to Sam's office around midnight."

"Safe?"

"The facility staff would all be gone by then. The two security guards we saw coming in will walk the perimeter of the building. We can make our way to Sam's office when they do."

"What about all the video cameras I've seen?"

"Nick, we are looking for something stolen from the lab. Sam is not alive to report it. No one will view the video footage for tonight unless they think something is wrong. I believe we will be OK wandering around. How do you plan to get us through that locked door?"

"When I was in Thailand, I learned the art of picking locks from some of the best. It came in handy when we needed supplies for the children. Don't worry, just get me there."

Elli opened her desk drawer and pulled out a deck of cards and a bottle of Buffalo Trace and asked, "Care for a sip to calm your nerves?"

"I'm not nervous, but you seem distracted. What's going on?"

"Have you talked to your dad recently?"

"I sent him a text Tuesday, letting him know mom is staying at her sister's. Why, is something going on I should be aware of?"

"Derek is missing. Nigel said Zhang and Gus might have kidnapped him. I didn't want to say anything to you and wanted to keep us focused on what we need to do here."

"I'm sorry, Elli, what is Nigel planning to do?"

"He is going to get him back, of course."

"And my dad?"

"He is going to help Nigel."

They both drank several shots; there was not much more to say. They passed the rest of the time playing cards. Elli was right; they had to stay focused. It was midnight, time to get started. They carefully left Elli's office and made their way down the stairs. Sam's office was on the first floor, not too far from the main entrance. Nick could see the two guards were not at their stations and must be walking around outside. When they got to Sam's office, Nick could see the lock would not be a problem. *Some security*, he thought to himself. He manipulated the lock with a pick as the door opened easily. Once in, they searched the office. Elli began at the desk while Nick searched the bookshelves and then made his way to the files.

"Nothing, how about you?" asked Elli.

"Nothing yet."

They both fell onto the couch, perplexed on where to search next. Nick carefully scanned the room, wondering to himself where he would hide a small thumb drive?

"Elli, did you look under the drawers to make sure nothing was taped to the bottom?"

"Yes, I did. Nothing there."

Nick looked over at the desk again and saw what was obvious, Sam's laptop.

"The laptop?"

"Nick, that is the first place I looked. There is no thumb drive other than one for the wireless mouse."

"I can see that, but where is the mouse?"

They both scrambled to their feet and made their way to the laptop.

"It couldn't be that simple, could it, Nick?"

"I don't know, but let's take it up to your office and plug it in. It's all we've got."

Backtracking back to their office wasn't that easy. One of the guards was sitting at his post. The other was still outside, making his rounds.

"What do we do now?"

"Elli, you belong here, just walk up to him and distract him as I go up the stairs. You hanging around the first floor can't be that uncommon, but with me, it may raise some questions."

Elli slowly walked up to the guard and tried to make small talk by flirting with the man. Nick sneaked around the corner to the stairwell. After glancing over, Elli could see Nick was in the clear.

"Hey, you leaving already? We were having a great conversation."

"Sorry, got get back to my office. I don't want to sleep here tonight; bye."

They both were back in Elli's office. She turned on her laptop. After it booted, she slipped in the thumb drive and opened the file titled "INSURANCE." In the file, she found what she was looking for. It was not the whole formula, but whoever had the formula would need this information to complete the task sequence.

"Whoever has the package would not be happy with this piece missing."

"What is it, Elli?"

"It buys us time, a good Biochemist would figure the sequence out with time, but it may take six months or more.

This thumb drive just has it already spelled out. Time is money; I believe Sam would sell this to the person who won the bid, making some extra money, and whatever Zhang paid him already.

"Let's get out of here. It's Friday morning, and we need some sleep. Nigel will be calling me sometime today. I will update him then."

CHAPTER 40

Saturday May 25, 11:00 AM - Shanghai,

Friday May 24, 11:00 PM - Bar Harbor

"Derek, I've meant to ask you something. Has your dad ever told you the story of him and your mom meeting, or said anything about their relationship with me?

"All I know about you is you are a cold-blooded killer who works for the bad guy that has the most cash."

"Good guy, bad guy; no difference from where I stand. Did your dad talk much about Argentina?"

"No. I know he was down there for the Falkland war, working on a gunship. He doesn't talk much about it. I don't know much about my mom's or dad's life from early on. They keep pretty quiet, and I figure they'd tell me about it when they wanted to."

"Any grandparents?"

"All dead. Two buried in Italy, two in England. Why are you asking me all this shit? All of a sudden, you're interested in me? Do you want me to start calling you Uncle Gus or something?" Derek could see he was getting under Gus' skin just a little bit, but he didn't care. It wasn't going to change the outcome of his situation.

"What if I told you, you had two grandparents on your mom's side growing old and rich in Argentina and your grandpa is one of the best winemakers there, possibly in all of South America? I bet you'd like to meet them before they die."

"Why would I believe anything coming out of your mouth?"

"Maybe you shouldn't. I can see I'm shaking you up. I guess if you don't believe that, you wouldn't believe the rest." Gus started to leave the room.

"What do you mean, the rest?" Derek asked curiously.

"I don't think I will tell you. Maybe if you are dying in your own pool of blood, and I have an opportunity to share it with you, I will. Before I leave, I think I'll happily share another, unrelated truth.

I rather enjoyed your comment to Wang about how your fingers are fine. Why would you share something like that?"

Hesitation… say something, Derek. "I had a previous hand injury that affected my ability to fish. Just letting dad know I didn't reinjure myself."

"You weren't letting your dad know; you were letting Jack know. I think there is something you want to tell me. Maybe a little secret I should know about?"

"Nothing I can think of."

"Well, I guess I can't believe anything coming out of your mouth either.

"I don't know what you are talking about, Uncle Gus."

"Yes you do, mi Sobrino (my nephew). When we got you in the car, we scanned you for tracking and listening devices. The belt was too obvious; we ditched it with your shoes a long way from here. The ring, though, is impressive, especially with such a powerful RFID signal. Unfortunately for you, we saw that coming. We electronically shielded the building from RFID readers."

"So why did you let me keep it?"

"To give you false hope. Those who have hope are always less troublesome than those without it. You have been very cooperative up to this point, so I guess it worked. I didn't know if I would tell you, but I just decided I didn't like your smugness when I tried to talk about your parents. Your situation should all be over in an hour. There's not much damage you can do from this room."

"Fuck you."

"Those sound like the words of a hopeless person Derek. By the way, next time you see your dad, if there's a next time, ask him about the time he shot me in the head and left me for dead."

The door slammed shut, and the lock clicked.

Saturday May 25, 11:00 AM - Shanghai

Friday May 24, 11:00 PM - Bar Harbor

On the way to the warehouse, Nigel grabbed his phone and entered Elli's number. It would be her bedtime. He knew how frustrated and anxious she had been the past few days and hated to make these calls, especially knowing he had to tell her Derek was still missing. He knew he didn't want to make this particular call, but Elli deserved it.

The calls always ended the same, with Elli telling him to get Derek out and get home. The research package would have to wait for another day.

The phone rang once when Elli picked up the call. "Nigel, please tell me you have Derek."

As much as Nigel wanted to give her good news, he hesitated to provide her with a false sense of reality. He needed to be as calm and honest as possible. "We don't, Elli, but think we are closer. We are checking out a good lead now and should know something by this afternoon. I wish I had something more reliable for you, sweetie, but I don't.

"By the way, how is Steph doing? I know she and Mack have been in contact, but he doesn't say much about their conversations, other than she's doing fine."

"She is still a little shaken up but overall she's doing good. Nick told me she would be staying at her sister's house until you guys get back."

"Where's Nick staying?"

"On the boat. We both felt Nick would be safer there, plus he's been a big help with keeping the FBI stalled, buying you guys some time. I do have to tell you; we won't be able to do it much longer. There are too many loose ends. I'll fill you in on it after you get things done today. I'm not going on to bog you down with anymore right now.

You also should know we found out Nick overheard a conversation where Sam mentioned he made copies of many documents before all my work was taken. We found some last night on a thumb drive from the computer, but we also found what I think are original saved documents. If they are the originals, it will be a game-changer."

"What do you mean by game-changer, and when did Nick hear this conversation?

"What we found won't make sense without other information and vice versa. It's possible Zhang didn't get all the information. Sam knew enough about what was going on to know what to take, especially if it would be an insurance policy for him. As for the conversation, it took place a while back. Nick heard and saw more than he told us, and he was tailing Sam because of other things he overheard. I have a gut feeling there's more to that kid than meets the eye, but right now it's just a feeling."

"Well, your senses have always been pretty accurate; Is there anything concrete you can put your finger on?"

"No, Just coincidences and my gut. I'm probably being irrational and creating conspiracy theories out of thin air."

"Like what?"

"Like, I thought I saw him at the diner with someone that looked like an old friend from years ago. Talia, my friend back before Derek was born, while I was alone in Bar Harbor and you were closing things out with MI6. We chummed around quite a bit, but she moved on with her life right after you were able to settle into Bar Harbor. I had to be mistaken; Talia would contact me if she were back; we were close."

"What do you mean together? Like eating together, holding hands, what?"

"Oh gosh, no. The two were standing in line, paying their bills. I couldn't even tell if they were together, to tell you the truth. Nick was behind her in the line. Probably just my imagination."

"Elli, that's scary paranoid. Try to get some sleep, and I'll call you back later once we have him. Eyes wide open, OK?"

"Please get Derek and bring him home..."

"I'll do everything I need to do."

"I know you will. I'll talk to you soon."

A long pause. Nigel wasn't sure if he needed to say anything more.

"Nigel, are you still there?"

"Yes."

"I love you. Please tell Derek I love him when you get to him."

"I will, Elli. I love you too."

The driver let Jack, Nigel, and Mack off at a location two blocks away from the small fabric warehouse Zhang had been seen entering. Andy stayed back at the office to continue his video searches. If Zhang or Derek were in the building, they were sure Zhang would have people posted on watch. They would need to be extremely careful not to be made.

They turned on their three RFID readers.

Jack knew they would have to get a little closer to the building to pick the signal up. "I'll move in closer to the building to see if I come up with anything. Mack, can I get you to circle to the opposite side of the building to scan from two directions? Be careful about being out in the open; there are probably people watching for us. Nigel, I need you to sit tight right now. Yours is the one face they will be looking for. I'm going to ask you to move back a few more blocks. Stay in the shadows. Here is my phone in case Andy calls. It's on silent, so keep your eyes on it."

Everyone went to their spots. Jack could see a few guys hanging out near the front door that didn't quite seem to fit in with the rest of the crowd. *That was a good sign something was going on*, Jack thought to himself, but there was still no signal.

Mack took a trip around a couple of big Shanghai blocks to get to the other side of the building. He was able to get close enough to pick up the signal but never got one.

Nigel was biding his time as instructed when Jack's phone started vibrating.

"Hello."

"This is Andy, who is this?"

"Andy, its Nigel. I have Jack's phone while he tries to get closer to the warehouse. Do you have anything?"

"Yes, we have gone through the footage from three different cameras and did not see Zhang come out. As far as we're concerned, he's still in the building. On top of that, one of the cameras picked up someone stepping out of the back door to relieve himself. We couldn't make out a face, but the guy was big and bald. He was not a Chinese either. We are quite sure it's that goon, Gus Peralta."

"Thanks, Andy. Good work."

Both Jack and Mack were on their way back. They could see Nigel waving his hands, telling them to hurry. *An excellent way to stay hidden*, Jack thought.

Saturday May 25, 11:15 AM - Shanghai

Friday May 24, 11:15 PM - Bar Harbor

Derek was shaken to his core. All the information and questions. They flew through his head, exploding like fireworks as they raced by. How much was true? (Boom) How much was made up just to torture him? (Bang) Did it matter if it was real? (Boom) There must be good reasons (Whistle). If dad shot that asshole in the head, why didn't he make sure he was dead? Then things started slowing down. Derek needed to think. What was he going to do now to get out of the situation?

New data requires new solutions; Derek couldn't rely on the RFID anymore. It was being blocked while he was locked in this room. There was no way of getting past Gus. He was too dangerous and formidable. Screaming would get him killed.

New data requires new solutions. New data requires new solutions. New data requires new solutions.

Socrates…

Derek knew he was in a basement and near an outside wall. The water stains on the walls and the dank smell of mold and mildew gave away the room's relative location within the building.

The traffic sound was muffled as if it moved downward towards him rather than carrying into the sky. Also, Socrates made his way in and out of the room easily where one of the walls met the ceiling, convincing Derek he was at an outside wall.

How was he going to get Socrates back into the room? For some reason, he had only visited at night. Here it was, late morning, as far away from nighttime you can be.

Could it be that the rat came not because it was night, but because that was when food was most available? Gus served his only meal later in the day, and his couple packs of crackers to get him through the next day came at the same time. If it was food rather than comfort Socrates was looking for, maybe he could coax him in. New data requires new solutions.

Derek hoped he was right. He reached to the side of his bed, grabbing a couple of crackers and squeezing his hand simultaneously. The crackers crumbled into small pieces and dust. He put some of the crumbs on the edge of the rat hole and sprinkled a trail to his bed. Hopefully, Socrates would smell the food, with the opportunity for some extra food outweighing any sense of danger.

Now, he needed to get to his next task. Slowly, Derek started picking at the corner of his blanket. Eventually one of the heavy woven threads came loose. Carefully he started pulling and manipulating the thread to come loose as one continuous piece. He was amazed at how little he had to unravel to get a length almost ten feet long. You wouldn't be able to see any evidence unless you carefully looked at the blanket.

Was ten feet enough? Derek hoped it was. The exterior of the building was probably no more than three feet away. This was no time to get greedy.

Gus said they had shielded the building. He didn't say they had stopped the ring from working. New data requires new solutions.

Derek gently pulled the ring from his finger, slipping the thread through it and tying a knot to hold it in place. He left enough thread at one end to fashion a slip knot with a loop big enough to get over Socrates' head. The rest would be for a leash if he were lucky enough to get Socrates to come.

He shook his head with wonder, thinking mom and dad spent all the money to get him through engineering school at MIT; all the courses he took to become a Mechanical Engineer, Statics, Dynamics, Fluid Mechanics, and Thermodynamics. The list could go on and on. Yet, here he was, fashioning a dog leash for a rat in an attempt to save his own life. This maneuver must have been something he saw on MacGyver when he was a kid, not an idea formulated by an MIT educated engineer's mind.

CHAPTER 41

Saturday May 25, 11:30 AM - Shanghai

Friday May 24, 11:30 PM - Bar Harbor

Mack and Jack ran to Nigel.

"Andy called, he verified Zhang hadn't left the building. He also found some video from this morning of someone who looked like Peralta, coming out the back door to take a piss. Any luck with the RFID?"

Both shook their heads no.

"Jack, are we missing anything? What are the odds of Derek being in there?"

"Honestly Nigel, I just don't know. They would have had to either scan him for signal producing electronics or look remarkably close to identify the RFID in the ring. It's also possible they simply took all his jewelry away."

"But if they took it off him, it's likely it's still in the building. Wouldn't it still be sending out a signal we'd pick up?"

"You're right, Mack. If he's in there and we're not getting any pings, there's a good chance they located the devices. Nigel, the next step is up to you. He's your son. We are thirty minutes away from the start of bidding, but I know the package is not our primary priority. I know this is a difficult decision. I wish I could help you."

"You can. Just answer my questions as honestly as you can. Am I wrong in thinking that even if we don't interfere, Derek is still in grave danger?"

"Judging by your history with Peralta, I'd say so. I have to be straight with you. It's not looking good for Derek. I'm positive the package is in there, but not positive Derek is. If we make a move, they are likely to have him killed once they know we have interfered. If he's in there, we will have a chance to get him, but not the package. If he's not, we won't be able to help him."

"Right now, the package is the last fucking thing on my mind."

Silence...

Saturday May 25, 11:45 AM - Shanghai

Friday May 24, 11:45 PM - Bar Harbor

Derek had his head down. If someone were to walk in, they'd think he was in deep prayer. In a way he was, but instead of praying, he trusted in some imaginary power and sent out his will in the direction of the street. *Come on, Socrates, be hungry. Come on, Socrates, smell the food. I know you can hear me, buddy. Come back to the room*. He had been trying to will Socrates for fifteen minutes, which seemed like only thirty seconds, when he was rousted out of his meditation by a scratching sound and then a plop as something hit the floor.

Looking over to the floor below the rat hole, he saw movement. He was expecting Socrates, but saw an ugly emaciated rat with deep-set, fierce eyes, nibbling at the food Derek had left as a trail. Derek immediately thought of Ted Bundy when he saw the menace in its eyes. When he got up to go check out this menace, it hissed and bit at him.

"Fuck, just what I needed, a flea-ridden, rabid, Ted Bundy looking badass that probably wants to hurt me more than Gus does, but you'll have to do."

He moved forward again. The rat version of Ted Bundy's back fur stood straight up as his body twisted in a corkscrew getting ready to pounce.

"Plop" as another mass hit the floor. Derek's companion, Socrates, jumped at the menace with the fury of a wolf going after the meat of its kill.

The two ferociously fought, but once Socrates drew first blood, badass Ted Bundy rat scurried through the hole.

"Thank God you showed up Socrates," Derek said as he held out his hand with a cracker cradled in his palm.

Socrates came over to the cracker and started nibbling. Derek reached out with the other hand that had the slipknot and thread in it. As he tried to slip the loop over Socrates' head, it startled him.

Socrates jumped and backed off about five feet.

"I'm sorry buddy, I'm not trying to hurt you. I need your help getting out of here. If I make it, I promise you'll get rewarded."

Socrates moved back towards Derek.

"C'mon buddy; you can do this."

As Socrates nibbled on the cracker, Derek draped and tightened the slip knot with the ring attached over Socrates' neck. The ring looked like the dog collars you get at the pet store to identify the owner's name and address. Hopefully, it would serve the same purpose here.

Derek flipped his hand up to the rat hole, waving it a couple of times. "OK buddy, scoot."

Socrates ran through the hole. The line was taut in less than five seconds as Derek could feel Socrates fighting the thread.

Saturday May 25, 11:58 AM - Shanghai

Friday May 24, 11:58 PM - Bar Harbor

The silence in the conversation among Jack, Nigel, and Mack ended when the RFID reader dinged. It startled all of them; then, it dinged again.

In tandem, Mack and Nigel both looked at Jack, "What's the location?"

"At the front of the warehouse, but outside." They all looked, but the only thing they could see were a few locals walking and the two guarding the front door.

I don't see my son; something's not right."

Jack reached into the side pocket of his cargo pants, pulling out a small set of binoculars, and started scanning the front of the building. What he saw next, not just surprised him, but shocked him. "Holy Shit."

Handing the binoculars to Nigel, he said, "Look at the building base at side-walk level near the second window from the right."

Nigel finally sighted what Jack had seen. A rat with a ring hanging from his neck came out of a hole in the exterior stucco. "Holy Shit." He said as he handed the binoculars to Mack.

Mack spotted it too. He too had only one response, "Holy Shit."

"Derek must be behind that wall, probably in the lower level, judging where the hole was located. I'm ready to go after my son."

The always diligent Mack brought up the obvious impediment, "What about the two guys out front?"

"It's taken care of Mack. I had Andy bribe the local police earlier. He's ready to send some plainclothes in to haul them off at our request. That's them over there. I just need to make the call."

"Let's do it then. The auction is about to start."

Jack grabbed his phone and made his call. They could see one of the plain-clothes answer his cellphone and shake his head yes. The four of them started walking towards the front of the building.

"I hope you two are ready. Use your guns only if you have too. All three slipped on the silencers they brought with them from the office arsenal and reached into their pockets to make sure their knives were easily accessible.

"Go!"

Saturday May 25, 11:59 AM - Shanghai

Friday May 24, 11:59 PM - Bar Harbor

Derek heard the sound of Gus coming down the steps. He still had a hold of the string, trying to control Socrates. *What in the hell am I going to do*, he thought? If he kept holding the string, Gus would catch him and probably shoot him on the spot. If he let go, Socrates would scurry off, probably leading everyone on a wild goose chase. He let go.

Gus entered the room as the last foot of thread went through the hole, slithering like a small snake. Gus didn't see it.

"Zhang wants you in the room with him in case your dad tries something funny. Vamoose!"

Dereck turned and deliberately walked to him.

"Are you getting sick, mi Sobrino? You are all pale and sweaty." Do you need to go to the bathroom to wet your face? At least it will be clean when they find your body."

"I thought you were going to let me go if my dad stayed out of the way?"

"I guess you better think again. I made a promise to myself and God almighty almost forty years ago, that if I ever tracked down your father and mother again, I would put a bullet in their heads, just like your dad did to me. Through the grace of your birth, you ended up on that list too. You will be first to go so they have the pain of your loss until the day I find them.

Do you see that scar above my ear? That is where the bullet went in. It never came out. It lodged in my jaw and damaged my facial nerves. The left side of my face has felt like it is on fire since that day, and if you noticed, I never smile; it's because I can't. When I look in the mirror each morning, your father is the first thing that comes to mind. Your mother is next. I was in intensive care for months under house arrest and labeled a traitor by the new government. I was planning on settling down with my wife at her parent's farm and raise cattle. Instead, I had to escape the hospital and Argentina for Cuba, with my dreams left behind. My hatred for your parents has grown each day."

CHAPTER 42

Saturday May 25, 12:00 PM - Shanghai

Saturday May 25, 12:00 AM - Bar Harbor

Four well-built plainclothes cops headed towards the front of the building in a two by two formation. They all wore brown suits with real designer ties (not the ones you buy at Pearl City). The two lookouts would have seen them coming under normal circumstances, but they were focused on spotting a couple of round eyes with a slick-looking Mongolian.

In precision, each set of two officers split apart to leave a three-foot space between them. As they walked on either side of the lookouts, each officer put one of their bent arms into the lookout's armpit and lifted, so their captured preys' feet were off the ground, kicking and dangling.

Both lookouts started to yell until one of the police officers gave them a look that said *this could end up with a bullet in your head or a train ride to a camp in the countryside, your choice.* Neither of the lookouts said anything more.

Once the police and lookouts were out of the way, Jack, Nigel, and Mack made their way to the front door. Jack took the lead.

"We are not going in hard. Zhang is not expecting us. The longer they don't know we are here, the better. Nigel and Mack, you head right towards where we spotted the rat with the ring; there should be a stairwell. If you run into a locked door, knock it down if you have to. We'll deal with the commotion if that becomes necessary. I'll head to the left to look for Zhang and Peralta. Be careful, they both could be anywhere, and they are both likely armed."

Zhang was in an office on the first floor to the left, in the direction Jack was headed, and was beginning the auction. Bids were coming in from IP addresses all over the world, but he knew it was unlikely they matched the country of the bidder. All that was important to Zhang was their bank accounts.

He had been surprised by all the interest in the product. The likely players, like Russia, China, Israel, and Iran, were there. Zhang wasn't expecting some of the others he saw like South Korea, India, and the UK. Each of these surprise players had a friendly relationship with one of the primary bidders. If the item being sold was going to be weaponized, certainly they would be protected by a benefactor, wouldn't they? Zhang concluded this was only more proof no one trusted anyone.

Zhang had set the bidding up so his team could verify each bank account ahead of time. They would then send an encrypted code to the owner of each account. Upon receipt, the account holders were to prove their legitimacy by entering that code on a site located on the dark web, along with an address, another encrypted code should be sent. That encryption key would then have to be brought to Zhang before he would pass off the package. Zhang would only know who won the bid after the code was brought to him. The plan was not foolproof, but would ensure a high degree of certainty a bad player would be flushed out quickly.

Jack was first through the door, followed closely by Mack and Nigel. The hallway was all clear. Jack pointed at the two and motioned for them to go to the right. All three had their guns pulled and ready for anything.

Saturday May 25, 12:03 PM - Shanghai

Saturday May 25, 12:03 AM - Bar Harbor

Jack proceeded to the left. As he approached another hallway on his right, he peeked around the corner and saw someone guarding a doorway. That had to be where the auction was being carried out, and probably where the package was. He had no idea if both Zhang and Peralta were there until he heard silenced shots ring out at the other end of the building.

The guard's instincts took over and he left his post, running towards the sound. He rounded the corner, expecting to see a long hallway with perhaps a gunfight going on at the other end. Instead, Jack met him with the business end of an 8" knife. It entered below the guard's ribs and was thrust upwards into his heart. The guard was ready to yell, but could only pull the breath in. It didn't come out as a yell, but with the sound you might hear if you let go of a full balloon that hadn't been tied off.

Zhang, on the other hand, was making sounds similar to someone having an orgasm, but more subdued. The auction had been going on for a little more than three minutes. The bidding was already up to $80 million.

Jack knew he promised Nigel he would take care of all of them, but he also knew his primary purpose was the one he was hired for; get the package. Jack was a businessman and beholding to the CIA for his success, but getting hold of this package would make the CIA, and many others, very beholding to him. He much preferred to be owed, than owing. Jack's conscience pulled at him to help with Derek's rescue, but in the end, he headed for Zhang's office to do what he knew had to be done.

Saturday May 25, 12:04 PM - Shanghai

Saturday May 25, 12:04 AM - Bar Harbor

As Gus and Derek made their way up the stairs, they could hear some commotion upstairs. Gus paid it little mind. He had two guys out front, so wasn't too concerned, but his instincts told him to put his hand on his gun.

Saturday May 25, 12:05 PM - Shanghai

Saturday May 25, 12:05 AM - Bar Harbor

Heading down the hall, Mack and Nigel could see a stairway to the right that led to the basement. Nigel held up his hand to signal to Mack to stop. He then motioned he was going to enter the stairway and whispered to Mack, "Cover me."

Nigel swung around the corner with his gun pointed down the stairs. Seeing nothing but a landing, he motioned Mack to follow behind as his cover. Before Mack made his move, a door opened and Nigel heard, "My hate for your parents has grown each day."

It was too late; Gus, with Derek in front of him, stepped onto the landing as Mack appeared in the stairway entrance. Startled, Gus drew his gun and fired, while at the same time pulling Derek closer to him to create a shield. The bullet hit the wall behind Mack as he dove for cover.

Gus then scanned the entrance of the stairwell and could see Nigel. He shot again, hitting the stairwell's wall close enough to Nigel's head that the explosion of plaster drew blood from his left ear.

At the same time, they all heard a shot ring out at the other end of the building, where Jack was supposed to be. Things might be unraveling quickly.

Nigel knew he needed to make a move. Gus was still imposing, even when he was trying to hide behind another person. At least 6" of his head was still towering over Derek. If he got any lower, he'd have to crawl.

As Gus was pulling back for retreat, Nigel swung into the stairwell and fired two shots. Both missed high. The combination of being out of practice and not wanting to hit Derek could prove to be his biggest mistake. It did get Gus to flinch.

Derek heard the bullets whiz over his head and felt Gus' hold loosen as he fell backward. He pulled himself from Gus' grasp as hard as he could, swinging his elbow into Gus' chin at the same time. Gus let loose.

"Run, Derek!"

Derek had only one choice, which was to run. He headed towards his dad, scaling the stairs two at a time. Nigel drew down on Gus again, but he had retreated into the basement.

Grabbing Derek by the hand, he pulled him to safety.

"We need to get to Jack, but someone needs to pin Gus down until we get the package."

"That would be me," Mack said as he got to his feet. "You two go see what Jack is up to, and I'll stay here. Whatever you do, be careful."

"You too, Mack. Keep your eyes wide open. If anyone else is in here, they can come from two other directions. Derek and I will check this end of the main hallway before heading toward Jack."

Mack and Derek made their way through the offices at the end of the hall, then up the staircase leading to the second floor offices. There was also a double-door to their left at the end of the hallway. It led into the main warehouse but was locked. They peered in through the window and could only see rolls of old fabric, some cut and sew tables, and a couple of old, broken down looms. Satisfied there was no one to be concerned with, they turned around and headed in the opposite direction toward Jack's location, passing Mack on the way.

"All clear this way. We'll be back as quick as we can. If that asshole even peeks around the corner, blow his head off."

"I will Nigel, but would prefer not to have to; please hurry."

While the shootout was taking place down at the other end of the hall, Jack moved slowly towards Zhang's office, expecting Zhang to come out to see what was going on. The bidding process had him hypnotized. The silencers muffled the sound of the gunfire enough that Zhang's trance wasn't broken.

When Jack got to the door, he heard Zhang yell out in Mandarin, that if translated, would say, "Holy Shit, $150 million." Or something similar.

Jack reached for the doorknob and slowly turned it to see if it was locked or unlocked. He was sure it would be the former but got a surprise when it turned all the way. *My lucky day*, he thought.

Jack had his gun drawn, slowly pushing the door open about an inch, taking in as much of the room through the slit as he could. He could not see Zhang so knew he'd have to throw the door all the way open. He took two deep breaths to steady himself. On his second exhale, he could hear Zhang say, "$190 million, do I have a higher bid?" Jack threw the door open, gun in firing position, and put a bullet into the middle of Zhang's forehead.

"No sugar for you tonight, Cyclops."

Jack quickly proceeded over to the other side of the desk. He saw the number of $200 come up along with an IP address on the screen. It was the same identifier of several other bids. Zhang had set up the auction to talk with the bidders on a microphone or type from the keyboard. Whoever had made this bid and all the other bidders, were holding their cumulative breaths, waiting for Zhang's response.

Jack reached down, muted the microphone, and typed the words, *we are* sorry, *but this auction has been canceled*, ending the sentence with a "mic drop" emoji.

His final act was to press the computer's off button.

Saturday May 25, 12:20 PM - Shanghai

Saturday May 25, 12:20 AM - Bar Harbor

When Nigel and Derek passed the front door, where they had split off from Jack, Nigel abruptly held up his hand. They both stopped running. Not knowing what they may be getting into, Nigel wanted to be stealthier than they had been while running down the hall. Nigel took the lead, reaching his index finger to his lips and giving the shhh sign; he then waved his hand to proceed. Slowly he and Derek continued to the hallway Zhang's office was on. They saw the door was open and heard Jack shout "Damn" in a very disgusted tone.

They slowly approached the open door. Entering the room with guns high, they immediately saw Jack with his back to them, hands on his hips and shaking his head side to side. They then saw Zhang lying on the floor in a pool of blood, staring up at the ceiling with what looked like three eyes.

Nigel asking in shock, "What's going on, Jack? What happened to Zhang?"

"Never mind him; when I got here he was ready to complete the auction. The only choice I had to keep him from doing that was to shoot him. The more important issue right now is I can't find the package."

"I was positive it would be here. Where else could it be?"

Jack was gazing at the wall behind Zhang's desk as if he were in a daze, "I don't know unless I'm just missing something obvious."

"Jack, you just aren't looking hard enough."

Flustered, Jack looked at Derek, "I don't know what you mean by I'm not looking hard enough."

"You of all people should know better. Look closer at the wall. What do you see?"

"A wall. What am I supposed to see?"

"Are you sure you're a spy, or are you just very forgetful about secret hiding places? There are two seams in the wall that don't look like they should be there." Derek walked toward the wall, rubbing his hand on the underside of furniture, mantles, and bookcases. "Ahh, there it is." They all heard a click, and the section of the wall Derek pointed at sprung open, revealing a large freezer. "A secret room Jack, imagine that."

Jack looked embarrassed but smiling, "Just like when I'm searching for my reading glasses. I look everywhere in the house, then realize they are on my head. Nice job, Derek."

They all walked into the room. Jack reached out and pulled the freezer door open, revealing its contents.

In unison, all three said, "The package…"

The temperature inside the freezer was much colder than normal. Nigel estimated it was -20C or lower. Elli had told him before he came the RNA samples needed to be kept at least that cold or they would degrade. Even at that temperature, some degradation would take place. They'd have to figure out a way of getting the samples back without a freezer.

After a couple of seconds, Derek came out of the joyous stupor everyone seemed to be in. "Damn, we need to pack up and go help Mack. We also need to decide what we are going to do with Gus. Derek headed towards the office door with Nigel close behind. Jack grabbed the package.

Saturday May 25, 12:30 PM - Shanghai

Saturday May 25, 12:30 AM - Bar Harbor

Mack was starting to get a little shaky. He had to make sure Gus stayed in the basement but was losing his concentration. The noise going on down the hall was pulling his attention in that direction. When he realized he had been looking down the hall too long, he turned his attention back toward Gus. He was too late; the collision was about ready to happen.

Gus had decided he needed to take a chance. When he heard the commotion at the end of the hall, he knew there might be a chance for Mack to look away. He was right. Gus had already decided that shooting a gun would be his last resort. If he was going to get a jump on the other group, he needed to take out Mack without firing. He decided to sneak up to the landing and make a rush toward Mack.

Mack was less than three feet away when Gus made a headfirst dive for his chest. It looked like he would get his clock cleaned much worse than the guy he tackled years ago in Boston. There was no time to get his gun up, and he braced for contact. The impact pushed all the air out of Mack's lungs. All he could do was gasp. There would be no warning yells. Mack knew he was going to die. He was positive Gus would have a knife, and either gut him or slit his throat.

Mack was losing his composure, then suddenly felt a wave of peace come over him he wasn't expecting. *Nick, Steph, I'm sorry. God, please take care of them.* Mack's peace was broken at the same time as his jaw. Gus didn't have a knife, so he decided to knock his Mack's ass out. The last thing Mack could remember before passing out was the sound of his jaw breaking.

Gus headed for Zhang's office.

Saturday May 25, 12:31 PM - Shanghai

Saturday May 25, 12:31 AM - Bar Harbor

Nigel and Derek exited the office heading towards Mack. Derek was in the lead. They weren't prepared for what they saw next.

Mack regained consciousness almost immediately. He was in a lot of pain but had to get it together to help stop Gus. He pulled himself up to his feet and headed down the hall, yelling from the back of his throat because of his broken jaw, afraid it was too late.

Jack, who was still in the office wiping down fingerprints, heard the commotion and ran for the office door.

Both Nigel and Derek saw Gus simultaneously, pulling up his gun, with his finger on the trigger. They also saw Mack coming around the corner. Nigel reached for the back of Derek's collar with his left hand. Grabbing on with four fingers, he pulled Derek backward, slowing his momentum down enough to get in front of him. Nigel drew his gun with his right hand, firing off one shot and heard three others. As Jack ran out of the office, he got hit by Gus as he sprinted past him to make his escape through the warehouse door. Zhang had previously unlocked this door as a precaution for escape if one was needed. When he did it, he was the one planning to use it, not Gus. Gus got through the door before Jack could do anything.

Mack yelled out he had hit Gus twice, once in the shoulder and once in his thigh.

"I heard four shots.", Jack yelled back as he went through the exit into the warehouse to follow Gus out or stop him.

"Where did the other ones end up?" yelled Mack. Mack stopped yelling when he saw a heap of two entangled bodies on the floor.

As Jack exited through the warehouse door, he saw a trail of blood expanding as it moved away from him. He ran in the direction of the blood, doubting Gus would be waiting for him. When he rounded the corner to head down the back most aisle, he came to a dead stop. The trail of blood had grown into a pool of blood.

Lying face up was Gus, Jack could see two bullet holes. The first was an exit wound in the thigh, with blood just trickling now, and an entry wound in his chest. Gus was looking at Jack with almost dead eyes. They closed a little more with each heartbeat that spat more blood onto the floor.

Right after his last heartbeat, Gus Peralta took three quick breaths and died.

Almost whispering, Jack leaned down to Gus' ear, "If Nigel didn't kill you, I would have eventually. I hope it was painful."

The heap Mack was staring at started squirming. Derek was crawling out from under Nigel, yelling and crying at the same time, "Dad? Dad? Dad!!!"

Nigel didn't respond. Derek, now on his knees, reached with both hands under Nigel to roll him over. "He has to be OK." He felt the wetness of Nigel's blood on his hands. Mack knelt to help Derek and to give first aid if he needed to. When they finally got him on his back, they could see the gaping hole in Nigel's chest.

Mack reached for his pulse. It was so shallow; there was almost nothing to feel. Nigel barely opened his eyes. He had remembered something Elli had said to him that had been bothering him since their conversation earlier that day. He mouthed some words, but Derek couldn't hear him. Derek bent over and put his ear to his dad's mouth. Nigel spoke two words. The first word Derek understood; it was "Nick." He wasn't sure about the second. He thought he heard "Tal."

Jack came out of the warehouse quickly, running over to where everyone was kneeling. He kneeled with them, looking at Nigel with the eyes of a confused man. Nigel didn't understand Jack's expression but didn't care too much at that point.

Jack continued to look at Nigel and spoke. "Nigel, you got that mother fucker, tore out a piece of his heart with your shot.

Nigel, in *a whisper, "I killed him? You sure?"*

"Yeah, Nigel, I'm sure."

Nigel smiled and took his last breath.

Mack put his arm around Derek, "I'm so sorry, Derek. I never expected this to happen. You know he saved your life, and the lives of many others by taking Gus down. Were you able to understand what he was trying to tell you before Jack got here"?

"Yeah Mack, he said he loved me."

Jack looked at his watch; it was 12:40 PM.

Derek then stood up, grabbed his dad's gun, and walked toward the warehouse door. "I'll be back in a minute."

He followed the same trail as Jack had, finding Gus' body at the end. Walking up to the body, he pointed his gun down and blew Gus' face entirely off.

"Just wanted to make sure this time, asshole. Now you can go to hell with two bullets in your head."

CHAPTER 43

Looking up from his watch, Jack implored the others, "We need to get out of here as quickly as possible. The authorities will be here in less than an hour."

"I thought you bribed the police." Mack shot back.

"Yeah, I did; to take care of a couple of goons out front, not to clean up a murder scene. If we are caught in here with the bodies, we can expect concentration camps for many years. Maybe even a firing squad."

"They can't do that. We were defending ourselves and freeing Derek. Plus, we're Americans. The consulate will protect us."

"Mack, you've been watching way too many movies. First, the consulate doesn't even know you are here. You could disappear for months before they stepped in. By then, they'd never find you, or your remains."

I'm not leaving my dad here; I don't care about this concentration camp bullshit. We need to get his body out of here before the authorities arrive. I'll drag him out myself if I have to."

"Don't worry, Derek. Talia told me she had a clean-up crew standing by. I'll call her right now. They'll have enough time to get your dad and Zhang out of here. Gus can rot in the warehouse for all I care. That should give us enough time to catch a plane out of China. Grab your dad's phone and identification, and take it with you."

"What's going to happen with dad's body?"

"We'll get him put on ice, then smuggle him out via airfreight to San Francisco. We'll have someone set up who will take him home from there. We'll also need to concoct a story about his death. We need to do anything possible to disconnect him from this incident."

"Let's get him out of here first. We can worry about the story later. Make your phone calls."

Jack walked away to make the calls. When he was done, he walked back over to Derek and Mack.

"They'll be here in less than fifteen minutes. In the meantime, we need to clean up any trail we may have left behind. The clean-up crew has been told to concentrate on Nigel and Zhang and destroy any DNA evidence they might leave. You need to take care of your part by removing any evidence you may have left behind. Be as meticulous as you can."

"What about Peralta? Will they be able to track him to us?" interjected Mack.

"I doubt it. If the police figure out what it is, it might even add some confusion to their investigation. Also, before we get out of here, leave your weapons next to Zhang's body so the crew can dispose of them. Head out to wipe down anything from the stairwell and basement. I'll finish up here, then start setting up plane flights. Be back in fifteen minutes."

Something Wang had just said, piqued Mack's interest, "Flights, as in plural?"

"Yes, we each need to take a different route back to the States. We shouldn't be traveling together. Under that scenario, if one gets detained, we all do. This way, we'll have a fighting chance for all of us to make it back."

"So, are we going to split the contents up in threes, too?"

"No, for several reasons. First, losing a third of that package will significantly delay implementing the research back in the US.

Second, if you noticed, the freezer we were storing the package in was icy, but only cold enough to keep the RNA samples safe. You can't keep the samples cold traveling around the world on domestic flights. We will send it with your dad's body. Talia's people will have a container just big enough to keep the samples cold which will make it much easier to move around when it gets to the US. As I said, your dad's body will be stored in refrigeration units on the planes. I will pick up the package at the Bar Harbor Airport. Arrangements will be made to send your father's body directly to the mortuary."

"My dad got killed for the package. How do we know we'll ever see it again?"

"You don't. You're just going to have to trust me. I'm sending it on the plane. No more discussion." Looking down at his watch, Jack said, "You now only have ten minutes left. Go!"

Mack and Derek headed for the stairwell. Derek sprinted into the basement, while Mack stayed behind in the stairwell, wiping things down and picking up shell casings.

Derek went into the room where they had detained him, which made him think of Socrates. Derek remembered thread was still tied around his neck, which was going to be dangerous for him. He needed to try to get him back in here. Derek recalled something he saw in Zhang's office, a half a case of the crackers he and Socrates had been eating. Derek also remembered a promise he had made to Socrates if he helped him get him out. Derek wiped down the room the best he could with one hand, returning to the group with Mack.

"OK, let's get out of here. Andy has already made the arrangements for flights. It's complicated, so listen close. Mack and Derek, we will take you by the hotel to get your stuff, then get you over to the Hongqiao Airport. That airport only accommodates domestic flights. Derek, you will fly to Beijing, transfer to a flight to Atlanta, then get to Bangor via US domestic flights we are setting up now. Mack, you will fly to Guangzhou, then take a direct to Chicago. Same instructions as Derek's on US domestic. Your tickets will be waiting at the hotel. I suggest you two check arrival times in Bangor and wait for each other so you can drive into Bar Harbor together."

"What about you, Jack?" Derek asked in a distrusting tone. I'll fly out of Pudong on a direct to LaGuardia. We should all be getting to Bar Harbor between 2:00 and 5:00 PM Sunday their time. I can fill your mom in on things before you guys get there if you'd like."

"You will not fill her in on anything! I will do that. Don't even think about it."

"Derek, I didn't plan on filling her in on Nigel. Talia and I already discussed how terribly upset she will be, especially with you not there to comfort her. It's up to you if you want to tell her before you get there, but you may want to hold off. She's expecting a call from your dad. You may want to make that call and cover for your dad."

"That makes sense, Jack; I'll make the call." Derek felt uneasy, but it wasn't the fact he would have to make the call. It was the name of Talia. He thought he must be getting overly paranoid.

"Let's get out of here now. We need to get everyone to the airport."

Derek yelled as he was running into Zhang's office. "I need five minutes, Jack. I have one last item to clean up."

"Jesus Derek, I told you we don't have the time."

"Sorry, five minutes max," Derek said, running past Jack and Mack with a half-case of crackers in his arms.

Hustling down the stairs, Derek set the box down and started tearing open packs of crackers with his teeth, while throwing them under the rat hole. When he was done, there was probably enough to feed Socrates and many of his friends. He then stood back and waited.

Within thirty seconds, he saw Socrates' head pop out of the hole then run down the wall to the pile of crackers. Derek walked over and gently started loosening the noose around his head, then taking it off. "Buddy, I told you I'd take care of you if you helped get out of this mess. It didn't quite turn out the way I wanted, but a promise is a promise. Thanks for sticking with me."

Socrates continued to nibble at the crackers as Derek tossed the thread to the side of the room, turned, and headed for the stairs.

When he got back Jack was talking with a group of men. They all were wearing hazmat gear and were carrying and rolling around a bunch of cleaning equipment.

"Derek, these are Talia's guys. (another uneasy feeling, but even more disturbing this time) They're here to clean up this mess and get your dad home."

"Thanks guys; please make sure you take good care of him."

"We will, son. Deeply sorry he has to return home this way. I wish we could have kept this from happening. Talia (Derek was starting to despise that name) told us both he and your mom had been courageous and loving their entire lives."

"Thanks again. Jack, can I have a word with you in private, in Zhang's office, please?"

"Sure."

They both walked into Zhang's office, Dereck in the lead, with Jack closely behind.

"Close the door Jack. I need to ask you a question. I've been hearing about this person named Talia since we got here. I know she has been supplying services to help us, and now the resources to get dad home, but who is she. What's her connection?"

"Derek, she is from the Mossad out of Israel. Have you heard of them?"

"They're like the Israeli CIA, correct?"

"Something like that. I understand Talia and your dad worked with each other in the late seventies, early eighties. She thinks highly of him."

"And my mom… Do you know how she knew my mom?

"Sorry Derek, I don't. That's something you'll have to ask your mom."

"I will. It's strange; I don't recall my mom ever bringing up that name. Thanks Jack."

"Welcome, now let's get out of here. The crew needs to get in here to clean up Zhang's mess."

Jack, Derek, and Mack exited the building from the rear. Two vehicles were waiting for them. Jack climbed into one. "See you guys in Maine." His black SUV drove off. Derek and Mack got into their SUV, headed for the hotel, the airport, and eventually their long journeys home.

On the way to the airport from the hotel, Nigel's phone started ringing. Derek had forgotten he had put it in his back pocket. Pulling it out, he saw it was his mom. "Damn!"

"What's wrong Derek?"

"It's my mom. With everything going on, I forgot she was waiting to see how things turned out. I'll need to answer this."

"Are you going to tell her?"

Shaking his head no, he answered the phone, "Hi mom!"

(Pause) His mom talked, but part of his mind was on what his dad's last words were; "Nick, tal." He knew he had an answer, but it just wasn't coming into focus in his mind.

"Yeah, it is me. I'm glad to be safe, too. Dad's busy finishing up some things with Jack and Mack. It has been very hectic. I'm sure he meant to call, but things kept coming up. He told me to pick up if you called and said to tell you he was extremely sorry he hadn't gotten back to you. I think he was hoping you'd fall asleep, and he'd be able to call later." Derek knew he was rambling and told himself to shut up.

(Pause) "Nick, tal" What was it?

"Yes, we did get the package, too. Jack said it was coming in a separate flight to Bar Harbor. He will pick it up and bring it to the lab for our review. They have set up cold storage to hold it until we meet. Jack also felt because he is Chinese, well, actually Mongolian, he'll have a better chance of getting it out of China without any hassles. He's also tied to the CIA, so he has connections there to help with safe passage."

(Pause) "Nick, tal," something was coming. He could feel it.

"He said they will keep the samples in a container holding the temperature below -20 degrees Celsius. I think he mentioned something about liquid nitrogen.

(Pause) "Nick, tal,"

Mom, he's been trustworthy up to now. Do I trust him? I can't say yes to that. I don't think I trust anyone involved in this situation."

(Pause) Think Derek. It's there. Quit trying so hard.

"We should be home Sunday afternoon to Sunday evening your time. I'll call when I arrive in Bangor, and give you something better to go on. Jack has someone working on our tickets there right now."

(Pause) "Nick, tal" Is tal the beginning of a word or a name?

"No, we are all traveling separately. Jack felt it would be safer that way. I'll fill you in on the details when we get back."

(Pause) "Nick, tal" Holy shit, it had been in front of him all along. It was the beginning of a name! No wonder he got uneasy every time he heard it. His soul had been whispering to him. Now it was shouting, "Talia." What else was dad trying to tell him when he said Nick's name with Talia's?

"I love you too, mom, I'll let dad know too. Oh, mom, I forgot something. Do you know anyone by the name of Talia?"

(Long Pause) …

CHAPTER 44

Elli was shocked by Derek's question. She had never mentioned Talia to Nigel or him. Since she had not seen Talia for some time, she kept their relationship somewhat private.

"Derek, how do you know the name, Talia?"

"Mom let's not play the question game; this is serious. Who is Talia?"

"She is an old friend of mine, someone I knew before you were born. She moved here from Germany when your dad and I were setting up house here. She and I become friends, and we were inseparable for a while. She had to move back to Europe. We stayed in touch for a couple of years, but we have lost track of each other."

Elli was losing her patience with Derek, especially after thinking she saw her the other day in Bar Harbor with Nick. "Derek, now you have to tell me how you know about this Talia, and whether we are talking about the same person, what does she look like?"

"Mom, I have not met Talia, but she knows dad."

Elli again in shock, "Derek, how does she know Nigel? Derek, tell me everything you know. This time I'm not playing the question game. "TALK.""

"Mom, Talia has been a big help to us in China. She has been providing dad intelligence on Zhang and China operations."

Elli was trying to put the pieces together. Can this be the same Talia I know? If it was, how can she be in China and Bar Harbor at the same time? The Talia she knows is a writer and photographer, not a covert spy.

More troubling, if it was Talia she saw with Nick, then what?

Elli wanted to believe that if Talia was in Bar Harbor, she would contact her. Why wouldn't she? They were the best of friends.

"Mom, I have to go, we can talk more when I get home. Got to catch my flight."

What about Nigel; is he OK?

It was too late; Derek had already hung up.

Elli was perplexed about the whole conversation and now worried about Nigel.

Nick was awake down in the boat's mid-cabin. He could vaguely hear Elli's conversation out in the wheelhouse, but figured she was talking to Nigel. Although he wanted to know what was going on in China, waiting until she was finished talking would be best.

After a few minutes, Nick went up to the wheelhouse to talk to Elli. He could see Elli was upset and asked, "So what's the news from Nigel?"

"I didn't talk to Nigel. He was unavailable or something like that. It was Derek who called me."

"Is everything OK?"

"I think everything went well; they got the package and are on their way home. I don't know much more. Derek said they would catch us up when they got here."

Nick, not wanting to upset Elli, knew his dad, Nigel, and Derek just didn't walk in there and get the package. There had to be some collateral damage, especially with Gus being there. He knew Talia would update him before they all got back. He was worried about his dad. Gramps would be able to handle these types of situations, but worried about his dad. No way, he is a pacifist, a liberal, wouldn't hurt a fly. Now he's saving the world.

"My dad, did you hear anything about my dad?"

"No, not directly. Derek said everybody's fine and they would be home Sunday. He also told me they had some help, some woman who helped them."

"A woman?" Nick asked.

"Yes, it was strange, Derek said she used the name Talia. I had an old friend named Talia; it just struck me weird."

Nick knew it was the same woman, but didn't want to say anything to Elli. "Yeah, that is weird. I'm sure it's just a coincidence." He also knew it would only be a matter of time before Elli connected him and Talia.

"Coincidence, how many Talias do you know?"

Nick knew one, but couldn't say anything, not just yet. Until he talked to Talia, the mission wasn't quite complete. The formula had to be brought back to the United States; the thumb drive had to be retrieved and tested. If it was all there, then the mission would be finished.

Nick asked curiously, "Elli, what did this Talia do for them?"

"She gave them China operations intel. She also provided security for them. It doesn't sound like the type of thing my friend Talia would be able to do."

"Nick, I must be out of my mind; I could have sworn I saw her with you in Bar Harbor the other day."

"Me and your friend Talia, that's impossible. Where do you think you saw us?"

"At a local restaurant, Side Street Cafe, I think. You were at the cashier, and I saw this woman who looked like her. She was standing behind you. I only saw her from the side. I'm sure I was mistaken."

"Elli, you have been under a lot of stress. With the break-in at the lab, having critical information stolen, the shooting at the cliffs, then at your house, and Nigel and Derek having to go to China with my dad. Geeze, how can anybody not be affected by that? You have a right to be a wreck."

"Nick, you have the same shit storm happening in your life. My God, your mom was shot, and your dad is taking such a huge risk going into China. His life is just in much in danger as Nigel's and Derek's. I'm so sorry I got your family involved in this. How do you do it?"

"Do what?"

"Remain so calm. You were so cool back at the lab; I felt like I was working with a professional. You're so young."

"Hey, don't give me all the credit, you were pretty cool in there as well. As far as my age, look at Derek. I'm sure he is not much older than me and had to keep his cool as well. Give your son a lot of credit. He and Nigel are courageous men."

"You're right; I miss them. I can't wait for everyone to come home safely. I'm going to give Derek the longest hug he has ever had."

"What about Nigel?"

"I will be relieved to see him, but I need to act pissed first. He put our son in danger."

The next morning Nick was correct in getting a call from Talia. It was short and to the point – "*Your dad is alive, they recovered the package, and Nigel is dead.*"

CHAPTER 45

Derek and Mack made their way into the Hongqiao airport and proceeded to navigate their way through the madness that seemed to be expected in all transportation hubs in China. Little could they tell that this dinosaur of an airport, which was ancient compared to most Chinese airports, still handled more yearly traffic than every airport in the United States, except Atlanta.

All they could see was mass hysteria. People were pushing other people out of the way, running luggage carts into each other, and line-jumping like it was no big deal. The most frustrating part was the Immigration Agents playing God with how much trouble they would give you before letting you through their booth.

Fortunately, both of them made it through relatively unscathed. The most problematic situation was Mack being held back for several minutes while the agent went through his passport, scanning page after page for his entry stamp. Mack knew the agent was giving him shit because there was only one other stamp in there from when he and Steph took a trip to France the previous year. He kept his cool, knowing he had shot a man while in Chinese territory just two hours ago.

Once they hit the main terminals, and before separating, Mack and Derek compared their arrival times in Bangor. They saw they'd arrive less than an hour apart, so they would wait for each other before heading to Bar Harbor.

Mack said he planned to sleep all the way if possible. Derek said he'd do the same, knowing it wouldn't be the case. Getting back home would not be a celebration but possibly one of the hardest things he'd ever have to face. How was he going to break the news to his Mom?

Both planes left for their first stops as close to on time as you can get in China, which is usually better than most US airports on their best days. Mack had two glasses of wine, ate his pork stir-fried rice plate, and fell asleep, getting an hour of nap time before hitting Guangzhou International. By the time he got on his flight to Chicago, he was ready for more wine and sleep, with maybe a few movies thrown in.

Derek's flight to Beijing was just long enough for him to catch a very restless cat nap. Things went better than expected in the transfer hall, which gave him a lot of time to spare before catching his flight to Atlanta. He decided to a little shopping in duty-free, picking up some good Cuban cigars to enjoy back in the States when he had the chance. He was doing his best to keep his mind off his mom and the next flight, which he was dreading. It would be seventeen hours of mourning his father while preparing to mourn with his mother. What was he going to say to her? *Dear God, please give me some words, please*, he shouted in his mind.

By the time Derek got to Atlanta, fatigue had the best of him. His mind had analyzed every scenario on how to handle the conversation. His mind was still numb from all the thinking and worrying. If anything about the flight was fortunate, it would be he finally realized there would be no right outcome. There was no planning for the circumstances. The words that came out would be the words that came out. Planning was worthless. Acknowledging this futility did give him some peace, but not enough to sleep much the rest of the way. He may have been out a couple of hours at most.

Derek made his way through Immigration and Customs, then onto the train headed for domestic concourses. It was early in the morning, so he had quite a bit of time to kill before catching his flight North. He was famished, so a few essential visits related to, food he needed to make.

The first visit he planned to make was to a Chick-Fil-A; the second would be a bar to savor a domestic IPA beer. Most of the restaurants and bars were still closed, but would be back open in an hour or two, so he tracked down the location of the Chick-Fil-A on the Concourse maps finding out he'd have to head back to another concourse. No problem, he thought. He'd grab a beer or two at Tap, which was in the same concourse and open, then go back to get his chicken and pickle piece of Americana. He couldn't wait. Other than seeing his mom, this sandwich delight had been the only other thing on his mind.

Derek saw the Chick-Fill-A physical location on his way up the escalators into the concourse so after his couple of beers and an hour, he quickly headed back that way. As he strolled down to the location, he could see and hear all the vendors opening up their storefronts, sliding up their entrances' security doors, and turning on the interior lights and whirly toys to draw attention. They were all such happy sights and sounds, just what he needed.

Getting to Centerpoint, where he entered the concourse from the rail system, he spied the Chick-Fil-A, but the gates were still down and locked. What the heck, he thought? He then realized, with the weight of that thought landing squarely on his shoulders, today was not going to be a good day. Karma was kicking his ass. It was Sunday, and his beloved Chick-Fil-A would not be opening.

Dejected, Derek decided the only thing he could decide at that point; he'd head back down to Tap for a few more beers and grab the next best thing on the way there, an Egg McMuffin at McDonald's.

Mack arrived in Bangor first, at a little after 1:00 PM. Derek was supposed to arrive at 1:25, but his plane out of Atlanta had been delayed. The delay was no shock to Mack. He'd get there around 2:30.

Jack had arrived at almost the same time as Mack, so they were able to meet up with each other in the terminal.

"I'm going to drive to Bar Harbor ahead of you and Derek to retrieve the package and check into check into the Bay Ledge hotel. When you are leaving the airport, let me know. You can come past the hotel and pick me up. We'll all travel to the Serendipity together to see Nick, Elli, and Stephanie, if she's up to it. I'll text Elli and let her know we'll be there around 4:30."

"Steph should be fine; I'm sure she'll be there. I'll sit tight until Derek gets here. Make sure you show us the container and its contents when we get to the hotel.

"I will. Don't worry. I told you I'd get it there" Jack headed for the rental cars in a foul mood because Mack kept calling him out.

Heading down Highway 1-A, Jack fiddled with his Apple Connect on the rental car. Once things were synched, he hit the speed dial for Talia.

"Hey, I'm on my way into town. Anything I need to know?"

"Not much right now. We still aren't sure if we've retrieved all the documents Sam Wilder copied. We found a thumb drive we hope has all the files he kept; some may be copied, and some may be originals. We can't be certain it's everything, and won't be until Elli gets to take an inventory with what we give her.

On another issue, I need to know what happened in the warehouse. No one was supposed to get hurt. That was one of your primary priorities. My God, I understand collateral damage, but letting Nigel get killed? How could you let that happen?"

"Talia, I'm so sorry. I let my guard down for just a minute. I thought everything was under control until I heard that crazy mother fucker Gus running down the hall firing off shots. By the time I got to the point I could do anything about it, he had already knocked me down and was on his way out the door, hightailing it to save his ass. Unfortunately, there is another piece of collateral damage you need to know about if you don't know already.

"Geez, things just keep getting worse. I sure hope what you are going to tell me nothing that has the potential to compromise the mission. Go ahead ..."

I realize we had partnered with Zhang to pull this whole thing off, but he put me into bad a situation I felt required necessary action."

"Spit it out, would you?"

"I had to kill Zhang. We both suspected he could go rogue, and he did."

"What did he do?"

"At the auction, per the plan, we would sell the copy of the package, containing the documents copied from the original package, collect the money, and keep the original package for ourselves. Things started going sideways for us when a Russian diplomat personally visited Zhang with an offer.

Based on the Russian offer. Zhang decided to pre-arrange the bidding with Russia. Iran had also indicated they were also interested; they'd be driving the price up too. He knew your organization would give him $150 million, no questions asked, but realized that number was so low in respect to what it was worth. He then figured he could auction off the original package, keep the money, and the altered package, for himself then make like Houdini and disappear."

"Houdini?"

"Houdini, he's a famous... never mind. Both Russia and Iran were ready to go just about as high as needed. Zhang suspected he could get $300 million or more. I saw the opportunity to let the rescue play out. I needed to make sure Nigel, Mack and Derek continued to trust me, so I worked out a scenario where I would go in Zhang's direction during the rescue and eliminate him. Fortunately, it worked out for our benefit." *My benefit* he was thinking.

"How'd you find all this out?"

"Some highly technical spying equipment called bugs, on his phone and office. Have you ever heard of them? Anyway, he never suspected a thing."

"Imagine that. Well, truthfully, it's good Zhang is out of the way anyway. I never trusted him. He's never been a team player. I'm glad you are, Jack. Aren't you? OK, where do we go from here? Do we let Elli look at the original or the copy you made in Shanghai?"

"We can do a couple of things; first would be to just get the hell out with what we have, but I don't recommend that. We need to see what's missing and what's not. Only Elli can do that.

Second, we give her the original. If we do that, but can't get it back, the worst scenario for us would be some loss of income, but at least we'll have most of the technology. Your people ought to be able to catch up simply because of American bureaucracy. Hopefully, we can switch packages after the review. If we can, we should lighten the fake's load a little more by removing a few other critical documents. Having the original will put your organization's research ahead of anyone by three to six months. We'll have to get out of here quickly once the switch is made. They will be pissed and liable to get the American Feds much more involved."

"You forget one thing, Jack. We also need a copy of the thumb drive, but I have a secret weapon named Nick to help us with that. Let's give them the original package and come up with an idea for switching them and disappearing."

"OK, I'll follow up with you tonight after our meeting at the boat."

Derek and Mack met up and got out of the airport as quickly as they could. The drive home was mostly silent.

"Derek, I'm so sorry about your dad. I wish I had the words. I know you having to break the news to your mom is going to be tough. Is there anything I can do to help?"

"No, Mack, but thanks. You have helped way too much already, putting your life on the line like you did and allowing Stephanie and Nick to stay involved even after what went down at my dad's place. My God, at the warehouse you were all in. You didn't have to come down the hall after Peralta, but you did. You had enough wits about you to shoot him twice while chasing after him. If you hadn't hit him, mom would be having a double funeral."

Well, I still feel like there is more I could have done. I hope you know me, Steph, and Nick will do what we can to help you get through this."

Derek thought to himself, *why did his dad say Nick's name with Talia's before he died? Was Nick playing a more significant role than he thought? Was he working with Talia? How could that be? Maybe Dad was just delirious. All he knew was he needed to pay special attention to Nick for the time being.*

"Thanks Mack." The conversation went silent again until they picked up Jack. He filled them in on the meeting set up at 4:30. Steph was on the way, and Nick would be at the boat when they got there.

Elli, Steph, and Nick were inside the Serendipity when they arrived. Even with her arm still bandaged up, Steph drove all night to be there when Mack arrived. The gravel parking lot of the marina had a distinct sound when someone was pulling in. Elli's demeanor was soft compared to Steph's almost jubilant state. She had not had a good feeling since talking with Derek the day before. She had always been a "worst-case scenario" type of person, so she kept telling herself to smile and quit being such a worrier.

When they heard the car doors slam, they all left the captain's quarters, Skipper's throne room, and the one place among many that would miss hearing his laughter and all the tall tales. They ran one by one up the stairs that led from the quarters to the deck. Nick first, then Steph, then Elli. Steph and Nick immediately saw Mack and ran to him as fast as they could. Elli got to the deck and surveyed the parking lot, scanning it from one side to the other in what seemed like slow motion. She first saw a rugged, Chinese looking man standing next to the car, scanned some more, then saw Derek standing alone, looking at her with tears in his eyes.

She knew.

All the words Derek had thought about saying to his mom over the past twenty-four hours, with none of them ever ringing right or true. What was he supposed to say? Would it make any difference? At that point, he realized pretty much the same thing that had come to him on the plane. He had circled back again. There were no words.

Elli came down from the deck slowly, but increased her pace as she got closer to Derek. She kept telling herself Derek had been through hell and needed her strength. Elli needed to be a mother right now. She could be a wife later, in private. She was steadfast until she was almost to Derek, but couldn't hold back anymore. The tears began to flow as soft sobs escaped her lips. She was broken.

Derek quickened his pace while agonizing even more for his mom. All the words, all the damn words. Derek grabbed his mom by the hand, pulling her close, then gave her the longest and most loving hug she ever had.

Mack, Nick, Steph, and Jack stood silent, looking on. No words.

CHAPTER 46

As Nick watched the reunion he was relieved his dad was safe, hugging his mom while wiping the tears from her face. Derek's and Elli's reunion was not as happy. Nigel was gone, and Elli was grieving his death, while embracing Derek's safe return. Nick liked the Skipper and enjoyed the time they spent together on the Serendipity. He would miss him as well.

Nick knew this was far from over and had a big unanswered question with Talia. Elli had shared that she thought she saw her old friend Talia with him and believed she must have been wrong. Nick knew she wasn't wrong; it was the same Talia. Why hadn't she mentioned knowing Elli; what was the secret she was keeping from him?

Talia was not a photographer or a writer; she was working for some government or private entity. She helped Nigel and his Mack and with Jack's help, got them out of China. Nick was being paid a lot of money, but to do what, babysit Elli?

Zhiban "Jack" Wang is a name Talia had never mentioned to Nick. They had to know each other, and they were both working to acquire the package, but for whom? Nick shook it off for a moment to go over and hug his dad and join the reunion.

"Dad, I'm so glad you're safe. I'm sure you have some stories to tell."

"Son, it seems we both have stories to share. I was so worried about you and your mom. Thank God, you two are safe; I'm happy for this to be over."

Elli and Derek were kissing each other faces. Although the death of Nigel overshadowed the reunion, Derek being home brought Elli much relief.

"Derek, I have to know about Nigel; what happened?"

"Mom, dad saved us. He gave up his own life for Mack and me."

"How did he die, Derek?"

"Gus, Gus killed him."

"He was working with Zhang, but he won't bother us anymore. Dad killed him, once and for all. I saw his dead body, and I made sure he was dead."

"If Gus had died years ago, your dad would be alive. I hope he rots in hell."

Jack was observing the reunion when he decided to walk up to Elli. "I want you to know how sorry I am for your loss. My team in China made the arrangements to get Nigel home. His body has arrived and should be on the way to the mortuary. Ma'am, I want you to know Nigel was a courageous man. He saved our asses over there and gave up his life for ours. I'm sure Derek, who is also an amazingly smart and brave person, will fill you in on the details."

"Thank you, and you are?"

"Zhiban Wang, my friends call me Jack."

"Thank you…"

Nick wanted to learn more about Mr. Wang and his involvement in China and his relationship with Talia. He knew this was not the time or the place, so he kept it casual.

"Hi Jack, I'm Nick, Mack's son."

"Nick, you don't have to introduce yourself. I know all about you."

Nick couldn't stop thinking, was this because of his dad or Talia?

"Your dad could not stop talking about you and how brave you are, staying here and helping Elli."

"Mr. Wang, I think we all stepped up to get done what was necessary."

"So, do you have the package?"

"Nick, do you have the thumb drive?"

Both men gave each other the stare down, waiting for the other to respond. Just as Nick was about to speak, he saw Agent Johnson walking towards them.

"Elli, we have company."

Mack and Stephanie noticed a man walking up to them and asked, "Who is that?"

Nick responded, "The FBI."

"Elli, Nick, good seeing you guys again. Who do we have here, and where is Nigel?" J asked, scanning the area.

Although Elli had worked with Agent Johnson and generally liked him, she wasn't ready for all his questions.

Nick thought he should interject, "Nigel is not coming back; he has had a terrible accident."

"Accident?"

"Yes, he's dead, who the hell are you?" Derek jumped in.

"I'm sorry to hear about Nigel. I'm Agent Johnson with the FBI. Tell me more about Nigel, what happened? Did he die on his way back or in China?"

In hearing this guy was with the FBI, Jack extended his hand, "Hello, I'm Jack, a family friend. Listen, the family has been through a lot. This is not a good time."

"Hi Jack, good to meet a family friend. I will tell you that Nigel's death is a matter of interest, and my asking of what happened will not stop. Nick, since Nigel is not the topic of conversation right now, will you introduce me to who I assume are your parents?"

Nick knew he couldn't hide the fact they were his parents. He just wasn't sure how much Agent Johnson knew.

"Yes, this is my Dad, Mack. You never officially met my mother while she was in the hospital."

"Hi, Agent Johnson. I'm Stephanie."

"Mrs. Griego, good to see you up and around and doing better.

Mack, you have a great family, glad to see you're all back together. Elli, Derek, sorry again for your loss. I came by to tell you I have a little more information about the break-in at the lab. The dead young man at the hospital has been traced to a group out of China. We believe he is associated with Zhang and his team. Based on this information, we can only assume they took something out and shot up your place. And oh, by the way, Sam, he was dirty, too. That's all I got. Is there anything you may have to help me fill in the gaps?"

Elli just wanted him to go, "No, Agent Johnson, we don't. We depend on you to provide us with the details.

If we learn anything, we will let you know. Now please, can you give us some private time? I just lost my husband."

"Yes, of course, I'm sorry. We can talk later."

Agent Johnson walked back to his car and drove off.

Elli and Derek went down to the captain's quarters to be alone for a while. Mack and Stephanie thought it would be best for all of them to go home.

Mack believed Jack would get with Elli after she had time to absorb the loss of Nigel.

"Nick, are you ready to go home?"

CHAPTER 47

"Dad, not quite yet. You and Mom head back to the hotel. I have to take care of something that shouldn't take long. I'll meet you there."

"Can't it wait? This reunion has been a long time coming. What could be more important than spending some time together tonight?"

"Nothing, mom, really, but if I take care of it now, it will give us even more time in the next few days. I'll pick up a couple of pizzas and some beer on my way back. It should be an hour or so. I'll text you when I'm on my way. We'll have plenty of time to talk."

Perturbed, Nick wasn't giving in to her motherly shaming. She grabbed Mack's arm and started walking to her car, "Well, if you have to. We'll see you later, and make sure you grab some good beer, not that rotgut from Milwaukee you drink with your buddy Casey."

Nick knew where Elli was staying; a place on the outskirts of town called the Bay Ledge, a charming resort out near Sand Point. That was going to be his first stop, and he knew it wasn't going to be pleasant.

He'd pissed off his mom, but this was something that couldn't wait. As he entered the Bay Ledge parking lot he glimpsed a lone figure carrying two duffel bags, and heading for the lobby. It was no surprise to see it was Wang.

Nick quickly turned into the first space he saw, jumping out as soon as the gearshift was in park. He knew he needed to follow Jack to see where he was headed. He was convinced Jack's first stop would be with Talia and hoped they'd be together for his questions. This encounter needed to be unrehearsed.

Jack headed straight for the stairs up to the second level of the magnificent, rustic lodge overlooking the bay. Nick knew he wouldn't be able to follow close enough to see what room Jack would go to, so he walked to the check-in desk.

A well-coiffed, pretty, twenty-something stepped up to the counter, "Can I help you?"

In as charming and helpless a demeanor as he could muster, Nick replied, "Yeah, I'm supposed to meet with a couple of your guests about possible employment, and really could use some help. I just saw Mr. Wang head in and we are supposed to meet in Ms. Levy's suite (Nick hoped she wasn't using an alias). I believe it's room two-eleven. I thought I had entered it in my phone, but I must have not. Is that the right room number?"

"I'm not supposed to give out information like this, but you look a little helpless. It's room 216. You didn't hear that from me."

"Hear what?" Nick knew that was a tired old line, but had gone into flirting mode, thinking that saying something that dumb might be endearing. He may have to come back to this place once everything was over.

"Thanks," yelled Nick as he sprinted up the steps to the second floor. At the top landing, he dialed Talia's number and walked towards her room. Arriving in front of room 216, Nick could hear Talia's phone ring and her pick up. Nick knew he had the right room.

"Nick, I'm surprised you called. I thought we were going to talk tomorrow after the package review?"

"Talia, I think we ought to talk now!"

"Nick, it's obvious by your tone, you're upset. Why don't you cool down and we'll talk in the morning?"

Knocking loudly on Talia's door, Nick hung up, but not before saying, "Too late."

Talia reluctantly answered the door. She knew this conversation was coming at some point but was hoping she would have more time to prepare herself. She certainly wasn't planning on having Wang as part of it. Even though he had done everything he was supposed to up to that point, Talia still didn't trust him. Now she would have to juggle her lies to match the picture she was painting for Nick, with the picture she was painting for Jack. This circus act was a most dangerous scenario for her. She hoped Nick would ask him to leave.

Nick entered the room and with an air of satire as he greeted them, "Talia, Mr. Wang, surprised to see you here."

"Nick, now may not be the best time to air your grievances but go ahead and sit down if you must. Is it all right for Jack to be here?" hoping for an answer of no.

Nick's head was looking down as he rubbed his chin. He couldn't wait to hear what kind of story Talia would weave, "I guess my first question would be, why did you break your promise to me?'

"I'm not sure I know what you're getting at. I mean, you always seem to think I'm breaking promises to you. We had a conversation like this in Israel, now again here. Tell me what you mean."

"What I mean is; you said you wouldn't hurt anyone close to me if I agreed to stay with you. I told you it would be a deal-breaker, if you remember correctly. You let Nigel get killed. What about him?"

"What about Nigel? When I gave you this mission, and a hell of a lot of money with it, you didn't even know who Nigel was except for the intel I gave you. He and Elli were simply people you were supposed to watch. We explicitly sent you to monitor the work Elli was doing to make sure it didn't get into the wrong hands. I told you that. You working on his boat was a means to the end. It is not my fault you got close to him. You were trained not to get pulled into a situation where your emotions would betray you. It's evident that part of the training didn't stick very well. I've kept my promise."

Nick knew she was right, but not getting attached to Skipper and Elli just didn't feel right, no matter what he had been trained to do. They were decent people, just like his parents.

She was also correct in assessing this talk was similar to other conversations they had in the past. Nick had a different reason for this one, though; it was to get information he didn't think had been shared with him. This time he was familiar with Talia's tactics of being calm under pressure while driving the conversation in the direction she wanted.

He'd play along for now, but with him pushing buttons and all his antennas up. "That could have easily been my dad. I sometimes wonder if I'll ever become as smug as you are about death. I hope not. My God Talia, I thought Nigel was an old friend and lover of yours, someone you respected and kept track of for over 30 years. Gus killed him under your watch, but here you are, acting as if it's just another day at the office. What the fuck is wrong with you?"

Talia turned towards Jack with a look that seemed to be a mix of disappointment and scorn, then looked back at Nick, "It wasn't supposed to come down the way it did. When I became aware your dad, Nigel, and Derek had gone to China to be some modern cowboy posse, I immediately called Jack, who was already talking with Nigel's MI6 buddies. My team could see what Zhang was up to when he started notifying buyers about the auction he'd be running. At that point I pulled Jack directly into my circle to make sure he helped them and, at the same time, protect them. I thought it was under control. Evidently, I was wrong. Your dad and his new friends should not have ever gone to a place they knew nothing about. They had other options; better options to help Elli and the lab get out of a bad situation. Sometimes there are consequences for bad decisions, even when they are based on good intentions. I am sorry about your parents' involvement, too. They wouldn't have been involved if the ambush had not happened at the cliffs, or if Elli and Nigel had been more astute in contacting them sooner about where you were. At the time we weren't aware of Zhang or Peralta, or they had someone inside helping them. We knew some other parties were conscious of the research and also wanted it. We also knew the longer the research stayed in the lab under lax security the more risk for someone else to get their hands on it existed. If Zhang was already on the scene, who else was?" Talia was aware she was telling a lie by omitting she contacted and partnered with Zhang when she found out it was him at the cliffs, and who now had the package.

"It's your job to know what people like Zhang do. I knew he was there, and that he had an organization of Chinese associates running a cell out of the Chinese restaurant. For all I know, your buddy Jack here is part of that group." (Button number one pushed)

Wang stood up to impose himself over Nick as he pulled his sunglasses down over his eyes like he was trying to hide something more than anger behind them.

"Sit the fuck down, Jack! Nick, then, why didn't you report that to me?"

Nick wasn't falling for that gotcha question right now, "Hell, come to think about it, I easily could've taken a bullet at the cliffs because of your lack of knowledge. It has me wondering if this all may be some elaborate setup." (Button two)

Nick was now taking control of the conversation without Talia even being aware of it. He watched closely for Talia's reaction to see some sort of "tell," like in a poker game, but she remained stoned faced. On the other hand, Jack looked up and fiddled with his sunglasses again, like he did when Nick suggested he may be part of the restaurant group. There was Jack's tell. What was he hiding?

"Let's talk about Elli. I know you told me the history of her and Nigel; why were you compelled to contact her again, or come into town? That was a pretty brazen move. You realize, she saw us standing in the diner together. She seemed pretty certain it was you. It has her wondering what's up, and if I'm somehow involved in something I'm not supposed to be. This is a tangled web you weaved, one that was entirely unnecessary. She's not sure she can trust either one of us now." (Button three)

Nick was looking for Talia's tell. Nothing, well, maybe something. Her right nostril flared just slightly. He'd have to keep an eye on that.

"You are right. At one time, I felt I needed to get back in touch with Elli to keep a close eye on things, I recruited you to do that, and should have backed off."

Talia knew she had been bullshitting and telling half-truths during much of the conversation, but knew this was a flat out lie. It may have been true at one time, but not as much anymore. After everything went down in China she had been given new instructions by her superiors. Getting the original package under her sole control was absolute. No other option would be viable.

Things had changed only slightly since the orders were handed down. Now that there was an almost identical package, obeying her order became both easier and more difficult at the same time. It gave her an option she didn't have before. Unfortunately, only one of those options would be in her best interest.

The worst-case scenario would be her not getting either one of the packages. In her mind that was not an option. If it did happen, it would be the end of her career, or possibly her life. The best case would be her getting the original and destroying the copy. An acceptable scenario might be to relegate the copy to Elli and the US. She would know more when Elli went through the package and the thumb drive in the morning. There was a lot to think about in the next twelve hours.

The one thing she would need to remain quiet about was her new instructions. She was also ordered to do anything necessary to get everything for herself, even if it meant killing Wang, Elli, or her prized pupil Nick. Wang would be an easy kill, but Nick and Elli would be a lot tougher. *Watch your emotions,* she thought. Talia's superiors had made their requirements crystal clear America was not to control the technology and couldn't be trusted to share it.

Looking directly at Jack, Nick sighed, "One last question before I go. It seems to me that Mr. Wang over there and your associates, who shipped the package, had plenty of opportunities to mess with it. So did you Talia, since you were the one to set up the flight. These facts are rather concerning. Jack should probably be at the review tomorrow so we can question him about his knowledge of the contents or lack thereof if it becomes necessary. I plan on taking the package to cold storage when I leave here. I also asked Elli to make sure someone was posted outside the lab and cold storage to be certain it's not touched by anyone else during the evening or disappear again. I'm sure this is acceptable to both of you. By the way, that duffel bag there looks identical to the one carrying all the samples and data. Wouldn't you agree, that's a little odd?" (Last Button)

Looking up and fidgeting with his shades again, Jack replied, "Yes, I'm good with your plan, and these are just my clothes. Here open it up and look through my underwear if it will make you feel better."

Nick gave Jack a sly smile he wasn't sure how to react to, "Not necessary Jack, I know what I need to know." He then looked over at Talia.

Talia, with her right nostril flaring even more, concurred, "I'm good too."

Nick reached out for the duffels as Jack handed him the original as he and Talia had agreed.

"Thanks. See you in the morning."

Nick shut the door behind him, leaving both Jack and Talia in a minor state of shock, and knowing both of them were up to no good, while he was being squeezed into an incredibly dangerous predicament.

"Jack, you are going to need to be my eyes and ears tomorrow. We need to know exactly what is missing from the package and the importance Elli places on it. If something is missing, we are going to have to take steps to track it down. I need everything to be there before we deliver it to my people."

"Don't worry; we'll get it all. I'll make sure of that."

"For lack of a better word, you're acting a little 'nervous' Jack. Is there something wrong, something you want to say?"

"I'm not sure what you are talking about Elli. I'm fine. I just think all the excitement has us both wound up. I'm going to grab something to eat. Do you need me to bring anything back for you?"

"No, thanks."

When Jack arrived at his car, the first thing he did was to turn on the AC. Was it him, or was Maine always hot like this in May? The next thing he did was throw the other duffel bag into the back seat, then he finally pressed speed dial on his phone, "Wǒ shí fēnzhōng jiù dào. Míngtiān huì fāshēng." (I will be there in 10 minutes. It will happen tomorrow).

CHAPTER 48

It was 10:00 PM when the phone rang. Derek and Elli were beat, but Elli went over to where she had it plugged in. Looking down at the screen, she saw it was J.

"Elli, I'm sorry to call so late, but I needed to. I have something important to bring over. It can't wait. At the Chinese restaurant, I was eating and observing when that girl Nick met at the hospital came over to wait on my table. I believe her name is Gen. She passed a photo to me in my napkin. It was of four men, one of whom was the guy that died at the hospital. Another may have been the guy I met at the docks this morning. I'm not sure."

"Do you mean Zhiban Wang?"

"I thought his name was Jack, anyway I'd like you to take a look to see if that's him."

"Did she tell you why she was giving it to you?"

"No, but I'm sure she wanted somebody to know that these four men were all together."

"You sure this isn't some type of set up or diversion?"

"Pretty sure. You could tell the girl was frightened. She kept looking around to make sure nobody saw her pass it to me. My guess is she knows more about what is going on at the restaurant than she's let on. She is scared, or her conscience is getting to her. In any case, you may want to take a look at it.

"Yes, come over; you have my curiosity as well."

"Mom, who have you been talking to?"

"Derek, it was Agent Johnson, he is on his way and wants to show me a picture. I need you to see it too."

"Picture of who?"

"Your friend Mr. Wang. Derek, you need to tell me everything you can about this Jack fellow.

I don't want to walk into a situation with him at the lab in the morning."

"Mom, all I know is he is on our side. He helped us secure the package."

"Derek, think, how did he know your dad?"

"Dad didn't know him but was aware he existed. Dad's friends at MI6, with the help of Talia, hired him to help us out. They felt they would bring too much attention if they were the ones in China. Plus, Jack was very familiar with Shanghai and Zhang. Mr. Wang also was with the CIA before becoming a businessman in Shanghai."

Inquisitive and frustrated, Elli asked, "CIA, why would your dad get the CIA involved?"

"Former CIA mom. He was sent to dad. He still does some consulting work with MI6, the CIA, and the Mossad."

"Derek, I hate to tell you, once in the CIA, you are always connected to the CIA. What about this Talia person? Did you meet her?"

"No, I have not. Again, another friend of dad's."

"Derek, do me a favor when Agent Johnson arrives with that picture, whether or not it is Jack in the picture, tell him it's not him. I don't want to let him know any more than he needs to for now."

"Sure, mom."

Elli could feel there was a piece missing here, but couldn't put her finger on it. "Derek, did your dad ever give you the names of the MI6 agents he had contacted for help?"

"I want to say it was Agents Crawford and Crews if I remember correctly." I remember him calling them, but never heard much about their involvement after that."

"I remember Jim Crawford from days past. Your dad stayed in touch with him, and I'm sure his contact number is still on the computer. I'm going to give him a call early tomorrow. It will already be the afternoon in London. I'll be interested in what he has to say. Also, I'm sure he'll want to be told about your dad if he doesn't already know."

Elli was trying to pull all the pieces together but all she had was how they helped Nigel and Derek. Still, if Mr. Wang was indeed photographed with those men who stole the formula, was he working for them, us, or someone else? She had to trust somebody, and although she was suspicious of Nick's newly discovered covert skills, she believed he was there to help. Nick would be accompanying her to the lab with Mr. Wang in the morning. It didn't take long for J to get to the docks to meet Elli."

"Permission to come on board?"

"J, I thought you were told you said that only when the Captain was here."

"Elli, now that Nigel is gone, I'm trying to be respectful to the new Captain."

"Thanks, J, I appreciate the respect. Now, you got something to show me?"

Agent Johnson showed Elli and Derek the photograph, "Is it him?"

"I recognize Sam, but I'm sorry I don't know the other men. Derek, how about you?"

"No, I don't either; not even that Sam dude. Sorry"

Agent Johnson was getting frustrated, "We know Sam Wilder, we know of Zhang Wei and, of course, the dead man at the hospital. Take another look, is this the same man I saw this morning with you, Derek?

"No sir, it is not."

Agent Johnson could spot a lie, but choose to let it go for now, "OK, thanks for your time. I will be in touch later." Sorry for coming so late at night, Elli. I know you are having a horrible day. Good night."

CHAPTER 49

The morning had broken on a glorious New England day, the palette of the sunrise was a mixture of thin white clouds, with just enough moisture stored in them to give off a purple hue when the orange-red light of the sun bounced off their soft curves. Elli couldn't sleep, so got up to watch the sunrise. It was about 5:00 AM. Looking at the sky, she couldn't help but think about the old sailor's lament of "red sky at night, sailor's delight, red sky in morning, sailor's warning." She hoped it held no truth for today.

After finishing her second cup of coffee, Elli rushed over to the computer and pulled up the contacts file. Typing CRAW in the search list brought up, The Crawdad House Seafood Restaurant, Marcus Crawell, a local attorney, and Jim Crawford. It would be about 11:00 AM in London. Elli dialed Jim's number.

On the fourth ring, Elli expected the voice greeting to come on, when Jim finally picked up the phone, breathing a little heavy from running upstairs to retrieve it. "Hi, this is Jim Crawford."

Elli hesitated for a second. Was this his message greeting or a real person? She realized which reasonably quickly when the rest of the message didn't come.

"Hello, Jim?"

"Speaking."

"Hi Jim, this is Elli Brunetta in Maine, USA. You may remember me through Nigel Shackelford."

"Of course, Elli, I remember you. How are you and that old goat of a sea captain doing?"

When Jim asked his question, Elli knew he wasn't aware of Nigel's death. She wanted to respond with some care to make sure she could coax as much information as possible. "I'm calling because Nigel is no longer with us."

"What happened, Elli?"

"I've been told he was murdered in Shanghai by a guy named Gus Peralta, who was working with another guy named Zhang Wei. My son was there with him when it happened. I have no reason to believe it isn't true. Do either of those names mean anything to you?"

"They do. Gus Peralta is an old-school gun for hire. You don't want to be near anywhere he is. Zhang is an international armaments dealer. We have some intelligence indicating he was running some sort of auction for a possible new bioweapon but it got shut down unexpectedly for reasons we do not know. Was Nigel part of that? Did he come out of retirement or something? Why would he be involved?"

"Jim, he was in Shanghai because of the auction… and to save my professional ass. My team and I created that supposed bio-weapon at the lab where I currently work. I created it to do good things, but as you know, if humanity can turn something good into evil, they will. Are you telling me you didn't know about Nigel being in China or who he was with?"

"Cross my heart. I knew Nigel was thinking about going, but wasn't sure when. He called Agent Crews and me a couple of weeks ago to see if we still had access to our resources in Asia, and if he needed them, would we share? Of course, we told him yes. He did mention Zhang and Peralta, but I honestly didn't connect the dots until right now. He said he'd get back with us, but he didn't. A couple of days later we were contacted by another asset who works with us occasionally. She told us she had it handled, but didn't say anything else. Damn Elli, we should have double-checked."

"She? Is her name Talia Levy?"

Crawford's silence answered the question.

"What about a guy name Zhiban or "Jack" Wang."

"We know who he is too. He was a CIA operative in China and continues to do freelance work for them out of his business there. He has citizenship in both the US and China, allowing him to go just about anywhere he needs to. I have never worked with the man, and probably wouldn't. He has a way of making everything happen to his advantage, which, as you know, in our game can be dangerous. I don't trust him. Why do you ask?"

"Nigel met up with him in Shanghai. Wang told him he would be the liaison to Levy. Only recently did I find out it was her and not you guys he was working with."

"Elli, for some reason, that's what Levy wanted you to think. Hell, she was playing all of us. We had no idea he had decided to go. If we had, we would've had his back. I am so sorry. If there is anything I can do, let me know."

"Thanks Jim, I will." Elli somehow knew this conversation would be their last.

Elli was still trying to put the pieces together when Derek walked in, "Sort of early to be on the phone isn't it? I'm sure you're ready to go to the lab and put this behind you as fast as you can. I talked to Nick to invite him. Weird, he acted like he was coming anyway. Said he'd get over here ASAP."

"Are we sure we want him there?"

"Yeah, I'm sure. Nick's been a huge help and knows a lot about what has gone on here. Is there something you're concerned about or not telling me?"

"No, maybe I'm just overly cautious."

"Well, I think having him there is a cautious thing to do." Onto a different subject now. Please think hard on the answers to what I'm about to ask."

"OK. Shoot."

"I had the distinct impression you guys were going to be meeting up with the two MI6 guys in Shanghai. Was that your impression?"

"It was my impression also, Mom, but then when we got there, Jack showed up at the airport and said Talia had sent him. I didn't think about it much at the time because dad didn't react much to him being there. He sure didn't act surprised if that's what you're getting at."

"I talked to one of those MI6 agents this morning and he told me they were called off by Talia, who told them she had it handled. Do you find that as odd as I do?"

"Yeah, I guess so. Maybe dad just wanted to leave her name out because of, um, past relationships?"

"That may be part, but not all. Talia has been inserting herself the entire way; in fact, she's been inserting herself into all our lives since 1982. I don't trust her any longer. She is responsible for your dad's death, and whatever she's up to, it's no good. I'm certain she's lurking around here just looking for an opportunity to take advantage of this situation, with no regard for our lives. That bitch either needs to have a collar put around her neck or be put down. What about Wang? He and Talia seem to be tight."

"They have been. Like I said before, Jack's done about all he can do to help, but I wouldn't put much trust in him considering the Talia relationship. I'm even starting to question where Nick's allegiances may be."

Derek wanted to put his trust in Nick and, was still puzzled about the role he was playing. He told his mom, "I've already wondered about Nick."

"I think something isn't right, but he has always had my back. Let's get going then. I need you to pack your dad's gun, and please ask Nick to do the same. If he doesn't have one, let him use my revolver. It and the holster are in the top drawer of your dad's dresser. I am very nervous about this meeting."

"Mom, are you sure you want Nick to have a gun?"

"What did I just tell you?"

Jack left for the meeting on time, but he needed to drop off something at the Chinese restaurant. That was going to put him behind schedule. He texted Derek to let him know.

Talia, deciding she needed to be in better control, tailed Jack. She knew she'd have to wait in her car outside the lab due to security, but it would be better than waiting for him back at the hotel. There was an unexpected event on the way to the lab. Jack stopped at the Chinese restaurant carrying in a duffel bag in one hand and a manila envelope in his other hand. However, he returned to his vehicle a couple of minutes later, empty-handed.

Talia wondered why he was dropping off, what she believed, were the copies. What was in the manila envelope? She also concluded at that moment; Jack was playing her as well. At some point unbeknownst to her, he had made a deal with the devil, although she wasn't sure which devil it was. Talia also understood better why Jack shot Zhang in Shanghai. More than anything, it got him out of Jack's way to prompt Talia to think Jack was loyal to her.

J knew he had been at arm's length the entire investigation. It was starting to get under his skin. He had done everything to get Elli and Nick to trust him, but they would always give him enough to keep him off balance. He knew he was into something pretty big, but didn't have enough information to get the Bureau more involved. As far as they were concerned, this was still a murder investigation.

He wasn't being told everything about Nigel's death, what was in the lab, who fired the bullet that killed Sam Wilder, why Elli and Derek were not telling the truth about recognizing Wang, or what role this Nick kid played in all of it. There were way too many questions.

He decided the only way to get more was to tail Elli and Nick. The time for questions was over, and something would be going down soon. He was not going to miss it. J decided to sleep in the car for the night and tail Elli in the morning.

Nick arrived a little after 7:00 AM, which woke up J. Around an hour later, Elli, Nick, and Derek came out together. He knew something was up now. He rubbed the sleep out of his eyes and turned on his engine. He was finally ready to be a part of the action, not the bumbling FBI agent he had presented himself. That didn't work. Maybe this would.

The trio hopped into Elli's vehicle and took off. Elli quickly made a call to lab security to pre-clear everyone coming to the meeting. She knew carrying guns into the lab would be impossible without special clearance, even considering the lax security there. The three of them arrived at the lab about ten minutes later. When J arrived right behind them, he looked around to see if he noticed anything unusual. He saw a car parked down the street with a woman in it, slinking low into the driver's seat, and observing everything. Ten minutes later, J saw Jack Wang arrive and let in through security. Why was Wang here?

Elli's office was small and not well equipped, so everyone decided it would be best to move into the central lab's large conference room. It had all the necessary A/V, an electron microscope, mass spectrometer, and other more technical equipment needed to analyze samples. Any other general equipment was just outside the door if required. The best part of the room was its lack of windows, which would be useful in this case, allowing for the review of everything without prying eyes looking in. She dialed down to the lab and asked the guard to get everything together out of deep freeze and deliver it to the conference room.

As the group walked down the hall, Nick took up the rear to observe as much as he could. Derek was wearing his gun well. Only someone looking for it would notice it. Wang was not hiding his weapon so well. His gun was strapped to his ankle, pushing his pant leg out into an unnatural shape. On the other hand, Derek had his tucked in his waistband, covered by a loose-fitting shirt. Elli had a small .22 pistol in her purse.

When they arrived Nick took a seat on the same side of the desk as Jack, which was on the opposite side of Jack's gun leg. His logic was if something went down, Jack would have to do maximum work to get his gun pointed at Nick plus turn away from Elli and Derek to shoot. Elli sat at the table's head to Jack's right, with

Derek to her right. Derek was sitting directly across from Jack. Nick was planning to make sure that if Jack fired his gun, it would be at him first.

Nick put on a pair of insulated mittens, proceeded to the bag, removed its contents and the contents of the refrigerated sample container. He placed them lightly on the table. Elli moved to put the thumb drive into her laptop's USB, then walked over to the items on the table, visually analyzing each test tube as Nick placed it out. She then turned on the microscope and spectrometer. When they were up and running, Elli started preparing samples of what was in each tube to be analyzed appropriately. She was very deliberate but efficient. During any free time created while the equipment did their jobs, she compared documents from the duffel bag to the hard drive. Derek was keeping one eye on Jack and one on Nick.

For over two hours, Jack, Derek, and Nick quietly watched the doctor do what she did best. Elli kept what she was observing very close to her vest, though, no smiles or scowls. When her work was complete, she sat down very erect in her chair and looked into each person's eyes, then down to her inventory sheet. "Gentlemen, I think we have some problems, but I should give the good news first."

Nick saw Jack fiddle with the sunglasses sitting on his head.

"Upon comparing the thumb drive to the package, I have confirmed Sam Wilder did keep parts of some critical formulations on the drive. We have been able to compare what he had to what was in the package. When you put them together, everything is there."

Jack's mind started racing, realizing the other duffel was not complete without the thumb drive. He would need to get his hands on it.

Elli continued, "Everything else seems to be here except for one crucial file. We had reached Phase 2 of testing and had some vital data on dosing and side effects to lead us into more intense testing and alternative dosing. We need that information or will have to start our tests again. It could delay our progress by at least a year."

Jack started fidgeting again. He knew his theft would eventually be discovered and needed to remain calm. No one was yet aware he had that information. Jack then thought back to the scene of the gunfight at the fabric warehouse in Shanghai.

Jack's plans had changed and didn't include Zhang or Talia. Zhang needed to be eliminated, and Jack needed to retrieve an essential file from each duffel bag without anyone observing him.

What fate presented to him that day was fortunate. The opportunity to eliminate Zhang couldn't be more perfect. If Mack, Nigel, and Derek survived, he would only need to tell them it was necessary to stop the auction and shooting Zhang was the most efficient way. Talia might be less responsive to Zhang's demise, but Jack was sure making a story up about Zhang double-crossing them would suffice.

His plan to retrieve files from each duffel bag could be problematic, but the gunfight at the end of the hall should give him ample time to steal and hide the files titled "Phase 1 dosing and side effect reports." He knew if everything went sideways those files would be leverage to cash in on some of the money.

When he completed both tasks, it was time to take his position. Moving to the center of the room, he positioned his body with his back to the entrance, arms folded with his head shaking in a confused manner, and yelled, "Damn" loud enough for anyone coming down the hall to hear.

Fortune also had Nigel and Derek be the ones to enter the room.

Jack then put on a performance that was Oscar worthy, which included confusion over not finding the package. The performance was so convincing he continued to the final act of directing them towards the hidden room and the package they believed was fully intact.

The double-cross was almost complete. Talia was next.

Jack continued to think through the dilemma. Although he needed the thumb drive, he was the only one with the missing files now. He had dropped both the original and the copy off with the other duffel at the restaurant. How in the hell was he going to get ahold of the thumb drive without creating a scene?

Jack was pulled out of his thoughts when Elli started talking again. "It also looks like some of our materials have been contaminated by all the world-hopping and temperature changes; we will have to synthesize new product. This situation is problematic, but it shouldn't delay us too much since we have these originals. Thank goodness for that. If they had been completely reacted, we'd be in much more trouble."

That last observation got Jack's attention. Up to that point, he thought he would only need the thumb drive. That wasn't the case any longer. His mind searched for an answer; *If I don't get those samples back, the entire project will be considered a failure. That is not going to be acceptable to my employers. Fuck, I will have to take the whole bag and get these damn RNA samples in a deep freeze. That's entirely different than just a thumb drive.*

Things were off the rail more than Jack thought they could ever be. He needed to act.

Jack was confident his position in the conference room would be his best defense should Nick retaliate, especially if he made the first move. His right hand reached for his right ankle and stayed there. "Elli, I'm sorry I will need those samples and the thumb drive, I'm taking them with me."

Derek drew his gun, shouting, "The hell you are!"

This outburst caught both Jack and Nick by surprise.

"Derek, no," screamed Elli.

Nick immediately reached behind his back, grabbing the butt of his gun, focusing on Jack. He knew Jack was armed but figured Derek would keep his cool. He should have known better based on the way Derek had been acting lately. It was evident to Nick now how unstable Derek could be. He had watched his dad die, and his mom taken advantage of by Talia, knowing she was still in grave danger from that woman. With Derek also being on edge about Jack's allegiance and his apparent mistrust of Jack, Nick knew he'd be armed for war and ready to shoot before talking.

Jack reacted to Derek's movements and reached for his gun. It was as if Nick was watching this thing play out in slow motion. Derek's movement was slow and awkward; he wasn't prepared for this scenario. Jack was well trained and pointed his gun at Derek, firing one shot hitting Derek in the right shoulder. Jack, who hadn't planned on Nick being equipped for situations like this, was surprised when he saw Nick's gun drawn. Before Jack could react, Nick fired two rounds into Jack's chest.

CHAPTER 50

About two hours into the wait, J was getting very bored and sore. He had spent the night in the car, which had flared up some old football injuries. He needed to be moving. Still intrigued by Wang being part of this meeting, he decided he would take some action to see what was going on behind the gates. The lady parked down the street wasn't moving, so he didn't have to worry about her. He also knew if someone approached him on the other side, all he'd have to do is show his FBI identification and flash his toothy smile.

J made his way around the perimeter of the fencing and found a spot he could get over. He wasn't as agile anymore but could still climb a fence. As he got to the top and struggled to get his second leg over, he heard the crotch of his pants split open and three gunshots.

J fell to the ground and quickly got up and examined his crotch area for damaged goods. "Thank God, all good," he murmured to himself.

He ran towards the building front entrance. "There's goes my attempt not to be seen or stopped by security," more murmuring.

The guard at the door held up his hand and motioned to J to stop. "Sorry sir, we are locking down the facility; you cannot enter."

J pulled out his credentials and showed it to the guard, "Officer Allen, I'm with the FBI, we have determined this facility's activity is a matter of national security. I heard gunshots; has your team responded?"

The young man stood there, speechless and scared. He thought this job was to be a piece of cake, slow and calm, not an international incident with gunfire. "No.., but we called the authorities."

"I am the authorities," J said as he ran into the building. Scores of people were making their way out of the building. J fought the rush of the crowd. He saw a man wearing a white lab coat, stopped him, and asked, "Where are the gunshots coming from?" The man wouldn't make eye contact. Without looking at Agent Johnson, he responded, "I don't know. From down in the labs, I think. Now let me go, please."

J let him go, then realized something, but it was too late, definitely, an ahh shit moment. He had seen this guy, several times before at the Chinese restaurant.

They called him Lin but was wearing a name tag with a different name on it. *What was it?* J thought. *I'm FBI; I'm supposed to notice things like that.* Then he realized the name on the badge was "Wilder." *Holy Shit,* he thought, *the guy wasn't supposed to be in here. That was a stolen badge.*

Even though J thought about turning around and chasing Lin down, he decided otherwise. J made his way to an area of the building that was oddly empty of any activity or movement. He could hear a woman screaming "Derek" and ran towards the voice. It was coming from a conference room. He drew his weapon, not knowing what was in store for him.

"One, two, three," he kicked the door open to find Elli holding Derek in her arms, crying and shouting, "I can't lose you too."

On the other side of the room was Nick with a gun in his hand, "FBI, drop it; damn it, I said drop it."

Nick knew better than to turn towards the man with a gun shouting at him. Nick dropped his weapon. Lying on the floor was the Asian man he saw at Nigel's boat. The Asian was the man J was asking Elli about. J could tell this guy was dead by the two wounds in his chest. Knowing that, J put his gun in his holster and cautiously walked over to where Elli and Derek were. However, he kept his eye on Nick. He could see Derek would need medical attention, but his wounds were not life-threatening.

"What in the fuck happened here, Elli?" Keeping his hand on his holstered gun.

"J, Nick saved us; you can take your hand away from your gun."

Her attention was back on Derek.

J slowly took his hand off his weapon and kneeled to give Derek aid. Nick walked over to help J as Elli looked on. Derek was still conscious but moaning due to the pain.

Elli cried while she wiped Derek's brow, "You're going to be alright; you're going to be alright."

J knew the local police would be there soon, but called 911 anyway to request an ambulance for Derek.

"Mom, I'm so sorry; I tried. Where's Jack, what happened?"

"It's going to be OK, Nick got him; he's dead. Jack is dead."

"Nick, really?" moaned Derek.

J heard footsteps approaching the conference room. Knowing it would be the police, he thought it would be best to meet them at the door and identify himself as an Agent with the FBI.

"Elli, the police are outside the door. I'm going to have them take Derek to the ambulance. I'm also going to make sure they know this is an FBI matter and

I will need to secure this room with both of you being in my custody. We won't have a lot of time; I'm sure other officials will be here soon. What I need from you is for you to tell me the whole story, no more fucking around."

J carefully opened the door and presented his badge, "We have a man hurt, another man dead. I need for you to take the wounded man out to the ambulance and remove the dead man."

One officer responded, "We can't take the body and disturb the crime scene."

"Oh, the hell you can't, this is a Federal matter and I'm in charge."

The Officers looked at one another, shrugged, and followed the Agent's orders.

Elli managed to give Derek one last hug before paramedics helped him out of the conference room.

"I'm going to be OK, mom," again with a moan.

Elli, Nick, and J remained in the conference room once it was cleared it out.

"OK, we don't have a lot of time. Elli, what has been happening here?"

"J, I haven't been completely upfront with you. You must understand I did this to protect my family and to protect any information leaving the lab and falling into the wrong hands."

"Elli, I hate to break it to you, but your husband is dead and your son shot. I'm not sure you have been protecting them."

"Easy, Agent Johnson, that is not fair."

"Quiet Nick; I will get to you later. Elli, please continue."

"J, you know about the break-in here at the lab, but you don't know what was taken. I could get into the details, but you said we don't have much time. Let's say it could have been bad."

"Elli, bad, how bad?"

"The research we do here is primarily on gene editing techniques. We have developed methods with this technique to help us fight viruses. It will also be invaluable in curing many chronic diseases. The current focus we have now is on viruses and developing medical treatments similar to vaccines that will keep them from reproducing in the body."

"Elli, what viruses?"

"There is not one specific virus we are targeting; we are targeting them all. Even the ones that are not out there yet. Research like this is being sought after at any cost. The reasons become obvious if you think through the consequences of someone having the ability to create or discover a virus and almost immediately have a cure. It will make the owner very powerful."

"You said it could have been bad, what changed?"

"Nigel, Derek, and Nick's father went to China to help re-secure the stolen research and samples. Nigel paid with his life to get these back."

"Nigel, how did he even know how to get these formulas back?

"Let's just say Nigel's past life prepared him for this moment."

"So, who took the research?"

"Zhang and some of his contacts in China, who were the shooters at the cliffs. It's my understanding they were trying to sell it off to the highest bidder before Nigel helped stop them."

"Stopped, how were they stopped if Jack was just here?"

"Jack believed there was one piece missing and came here to get it. His partners were killed in China; Zhang, by Jack's hand, and Peralta by Nigel's. We are also certain he was working with an alleged Mossad agent named Talia Levy. Nick killed Jack when he attempted to take the research today, after he shot Derek. Nick was protecting us."

J was listening but shook his head in a confused manner. "I just can't wrap my arms around this young kid being a hero, but I'll take your word. Was there a missing piece?"

"Not really, we have everything but one file.

The rest is safe now; no more missing pieces, right, Nick?"

Nick walked over to the computer that had been knocked off the table during the commotion. He reached to pick it up, grab the thumb drive, and say "Right" when he noticed the thumb drive wasn't there.

Elli could see the look of horror in his face, "What's wrong?"

"There's no thumb drive Elli. I don't see it in the USB port or on the floor. Do you have it?"

"No, it was in there before all this happened."

J jumped into the conversation, remembering the guy in the lab coat running past him wearing Wilder's badge. "What happened immediately after the shooting? Was anyone else in the room?"

"No, No," Ellie replied.

"You're wrong, Elli, there was. Right after the shots, a lab tech ran in to see if he could help. He caught his foot on the power cord to the computer, which knocked it to the floor. A lot was going on then. He reached down to pick the computer up, and I yelled for him to get help. He had to be working with Jack and must have grabbed the drive while our attention was elsewhere."

"Shit," J screamed. "I saw the SOB leaving the building, but didn't realize why he was here until right now. He was an Asian guy I occasionally saw hanging out of the Chinese restaurant, but he was wearing Wilder's work badge."

"God, you all have shitty security here," Nick couldn't help saying." Elli, did you close the file before the shooting started?"

"Nick, I don't think so."

Nick picked up the computer and hit the space bar, not sure what he would see. It was a dead screen. Power had been drained.

"Shit. Plug it back in and turn it on." Elli screamed.

Derek followed Ellie's instructions, booting up the computer. "Nothing came up, Elli."

"OK, pull up my file list. Scroll until you see the temporary file location and click on it. My software is supposed to download any new file it sees on any of the drives as a temporary file.

There's a bunch of stuff with file names are combinations of letters and numbers."

"That's because my system automatically encrypts their names. Is there a recent one?"

"Yeah, one from about thirty minutes ago when we started the meeting."

"Click on it. It will ask for a password. It is "winemakergiulio," one word, all small letters."

Derek clicked, entered, and smiled. He quickly clicked on "save as" and named the file "Nigel" before saving it to the C: drive. He turned to Elli, showing her the screen, "I named the file Nigel."

"Thanks, Nick. I guess I can breathe now. They got away with something, but it doesn't hurt us as much as they think."

Agent Johnson also breathed. He knew he had enough information, for now, to speak to his superiors before a full-blown investigation would begin. J asked Elli and Nick to make themselves available and allowed them to leave the scene. He knew he also had a visit to make to the restaurant but didn't expect to drive there that day.

Lin exited the lab, hopped onto his Kawasaki, and headed straight to the restaurant. He was met outside by a man in a pin-striped suit. Lin handed him the drive. Not wanting to be there any longer than he had to, or caring who he had just given something so valuable to, he grabbed an envelope of cash from the man, leaned over his bike, and had it to full throttle, fourth gear in less than 8 seconds. Within a minute, the suited man exited the restaurant, with a duffel bag in hand, jumped into an Uber, and headed to the airport for an unknown destination. He would be made aware of where he was going when he got on the private plane waiting for him.

Talia's cell phone began to ring. She could see it was Nick.

"Talia, we need to meet."

"Meet, what happened? I'm in my car outside the lab. I can see all the commotion."

"I can't talk now, but there's a place I know we can talk. We need to be very discreet. The FBI is heavily involved in this now. Get a map of Bar Harbor and find Eagle Lake. You will take State Highway 233. When you enter the area, you will find a turn off about half a mile past the welcome to Acadia National Park sign. There is a parking lot that is under repair, construction signs mark the entrance. There should be no other cars there; the lot should be empty. Meet me at 11:00 PM. I will be in my blue Ford near the bike trail entrance. See you then."

Nick hung up and turned to Elli, "It's done. She will be there, take my car and my gun."

CHAPTER 51

Talia had been given some unsubstantiated information about what happened at the lab, so she slowly approached the parking lot. It was dark that evening, with only a sliver of a moon landing its light on the trees' highest branches. Once Talia could see Nick's blue Ford, she stopped and turned her headlights towards the front of his car. Of all places, she wasn't sure why Nick would want to meet her here. It didn't feel right, but she weighed her options and stepped out to the driver's side. The beam from the headlights shining towards Nick's car did a more than an adequate job of making it difficult for the occupant to see anything other than her dim silhouette.

Talia waited. All she could hear was the chirping of crickets, the deep croaking of bullfrogs, and the sound of her heartbeat. In what seemed like an eternity, she heard a click. Was that a gun being cocked or the sound of the handle disengaging on the car door, or both?

Surveying what she could see, nothing seemed out of place, then the car door of Nick's car opened, and Elli stepped out.

Talia immediately knew who it was. "What are you doing here, Elli? I was expecting someone else."

The tears on hold now, Elli forced the quiver of her voice to subside. "I could ask you the same thing. I assume you were expecting Nick, but he won't be making an appearance tonight. He has finally come to the same conclusion as I have; you are not what you seem."

Talia moved straight into her pattern of breaking down conversations into elements that fit her viewpoint, handling her debate opponent like a potter with clay on her wheel. "What do you mean by I'm not what I seem? That must mean I seem like something."

"You seemed like a friend back in the eighties. We were inseparable, and I had grown so fond of you, only to find out you were using our friendship to spy on Nigel. Then you seemed to be an ally of Derek and Nigel while they were in China, to find out you weren't. You teamed up with the people that gave you the best chance of getting the research. You were working with Wang to get the package for yourself, but evidently, Zhang had different ideas. He ended up dead, and by the end of the day, Nigel was dead too. How long would it have taken you to kill Nigel if Peralta hadn't done it for you? Judging from some of the things Nick told me, you seemed to be a friend and mentor to him, but just used his anger about his brother's death, topped off with some cash, to make him feel better about doing your dirty work."

Don't be silly, Elli; I wouldn't have ever shot Nigel. He brought it on himself by going to China. Nigel easily could have brought death onto Derek and Mack too. You became complicit when you allowed them to go. You had to protect your and the labs reputation. You've been so immersed in your research and self-worth for all these years; you found them more important than both Nigel and Derek. By the way, how has that worked for you so far?"

Elli's grief turned on a dime into deep anger and a strong sense of wanting revenge, culminating with Talia's death. "You are not going to get away with the research Talia. We have it. Jack did his best to take it from us but ended up on the wrong end of a bullet for it. Now you are responsible for another death, and Derek being shot. I'm sure you'll find it disappointing to know it wasn't fatal."

Talia stepped sideways toward the car; she didn't have the time to explain to Elli she didn't give a fuck about Jack. He had double-crossed her. She considered telling Elli she didn't give a fuck about either her or Derek but decided to control her tongue. Elli was wrong about how Talia felt about Nigel. Talia was deeply saddened by what happened to him.

Right this moment, all she knew was getting to the restaurant to retrieve the other package was her priority. It would be gone by morning. Other than the guys at the restaurant, she was the only person to know about it. She then stepped as close as she could get to the driver's side door, reaching her hand in towards the steering wheel.

Before Elli knew what was happening, Talia turned her headlights off. All Elli could see was Talia's muzzle flash as she shot towards her. The reverberating sound of the shots echoed over the lake, drowning out the crickets and bullfrogs. Elli hit the ground and belly crawled for her open door. When she got there, she knew she had one of two choices, leave or fight.

In a microsecond, her decision was made. While still on her belly, Elli fired two rounds in Talia's direction. She then got up and turned on her car's headlamps, not to escape, but to better see her target.

When the beams went on, it seemed to Ellie the light traveled through space in Talia's direction, as if time were slowing down. She leveled off her arm and gun on the door's top, using her car door as a shield. She cocked the trigger of her gun and waited for the light to get there. When the beams finally hit the spot where

Talia was standing, she took a quick breath in, steadied herself, and then saw something she didn't expect.

Nick's silhouette had replaced Talia's as he stood over her crumpled body, with his gun pointing down at her. Elli realized he had followed her in.

Nick looked at Elli with forgiving eyes, as Elli looked back at him with thankful eyes. She didn't have to be the vengeful killer. A boy younger than her son had taken on that sin on for her. She started weeping again as Nick walked towards her.

"I guess we both have been redeemed now."

EPILOGUE

It was winter semester, and Nick was sitting in class, shivering. He felt cheated choosing Oklahoma, and wondering how it could be so cold compared to Massachusetts. He couldn't help but also wonder if the building's heating system was broken, everybody else in class looked frozen, too.

Nick was in his freshman history class. It was just the beginning of his formal education. He was probably missing much of the lecture thinking about the last few years, especially the past eight months.

Although his parents wanted him to go to school closer to home, Nick treasured the distance from Boston. Besides, the University of Oklahoma had a great program in Global Studies, which, along with an undergraduate minor in Criminal Justice, would prepare him for law school, or whatever activity knowledge of the law could prove valuable.

Although Nick fought it for a long time, He finally brought himself to grieve his Captain's loss. Talia introduced Nick into a life that was indirectly the cause of Nigel's death, but Nick was now reluctantly understanding in doing good, sometimes evil things happen. Nick knew he wasn't finished with this new life. The world was full of people who needed an advocate to fight institutional inequities brought on by medical and pharmaceutical overreach. He had also learned from Talia there were many other "bad guys" hiding in the halls of power who needed to be dealt with. Nick owed this change in his life's direction to his brother, whose death led him to take on his more relevant spot in the big picture. Nick did know one thing for sure. He would only do it on his terms.

Of all of Nick's other newfound certainties, he knew he would carry one secret from that night in the parking lot with Talia and Elli to his grave. When Nick saw the sadness in Ellie's eyes that night after all the shooting had ended, he knew she didn't want to be a killer. Nick couldn't tell her it was one of her bullets fired off in a rage that killed Talia. Nick wouldn't let Elli live with the knowledge she had killed someone she once loved as a sister. He was willing to carry the burden with him. That secret would be his gift to Ellie, Derek, and most of all, Nigel.

Mack went back to teaching and when he could, helped Stephanie at the coffee shop. Nick was proud of his parents and always knew there was a little bit of Gramps in his dad. How else could he have handled himself so well in China?

J moved up at the FBI after the investigation was complete. He, along with Derek, Nigel, and Mack, became local celebrities. J had spoken on everyone's behalf during the inquiry, concluding Talia Levy must have been killed by an unknown person or persons outside the investigation. No weapons were found to match bullets shot, and forensics at the site were inconclusive as to who was responsible.

J also concluded Elli, Derek, and Nigel hadn't broken any laws, although their actions were probably not the wisest. Ultimately, they retrieved most of the documents. In the end, they delivered three unfriendly foreign agents, albeit dead, while eliminating a piece of shit by the name of Gustav Peralta. The investigation was dropped with a stern warning, as well as a commendation from the mayor.

Derek took over Nigel's boat, wanting the quieter life of lobstering. He renamed the boat "Nigel's Dream of Serendipity" in honor of his father. The pain of Nigel's death still lingered with him and his mom, but time and lobstering were doing some good in healing the pain.

In November of 2019, Elli went back to the lab, working with the I-CRISPR program, and ran it at a more methodical pace. She felt if she was sure and steady early, more time would be gained back on the back end with approvals. The pace stayed on track until a significant news story about a new coronavirus infection in Wuhan, China, made the internet. This development pressed the lab to react with an elevated sense of urgency.

Although reports from China and the World Health Organization indicated neither had concern about widespread infection from human to human, Elli decided to ignore them. She, of all people understood why quick action might be required.

The temporary shutdown of travel from China to the US put Elli and her colleagues on high alert. The spread of the virus to Europe and North America terrified them. Many medical experts and countless world leaders continued to ignore the signs of impending danger. On the other hand, China portrayed a national emergency in their own country but continued to play the global risks down.

Fortunately, Elli had already pieced together most of the lost data. Unfortunately, she and the world had squandered valuable time. Completion of Phases Two and Three of patient testing by the end of 2019 had been a reality before the package was stolen. It would now be delayed twelve to eighteen months at best.

February 7, 2020 - Norman, Oklahoma

For now, Nick was content having the life of a student, making good grades while chasing young coeds. On that winter day, after class, Nick made his way to the student union, where he saw a group of students standing in front of a TV screen. He jostled his way to the front to hear the commentator better. At the same time, almost 2,000 miles across the country, Ellie was in the cafeteria at the lab looking at her television, watching the same announcement.

Both had been closely following the story about the coronavirus, found in Wuhan China, and now called Covid-19. This announcement was different on an entirely different level, but received much-added attention from both of them. It didn't have much to do with the spread of the virus, but with the spread of information about the virus. At that moment, they both knew their instincts about a much more sinister agenda were right. Flashing across the bottom of the screen underneath the photo of a doctor from Wuhan was:

"Chinese Dr. Li Wenliang died due to complications of coronavirus. The doctor originally reported the new coronavirus to his colleagues in a Beijing media chat room on December 31, 2019. Several different sources have reported that after the incident, he was arrested, reprimanded by local authorities, and threatened jail time for "severely disturbing social order" and using ***"untruthful speech."***

POST NOTES:

Although all characters and events depicted in this book are entirely fictitious. Any similarity to actual events or persons, living or dead, is purely coincidental. However, the following information concerning COVID 19 in the United States and the rest of the world has been reported by the Center for Disease Control (CDC) and the World Health Organization (WHO):

- January 19, 2020: First reported case of COVID 19 in the United States.
- February 2, 2020: Travel ban from China to the United States
- February 6, 2020: First official death due to COVID 19 in the United States.
- February 26, 2020: First case of Community transmission in the United States
- March 1, 2020: New York announces its first case
- March 9, 2020: Nationwide lockdown of Italy
- March 11, 2020: WHO announces worldwide pandemic, 37 US deaths, 3173 China reported deaths
- March 13, 2020: Travel from Europe into the US halted. President declares a national emergency. The economy begins shutting down.
- April 1, 2020: Briefing from the US Intelligence community reported Chinese cases and deaths were much too low. 2850 US deaths, 3321 China reported deaths
- November 20, 2020: Several independent news sources report China vaccinating over one million citizens with product that hasn't finished phase III testing.

- **December 11 and 18, 2020: The FDA approves two COVID vaccines**
- **December 21, 2020: A New, more contagious COVID-19 strain reported in the U.K.**
- **January 10, 2021: 1,936,000 worldwide deaths, 381,480 US deaths, 4,634 Chinese deaths (unconfirmed)**

Thank you to our wives Linda and Sue
for being patient with our first endeavor writing our book.

Thank you to our friends and family, who took time from their busy lives
to read our manuscript, prompting many changes and improvements.
You know who you are.

A special thank you to Toni Nix for your help in editing
and proofreading our work.

REFERENCES

"Harnessing CRISPR to stop Viruses." *Harvard Health Letter*, Jan. 2020.

Steiner, Jason. "How CRISPR can help us win the fight against the pandemic." *Medcity News*, May 2020.

Weintraub, Arlene. "Stanford team deploys CRISPR gene editing to fight COVID-19." *Fierce Biotech*, 5 Jun. 2020.

Lewis, Tanya. "Scientists Program CRISPR to Fight Viruses in Human Cells." *Scientific American*, 23 Oct. 2019.

Leitch, Carmen. "How Cas13 Works in Bacteria." *Labroots*, 01 Jun. 2019.

Zhang, Han "Grief and Wariness at a Vigil for Li Wenliang, the Doctor Who Tried to Warn China About the Coronavirus." *The New Yorker*, 11 Feb. 2020.

Hegarty, Stephanie. "The Chinese Doctor who Tried to Warn Others about Coronavirus." *BBC News*, 9 Feb. 2020.

MAGNIFICENT
BASTARD
MAGNIFICENT
BASTARD

ABOUT THE AUTHORS

Ron Cisneros is a graduate of University of Central Oklahoma with a BBA. Ron has spent most of his career working in Human Resources specializing in Employee Relations and volunteering with numerous community service groups. He is a member of the Society of Human Resource Management and served as President of the Oklahoma City Human Resource Society and the Oklahoma Hispanic Professional Association. Like his co-Author, is a native of Utah but now resides in Oklahoma with his wife, Linda.

Michael Padjen is originally from Utah and a graduate of the University of Utah. Michael spent the majority of his professional career in international manufacturing and sales for the Home Furnishings industry. A Multiple Myeloma diagnosis ended that career but created an opportunity for him to continue his life as an advocate for the blood cancer and immunodeficient communities through blogging, coaching, and the founding of a nonprofit advocating those communities. Michael also has a keen interest in genetic research as applied to curing chronic illnesses and treating viruses. He now resides in North Carolina with his wife, Sue.